Love-shy

ALSO BY LILI WILKINSON:

A Pocketful of Eyes

Pink

Angel Fish

The (Not Quite) Perfect Boyfriend

Scatterheart

Joan of Arc

Acknowledgements

As mentioned in the dedication, I came up with the idea for *Love-shy* while on holiday with my dear friend Sarah Dollard. As well as being an excellent friend, she is also an excellent writer and story-doctor, and her wisdom and advice helped shape this book from beginning to end. As always, thanks, Snazzy.

Not to sound like a broken record, but I am so totally lucky to have editors like Jodie Webster and Hilary Reynolds, whose unflagging enthusiasm and careful attention to detail make all my books approximately one million times better than they are in first-draft form. Many thanks to them and to all the other Onions.

And of course thanks to my wonderful friends, my parents and Michael – thanks for listening to me rabbit on about love-shyness and Rhesus monkeys and Stepford mothers and all the other nonsense that fills my head. I am a lucky girl indeed to be surrounded by such wonderful people.

The very first draft of this book was written in November 2009, for (inter)National Novel Writing Month. NaNoWriMo is a wild, crazy project where participants attempt to write a 50,000 word novel in thirty days. It's very intense, but lots of fun. You can find out more at nanow-rimo.org.

Finally, love-shyness is a real thing. There are real people who are love-shy. Some of them just need a little confidence-boosting, but for others, like Nick, it's a serious psychological condition. Anxiety disorders of all types can be very isolating. If you think you have an anxiety disorder, or you know someone who does who you think might need some help – tell someone, and check out these organisations for more information:

HEADSPACE

www.headspace.org.au

—

ANXIETY TREATMENT AUSTRALIA

www.anxietyaustralia.com.au

—

SANE AUSTRALIA

www.sane.org

About the author

LILI WILKINSON WAS BORN IN Melbourne, Australia, in the front room where her parents still live. She was first published when she was twelve, in *Voiceworks* magazine. After studying Creative Arts at Melbourne University, Lili worked on insideadog.com.au, the Inky Awards and the Inkys Creative Reading Prize at the Centre for Youth Literature, State Library of Victoria. She now spends most of her time reading and writing books for teenagers. She's won awards for the writing part, but not the reading, unless you count the stopwatch she won once in the MS Readathon.

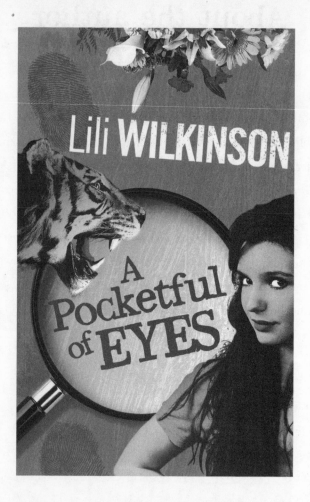

Lili WILKINSON

A Pocketful of EYES

'Wry, sly, funny, smart, and very entertaining.'
JACLYN MORIARTY

'Lili Wilkinson is like a coolgeekgirl Agatha Christie.'
SIMMONE HOWELL

Love-shy

Lili WILKINSON

ALLEN&UNWIN
SYDNEY·MELBOURNE·AUCKLAND·LONDON

First published in 2012

Allen & Unwin
83 Alexander Street
Crows Nest NSW 2065
Australia
Phone: (61 2) 8425 0100
Fax: (61 2) 9906 2218
Email: info@allenandunwin.com
Web: www.allenandunwin.com

A Cataloguing-in-Publication entry is available from
the National Library of Australia
www.trove.nla.gov.au

ISBN 978 1 74237 623 3

Cover photos © iStockphoto; Ada Summer / Corbis;
Patrick Moynihan / Getty Images
Cover and text design by Lisa White and Jade Raykovski
Set in 12/18 Adobe Garamond
Printed in Australia by McPherson's Printing Group

10 9 8 7 6 5 4 3 2 1

The idea for this book was born over breakfast in Tenby, Wales, sitting opposite one of my dearest friends, Sarah Dollard. Without her storytelling madskills, all my books would have ambivalent characters and unpunchy climaxes, and without her friendship, life would be significantly less awesome. This one's for you, Snazzy.

PRINCIPLES OF JOURNALISM

1. Journalism's first obligation
   is to the truth.

2. Its essence is discipline of
   verification.

3. It must strive to make the
   significant interesting and relevant.

4. It must serve as an independent
   monitor of power.

5. Its first loyalty is to the citizens.

6. It must keep the news
   comprehensive and proportional.

7. Its practitioners must maintain an
   independence from those
   they cover.

8. It must provide a forum for public
   criticism and compromise.

9. Its practitioners must be allowed to
   exercise their personal conscience.

*Energy rightly applied
and directed will
accomplish anything.*

NELLIE BLY
pioneer female journalist

1

I FOUND A STORY.

Before I joined the team, our school newspaper couldn't really be called a newspaper. It wasn't fit for wrapping fish, and not just because it wasn't printed with organic inks on unbleached paper. The typical headline was generally something like SOCCER TEAM TRIUMPHS AT REGIONALS or YEAR ELEVEN ADVENTURES AT ULURU. Nobody was interested in serious journalism. Except for me.

Since I came along, I'd written an analysis of the contents of the chicken-and-corn-in-a-roll sold at the school canteen (trust me, you don't want to know – suffice to say it didn't come from a chicken), an investigation into literacy levels in Year Seven, an exposé on the teachers who smoked outside the back door of the staff room, and a variety of penetrating interviews, unflinching reviews and frank profiles.

Nobody cared, of course. I was pretty sure nobody even *read* the *East Glendale Secondary College Gazette*. But it was all I had, until I could get out of this dump and go to university and then become a *real* journalist. I was going to be one of those freelance journalists who wasn't tied to a paper. I mean, sure, the hustle and bustle of deadlines and copyedits and that whole sense of camaraderie was alluring – drinking hard liquor at one's desk late at night and exchanging stories of adventure and intrigue while clustered around a single television watching some massively significant piece of breaking news. But I wanted the freedom to travel the world and write about whatever I felt like and then sell it to the *New York Times*, the *Guardian*, *Vanity Fair*, *TIME* Magazine. Penny Drummond was going to be the next Nellie Bly or Christiane Amanpour.

It was hard, developing one's writing skills on a school paper. I had to go deeper than the Drama Club's premiere of *Equus*, or the fact that our hockey team had once again failed to win a game this year. I needed something grittier, more compelling, more personal. I needed to climb inside somebody's life and report back from within their soul. I needed to get my teeth into some real long-form investigative journalism. I needed a story.

And then I found it.

It was a Tuesday, so I'd had Debating at lunch. We were practising for our next round of regional finals. We'd win, of course, because I was third speaker on our team and I always win. Last month the third speaker from the other team didn't even present his case. He just stood up after me, looked down at his shoes and burst into tears.

Anyway, I stupidly left my diary in the library after Debating and didn't realise until I was on my way to English for fifth period. I turned and headed back to the other side of the building, cutting through the Year Twelve lockers and up the stairs to the library. Mr Gerakis wouldn't mind if I was a few minutes late for class. I was his best student, after all. So I slipped into the library and through to the little room where we had our Debating meetings. My diary was there, right where I'd left it. And then it happened.

The security gate by the library exit door whooped. I turned around to see who had set it off, but all I saw was the big wooden door closing.

'Hey!' I shouted. 'Wait!'

Was someone stealing library books? Mrs Green, the librarian and one of the teachers outed in my piece on staff smoking, was nowhere to be seen. In fact, the library was completely empty.

One of the nearby computers chimed a shutdown tone. Was it the library book thief? What had they been doing on the computer? And why had they shut it down instead of just logging out? Maybe they were running a stolen-library-book cartel.

Every journalistic bone in my body started to hum. Maybe this was it. Maybe *this* would be the key to my next big story. I booted up the computer, all ready to undertake a browser-history search, or, if the cache had been emptied, do something tricky and clever involving the ISP. But as I double-clicked on the browser icon, a window popped up. 'Firefox closed unexpectedly. Would you like to open the most recently viewed tabs?' Too easy.

There was only one tab. And it wasn't at all what I was expecting.

'Loveshyforum.com?' I said out loud. 'What on earth…?'

It was a very simple website containing a home page, an FAQ and a forum. The homepage had a short paragraph and list in what I felt was an ill-chosen font.

This website is a resource for men suffering from love-shyness. Love-shyness is a debilitating psychological condition afflicting men all over the world. Do any of the following describe you?

1. You are a virgin.
2. You have never dated, or rarely date.

3. You have never had a romantic or sexual relationship with a member of the opposite sex.
4. You long for female companionship, and suffer without it.
5. The thought of approaching a woman in a casual, friendly way makes you extremely anxious.
6. You are heterosexual.
7. You are male.

If you answered YES to most of these points, you may be love-shy.

This was *so much better* than a library-book-smuggling racket. Was someone from this school *love-shy*? I clicked on the forum page and skimmed a few posts.

Shyguy72   I'm forty years old. The only physical contact I've ever had with a woman other than my mother was shaking hands at a job interview once. I didn't get the job.

Ruthv3n   I haven't left my house for two years. I couldn't handle it if I ran into a woman. The very thought makes me too anxious, it's better to stay here where I'm safe.

PEZZimist There's a girl at my school who I like. But I don't know if I'll ever be able to talk to her. I'm so lonely.

VirginBlues Why don't we have arranged marriages in this society? It's so unfair that if you're shy and can't approach a girl, that's it. Why can't they come and talk to us? Girls have it so easy.

'Penny?'

I closed the browser window hurriedly. It was Mrs Green, a haze of cigarette smoke still clinging to her.

'Penny, what are you doing in here? Shouldn't you be in class?'

I explained that I'd left my diary behind after my Debating meeting, and before she could ask what I was doing at the computer, I gathered my books and sprinted off to English.

Mr Gerakis raised his eyebrows when I slipped into the classroom a quarter of an hour late, but didn't say anything. It wasn't like being fifteen minutes behind everyone else in my class was going to put me at any kind of disadvantage. If anything, it might even the playing field slightly. The other students at my school were total Neanderthals.

Or so I had thought.

6

While I pretended to work on an essay about Malice and Intent in Shakespeare's *Othello*, my eyes darted around the room.

Was it one of these boys? Could one of them be posting on the love-shy website?

I considered each of them with my keenest journalistic eye.

Second row from the front was where all the smart kids sat (myself included). Perry Chau was quiet, but he'd come frighteningly close to kicking my arse in Year Eight Debating, so he clearly didn't have any fear of women. Max Wendt was going out with Arabella Sampson, so that ruled him out. Clayton Bell was gay, and Peter Lange had been spotted kissing a girl from St Aloysius at the last Maths Tournament.

In the middle of the classroom Andrew Rogers, Con Stingas and Luke Smith threw wads of paper at each other and giggled. Surely none of them were mature enough to even have girls on their radar.

James O'Keefe and Rory Singh were asleep up the back. Probably not them, as I'm sure if they were terrified of being around girls, they wouldn't be *able* to fall asleep if girls were in the same room. Next to them was Nick Rammage. He'd only arrived at our school at the beginning of the year, and he was deeply, deeply cool. The adorable black curls that spilled over his forehead had every girl at school planning to jump him at the upcoming social. I'd heard that he'd pashed Olivia Fischer in the girls' toilets his very first day here. Definitely wasn't him.

That left the front row, where all the dorks sat. Frankly, any of them could be love-shy. Youssef Saad and Florian Lehner were definite possibilities, but maybe they all were.

It couldn't have just been curiosity that led someone to that website. Surely whoever was in the library was a regular visitor. And what reason would you have to visit a love-shy forum unless you were love-shy yourself?

But who *was* it?

I puzzled it over all the way through English and Italian. I was tempted to pull out my phone in class and continue investigating loveshyforum.com then and there, but I didn't want to push my luck. I got along well with all the teachers at my school – they couldn't help but respect me, because I was by far the smartest person there. But mobile devices were strictly forbidden and I didn't want to risk having my iPhone confiscated.

So I continued my investigation on the train on the way home from school. I read page after page of forum posts. I was so engrossed in the lives of these weird people, I nearly missed my station. Hurrying through the train doors just as they closed, I realised that I was also missing my prime objective. I needed to figure out which poster was the one from my school. Surely he'd leave some kind of identifying clue. I was a *journalist*, after all. I just had to read between the lines.

I continued to read as I entered our apartment building and pushed the button for the lift. An Asian girl of about my age stepped into the lift with me.

'Hi,' she said.

I nodded at her and went on reading. The lift pinged and the doors opened. I wandered out, vaguely aware that the girl was following. I frowned as I pulled out my keys.

'Can I help you with something?' I said, turning to her. She was tiny, with long, glossy black hair, but who knew what muggers disguised themselves as nowadays? She could totally have a knife concealed in that Hello Kitty backpack.

The girl shook her head and smiled, shrugging off her pink backpack and opening the front pocket. I saw the glint of metal. She *did* have a knife! I wondered if I could open my front door and get it shut before she came at me. No sudden movements, though. I didn't want to startle her into action. She came right up to me, her hand still digging inside the pocket...

And kept going.

The blood pounded in my ears as the girl continued down the corridor. With a tug and a jingle, she pulled out a keyring adorned with pink plastic characters.

'See you,' she said, as she unlocked the apartment door next to mine.

'Yeah,' I said, weakly. 'See you.'

Dad worked late on Tuesdays, so I had the apartment to myself. It was a cool apartment, all cream leather and soft carpet and stainless-steel appliances. We moved here three years ago, after Dad came out and Mum left. We used to live in a big house in the suburbs. I liked it here, although I did miss having a garden. Still, we had a great view over the city from the twenty-seventh floor. I could see the silver glint of the bay from my bedroom window, curving around all the tightly packed buildings.

Plus, being in the city we had access to all the best take-away food, which was just as well, as neither Dad nor I were particularly big on cooking. Dad's boyfriend Josh said that we were both disgusting and would die of malnutrition. But it wasn't as though I didn't order plenty of veggies and sal-ads. And anyway, by ordering all our food, I was creating jobs not only for the people who cooked the food, but also the people who delivered it. And I was giving myself more time to spend on the important things.

Like thinking about love-shyness.

I ordered duck penang and coconut rice from the organic Thai place around the corner, and settled down on the sofa with my laptop and a glass of iced tea.

I'd found the perfect story. It had human interest, mystery, science, medicine. It was about the way our society operated, and who it was failing. My feature would have heart and guts and plenty of facts and research.

But I needed to find him. I needed to find the love-shy boy.

I needed to find him, observe him, study him. I needed to figure out what made him love-shy. I needed to know what he wanted. What were his dreams? What was stopping him from achieving them? I needed to learn about his childhood, his parents. I needed to know if he had any pets. I needed to know if he was bullied in primary school. I needed to know it all, so I could fix him. I was no cheap tabloid paparazzi phone-tapper. I knew that the best journalism made the world a better place. I could really *help* this guy.

This would be the best story ever. Forget the *East Glendale Secondary College Gazette*. With an article like this, I could be published in a *real* newspaper. And not just the local *Leader*, either. Maybe the Sunday magazine of a national paper. Or in one of those journals like the *Monthly*. It'd be the story that would catapult me into my career. I'd make a real name for myself.

My favourite journalist, Nellie Bly, started out the same way. Because she was a woman, she was only ever assigned to write gossip and weddings and fashion. But she knew journalism could be a force for good, and she wanted to change the world. So in 1887 she pretended to be crazy and was admitted to a mental asylum, so she could investigate reports of cruelty and neglect. She wrote a book about the horrendous conditions, which prompted a grand jury investigation that totally overhauled the US mental health system. After that she was so famous that she got to do really interesting assignments, such as try to beat the record of going around the world in eighty days (not that it was really a record, as Jules Verne's *Around the World in Eighty Days* is a novel and never actually happened). She did it in seventy-two days, alone, with only one dress and some toiletries. *And* she bought a monkey in Singapore.

This love-shy boy could make me famous.

But I had to find him first.

I needed a plan.

2

My alarm woke me at six, and I headed downstairs to the pool.

Sometimes I thought I preferred swimming laps alone to competing in the actual races. It was good exercise and it cleared my head and I didn't have to talk to anyone. I didn't particularly like team sports. I wasn't very good at them, and I didn't like anything I wasn't good at. Also, I didn't like having to rely on other people in order to win. Debating was bad enough, but at least I knew that as third speaker, no matter how utterly rubbish my teammates were, I could always bring it home in my closing speech. I especially liked being able to pull us up from whatever quagmire the others had sunk us into, and save the day. It was much more satisfying to win from behind than to just win because we were all good. I wanted us to win because *I* was good. And team sports don't really work that way.

But with swimming, I was on my own. Just me, the water, lane ropes on either side, and the ends of the pool receding and approaching behind and before me. When my head was underwater, all the screaming and splashing and tinny music piped over the PA system became muffled and distant. And I felt completely alone. It was very calming.

I did freestyle for ten minutes, then backstroke, then breaststroke and finished with four laps of butterfly, which was my favourite because it requires total perfection in order to enable synchronous over-water recovery – and I enjoyed perfecting things.

When I arrived back upstairs at the apartment, my eyes stinging from chlorine, Dad was chopping fruit. On weekends we went out for breakfast, but on weekdays we actually got out knives and bowls and did it ourselves. I spooned yoghurt onto my muesli and then scooped strawberries, banana and blueberries from Dad's fruit salad.

'How was work last night?' I asked.

'Meh,' said Dad. 'First Tuesday of the month is always party time over at the office.'

'Tax stuff?' I asked.

He nodded and poured us each a steaming mug of freshly brewed coffee. Dad used to be a plumber, but now he owned a plumbing business and had a whole bunch of staff to get their hands dirty for him. He spent all of his time in his office, doing paperwork. It was weird, because Dad didn't look at all like a plumber. He looked like the kind of man who had a skincare regime and wore Calvin Klein underwear. He *was* that kind of man. He went to the gym regularly. He did Pilates. He was interested in interior design. And he happened to be a plumber. Who earned *a lot* of money.

'Dad,' I said, watching him shake open the newspaper.

'Hmm?'

'Did you ever have any trouble talking to girls at school?'

'What do you mean?'

'Were you shy around girls?'

Dad took a sip of his coffee. 'Not really,' he said. 'I was shyer around *boys*. I always found it very easy to talk to girls. Most of my friends in high school were girls.'

I realised that asking my gay father about liking girls was probably not going to be useful.

'Why do you ask?'

I shrugged. 'Just for an article I'm writing.'

Dad regarded me across the breakfast bar. 'Penny,' he said, his carefully groomed eyebrows raised, 'have you spoken to your mother lately?'

'Nope,' I said cheerfully.

'You really should call her.'

'I will,' I told him. 'I'll call her on the weekend.'

I took my coffee into my room. I didn't want to talk about Mum.

I opened my laptop and brought up loveshyforum.com, checking for new posts.

And I found him.

PEZZimist   If you force a computer to shut down, will your browser reload when you switch it back on? Can someone figure out who was the last person to log on? I think I might have been busted today at school.

The post had no replies. I clicked on the username and it took me to a profile page. PEZZimist, 16, had posted eleven times over the past six months. Short posts, usually asking simple questions about how to approach a girl. There was one intriguing question about what constituted stalking, but it wasn't enough. I wanted more.

I typed 'pezzimist' into Google. Jackpot.

PEZZimist.blogspot.com.

My love-shy boy had a blog! I clicked through, my hands trembling.

18:13

Today I was nearly discovered. My heart is still pounding thinking about it. I was in the library at lunchtime. It's safe in there, the books are like a fortress. When the bell went, the teacher disappeared and I was on my own. I didn't feel like going to class, so I went to check the love-shy forum. But I wasn't alone. Someone appeared – a girl, I think, I didn't stay to find out. What if she saw what I was doing? I turned off the computer in a panic and ran. Except I had a library book that I hadn't checked out, and it set off the alarm. Betrayed by my own fortress. It felt like a mutiny. I just hope the girl didn't see me. What if she thinks I stole a library book and tells someone? I don't want to get into trouble again. I can't.

I had all the information I needed. He was a sixteen-year-old boy, who went to my school, and tended to overwrite. He was almost certainly in the same year as me.

I dug around in my filing cabinet until I found last year's yearbook. A systematic approach was required. Scientific. Methodical. Last year I'd written an article comparing the school's demographics to those from the last census, so I knew there were about a hundred and fifty students in Year Ten, and the school's gender breakdown was actually very much in line with the Australian Bureau of Statistics: 50.2 per cent women to 49.8 per cent men. Which meant that there were only seventy-five boys in my year level. That didn't seem like so many. I'd just talk to every single one until I found PEZZimist. It'd be an interesting social experiment. I'd even document the process, so that once I did find him, I'd have an excellent basis for comparison to the other boys at school.

I downloaded a Dictaphone app onto my phone, selected a crisp, fresh notebook, and laid them out carefully on my desk along with the yearbook, two HB pencils, pink, yellow and green highlighters and a blue ballpoint pen. Then I had a shower and got ready for school. Today would be an excellent day.

'Penny?' Dad stopped me as I came out of my room. He was dressed in a typically immaculate grey suit, pink and white-striped shirt and a pink and olive tie. He was probably the best-dressed plumber in the universe. I could see my face in his shoes, they were so shiny. 'Do you mind if Josh comes over tonight?'

Dad and Josh had been dating for six months, and it seemed pretty serious. Josh was okay, although I kind of missed it just being me and Dad.

'Sure,' I said. 'Can we get that Malaysian banquet again?'

What I did like about Josh was that he gave us the numbers to be able to order from the banquet menu.

'Sure,' said Dad. 'And you can pick the movie.'

'No,' I told him. 'I pick dinner. You guys can pick the movie.'

'Sounds like a plan.'

I leaned forward on tiptoes to kiss him on the cheek. 'Don't fall down any toilets today and spoil that fancy tie!'

Dad cuffed me lightly over the back of the head as I headed out the door. 'Enough of your cheek.'

Weirdly, the not-a-knife-wielding-mugger girl from last night was opening her door at exactly the same time. She blushed and smiled at me, and I smiled back, safe in the knowledge that she wasn't going to cut out my spleen.

'Hi,' she said. Her voice was barely a whisper, tiny and high-pitched, like the rest of her. Her hair was dead-straight and perfect. She wore a white shirt, pleated skirt and knee-high socks. It looked like she shopped in the children's section of department stores. The Hello Kitty backpack once again sat perfectly positioned between her shoulderblades.

'Hey,' I said. 'Have you just moved in?'

The girl nodded. 'A few weeks ago.'

'It's nice here,' I told her. 'The pool downstairs is good.'

She smiled and ducked her head. She was like a teeny mouse, which made me feel like an elephant. I wanted to make her laugh or do something unexpected to prove she was a real person and not just an exquisitely detailed miniature robot.

'I'm Penny,' I said.

The girl frowned a little, still smiling. 'I know,' she said, and it sounded like an apology. 'Everyone knows who you are. And we were in the same Maths class last year.'

She went to my school? I swear I'd never seen this girl before. 'Oh!' I said. 'Of course you were, sorry.'

Her smile widened into a proper grin. 'Don't worry,' she said, looking up at me. 'My name's Rin.'

I smiled back. 'It's very nice to meet you, Rin,' I said, and made an apologetic face. 'Again.'

We walked to the lift together, and Rin told me about her twin brothers, who'd moved out of home a few months ago to be closer to their university. She told me how huge and empty her old house felt without them, and how glad she was when her parents decided to move somewhere smaller in the city.

'It takes longer to get to school,' she said. 'But I love being in the city all the time.'

'Do you go out much?'

Rin shrugged delicately. 'My parents don't like me going out socially,' she said. 'But most of the time I just tell them I'm going to the library and then meet my friends and see a movie or go shopping. And sometimes my brothers come into town and take me out. My parents don't mind if I'm with them.'

I was hoping to spend the train trip to school reading more about love-shyness. I'd found some articles online about the condition, and was keen to have a full psychological profile of the kind of boy I was seeking. But although Rin was tiny and soft-voiced, she wasn't silent. She chattered happily all the way to school, telling me about her brothers, her parents, her friends, how much she'd love to have a dog. As she talked, I touched the screen of my iPhone through my bag. I was itching to pull it out and start reading, but I didn't want to be rude. Anyway, Rin might be a useful tool when it came to tackling the Asian boys I didn't know very well.

The thing that was really blowing my mind was that boys even *cared* enough about girls to be love-shy. I mean, after yesterday's assessment of the boys in my class, it was hard to believe that any of them even *thought* about girls. I knew that girls spent a lot of time thinking about boys, because that's all they ever talk about. Not me, obviously. I didn't really care about boys. I mean, I was pretty sure I wasn't a lesbian. But I had better things to do than fritter away my high-school years mooning over some dumb boy who was only interested in sport and cars and beer. Smart boys were marginally better – and usually made better competition than girls because they were less likely to cry (last month's Debating final notwithstanding). Girls cried a *lot*. And went on and on about hair and makeup and clothes, which were all things I did not care about. I swam three mornings a week and one lunchtime, so I kept my hair short (so I wasn't always having to dry it) and I didn't wear makeup. I chose clothes that were comfortable. I didn't own any high heels. I'd never painted my fingernails. I just didn't see the point. So I suppose I wasn't crazy about girls or boys – or really teenagers in general. Either way, I had absolutely no desire to *touch* any of them. It just seemed so *boring*.

And it wasn't like boys got any better with age. My second-favourite journalist, Katharine Graham, was in charge of the *Washington Post* during the Watergate scandal in the 1970s. She had a totally useless husband, who was her boss, and cheated on her and then went crazy and killed himself. And it wasn't until he was out of the picture that she could really pursue her career without everyone assuming that all her success was due to him being in charge because she was a woman and therefore incapable of being talented.

Anyway, I didn't have any horrible cheating men dragging me down, so I was ready to go. I was going to start with what I knew. The boys in my homeroom, my classes, my clubs and lunchtime activities. From there I'd spread out into other lunchtime clubs and societies, and then see what gaps were left. Every time I spoke to a boy, I'd record the conversation and later transcribe it. I'd take notes and pay special attention to whether each boy made eye contact, and whether he had any overt signs of shyness, such as sweating, fiddling or nailbiting. Luckily I'd had heaps of practice interviewing people for the newspaper, and I knew the four most important rules of interviewing:

1. Let the interview flow naturally, like a conversation.
2. Listen to the subject's answers.
3. Leave a long pause after each answer, in case something interesting slips out as they try to fill the awkward silence.
4. Be ruthless. Revisit questions that haven't been answered properly.

Once the interview had been completed, I would classify each boy into one of three groups and highlight their picture in my yearbook: Non-shy (pink highlighter), Possibly Love-shy (yellow highlighter), Likely Love-shy (green highlighter). This would give me an instant visual code, so I could tell at a glance how many boys I had spoken to, the ratios of shyness to non-shyness, and how far I had to go before I could safely predict which boy might be PEZZimist.

It was an excellent plan, neat and methodical. It couldn't fail.

3

I SPENT THE MORNING PREPARING MYSELF to start my
interviews. I was going to speak to the first boy at recess, but
after Media Studies, Ms Tidy kept me back to discuss an
article she'd read in the newspaper that morning about the
way young people were using technology to experiment with
language. I agreed that it was a very interesting article, and
informed Ms Tidy that it had originally been published in
the *Guardian*, and that our paper had clearly just bought it.
I then told her my opinions on the financing and structure
of newspapers, and how the notion of a 'free' press had been
totally compromised by the fact that all our news outlets
were owned by the same handful of media conglomerates.
Ms Tidy seemed interested at first, but after a while she
started checking at her watch and peering over my shoulder
at the classroom door.

Anyway, by the time I'd finished there, it was practically time for third period. I had to give a speech about my favourite animal in Italian, so I didn't have time to interview anyone until lunch, when I also had band rehearsal.

Of course, now that I'd properly met Rin, I saw her everywhere. We didn't have any classes together, but I passed her in the corridors and the canteen, and she was in the orchestra as well, in the string section. I'd just never noticed her before. The Asian kids all hung out together and didn't really associate with the non-Asians. They mostly had the same hair and eye colour, and similar-shaped faces. I supposed that made me seem horribly racist, but everyone else was such a riot of different hair and eyes and freckles and stuff that it was easier to tell them apart.

As I sat down in the wind section and opened the snaps on my oboe case, Rin gave me a little wave from behind her viola. I waved back and assembled my oboe. Now was my chance. It was time to put my plan into action. Subject Number One.

I turned to Jamal, the other oboe player, careful to make eye contact.

JAMAL ZAYD
Eye contact: Yes.
Overt signs of shyness: No.

ME: Hi, Jamal.

JAMAL: Hey. Wait, why are you pointing your phone at me?

ME: It's a Dictaphone app. So. What do you think of this Tchaikovsky piece?

JAMAL: Um. It's okay. A bit tricky with the key-changes. Why are you pointing that at me?

ME: Do you have a girlfriend?

(SUBJECT SHOWS SIGNS OF DISCOMFORT)

JAMAL: Um. Why do you ask?

ME: Just making conversation. You seem like a nice guy.

JAMAL: Oh, Ms Darling is here. We'd better pay attention.

ME: So I'm taking that as a *no*. Why? Do you struggle talking to girls?

JAMAL: She's banging her baton on her stand. I think she wants us to start.

ME: Have you ever kissed a girl, Jamal?

JAMAL: Look, do you think we could talk about this later? We're supposed to be tuning.

ME: Am I making you uncomfortable? Does talking to me make you feel anxious?

JAMAL: Well, now that you mention it, you're being a bit—

MS DARLING: When you're quite done there, Jamal.

JAMAL: Sorry, Ms Darling.

Verdict: Not love-shy.

In the breaks between pieces I also interviewed the bassoonist, and two of the male clarinettists. No joy there. The bassoonist assumed I was doing an article for the paper, and droned on and on about how the bassoon was such an overlooked instrument, yet essential to the overall tone and timbre of an orchestra. The two clarinettists had nothing of interest to say, but they didn't seem uncomfortable talking to me, and judging by the obscene gestures they were always making with their clarinets, they were definitely not shy about expressing their alleged familiarity with the female anatomy. As everyone packed up their instruments, I pulled the yearbook out of my bag and drew big crosses in pink highlighter over the faces of Jamal, the bassoonist and the two clarinettists. Not even one yellow 'maybe'. Still, each face I highlighted in pink was one face closer to PEZZimist's true identity.

I had a free period after lunch, so I headed to the library to finish an article I was writing for the school paper about gender imbalance in our English syllabus. I picked a seat where I could also stake out the computer where I'd first discovered the love-shy website. Maybe PEZZimist would come back.

I scribbled a few sentences for my article in my notebook, then googled 'love-shyness' on my phone. I could write the gender imbalance article later.

I wanted to know why love-shyness only applied to men. Didn't women get love-shy too? The article explained that the *effect* of shyness was different for women, because society had determined ages ago that men had to be the proactive partner in relationships. Equal rights were swept aside when it came to dating. It was the guy who was expected to ask the girl out – and it was also the guy who was supposed to *propose* to the girl. So shy girls would still get asked out and proposed to, but shy guys wouldn't.

The article also claimed that relationships were more important to a man's wellbeing than a woman's. A study of male medical students showed that the ones who got married in their early twenties were happier and more successful than those who were single throughout university. Another study took married and unmarried men and women in their fifties, and found that the unmarried women were the happiest, and the unmarried men were the least happy. This was because women had nurturing, emotional relationships with their friends, and could have proper deep-and-meaningfuls with them while eating ice-cream, whereas men were rubbish at talking about their feelings.

Fair enough, I supposed. Although I wondered where men like my dad fitted into this theory. He was sustaining an intimate, personal relationship with another man. Could gay boys be love-shy?

'I hope you're working on the introductory speech for tomorrow night, Penny.'

I glanced up to see Hugh Forward, my Year Ten co-captain and fellow debater, with a Biology textbook in one hand and a battered paperback of Walt Whitman poems in the other. He was automatically crossed off my love-shy list because at a cast party for the school play last year he'd tried to stick his tongue in my ear. I'd politely convinced him that this was not a good idea. With my knee. His eyes still watered a little whenever he looked at me, but that was a good thing, because it made him a total pushover when it came to drafting class policies or allocating budgetary resources for social events.

'What?' I said, craning past him to see if anyone had sat down at the love-shy computer.

'Tomorrow night,' he said. 'The Debating semifinal. You didn't forget, did you?'

I laughed with just the right amount of scorn. 'Don't be

ridiculous. It's all under control.' I was pretty sure I could walk in there totally unprepared and still debate the pants off everyone else.

I expected Hugh to walk away, but annoyingly he didn't. 'What are you doing?' he asked, trying to see the screen of my phone. I quickly turned it over.

'Writing an article for the *Gazette*,' I said. 'Did you know that in Year Ten we only study one text written by a woman? And there are no female protagonists on the syllabus from Years Eight to Ten. I mean, what kind of message does that send to our students? Are women's stories not worthy of study? Are the works of women writers not interesting or brave or strong?'

Hugh's eyes began to water at the word *strong*. 'Yeah,' he said. 'Fascinating. Er, I'd better go.'

He scuttled away as I rolled my eyes. Boys. So predictable.

Nobody came to use the computer I was watching.

We were paired up in Chemistry to make formic acid out of oxalic acid and glycerol. I made sure I was paired with a boy.

JESSE KING

Eye contact: Sporadic.

Overt signs of shyness: No.

ME: Have you ever had a girlfriend?

JESSE: Yes. Pass me the filtration flask.

ME: You're doing it wrong. The condenser goes in like *this*. Do you ever experience feelings of anxiety or depression? Do you have any allergies or sensitivities?

JESSE: I'm allergic to onion. It gives me a rash.

ME: How many hours a day do you spend day-dreaming about girls?

JESSE: Um. I thought this was Chemistry, not Psychology. Where's the distillation flask?

ME: You're putting in too much oxalic acid! It's only supposed to be 10 mg. Let me do it.

JESSE: Give it *back*! Are you seriously going to do this entire experiment on your own?

ME: I think that would be best, don't you? I mean, if I do it, it'll be *right*. Everybody wins.

JESSE: I think the point of this experiment is to *learn*, not to *win*.

ME: And that is exactly why I am going to go on to have a fabulous career, and you will probably end up underpaid in a dead-end job, too overwhelmed by the bitter reality of your existence to even work up the energy for a mid-life crisis.

JESSE: Hang on. Is that a Dictaphone app? Is it recording? What's going on?

(INTERVIEW TERMINATED BY SUBJECT)

Verdict: Not love-shy.

When I got home, I checked PEZZIMIST.blogspot.com for new posts. Nothing.

I sat at my desk and transcribed today's interviews. Then I pulled out my diary and recorded today's summary:

Interviews: 5

Possible love-shys: 0

I considered adding a third column entitled Brain-addled Morons, because clearly I would be meeting plenty of them. But it was a journalist's job to remain objective, so I would just have to rise above the idiocy of my male classmates and continue my search. I felt sure I knew PEZZIMIST now, from his blog posts. I knew he was different. He wasn't like the rest of the monkeys at our school. *He* lived on a higher plane as well. If only I could *find* him, then I could rescue him from his loneliness. I'd bring his condition to the attention of the world, and when I became rich, maybe I could start some kind of charity or foundation for helping other love-shy boys.

I pulled out my Maths textbook, but I couldn't concentrate on integers and tangents. I kept refreshing PEZZIMIST's blog and the love-shy forum for new posts. I needed a clue.

The sound of the front door opening, combined with the aroma of a Malaysian banquet, lured me out of my room and into the kitchen. Dad was opening plastic containers and getting plates and chopsticks, while Josh poured two glasses of wine, and a mineral water for me.

Josh looked up as I came in. 'Hey, Penny.'

I waved at him and grabbed a spring roll to chew on while he and Dad finished unpacking dinner.

'How's life?'

'Interesting,' I told him. 'I'm doing a story for the *Gazette* that involves interviewing every boy in Year Ten.'

Dad and Josh exchanged a Look. 'Are you hoping to find something in particular?' Dad asked.

I didn't really want to tell them about the whole love-shy thing. Not until I had a better handle on it. 'It's a sort of anthropological study,' I said, spooning kung pow chicken over my combination fried rice. 'Just trying to get a breakdown of what makes the Teenage-Boy mind tick.'

'And it's just boys?'

I nodded.

Dad narrowed his eyes at me. 'Penny?'

33

'Yes?' I snagged a couple of chicken wings. My plate was growing dangerously full. The problem with banquet meals is there's too much deliciousness, and you have to sample all of it.

'Are you trying to find a boyfriend? Because in my limited experience, shoving a dictaphone in a boy's face is not the best way to get him to like you.'

I grinned as I carried my teetering stack of banquet to the couch. 'No, Dad. I'm not trying to find a boyfriend. If there's anything I've learned from my first day of interviews, there is no creature more utterly uninteresting than the Teenage Boy. With a *single exception*,' I added, as Dad and Josh exchanged another Look. 'And that's the Teenage *Girl*.'

After dinner, Dad and Josh settled on the couch to watch *Iron Man 2*, but I pled homework and escaped to my room. I refreshed PEZZimist's blog. Bingo!

19:22

There's a girl. I know what you're thinking. There's always a girl. But this one is different. There is no girl like her. I live and breathe her.

She's the prettiest girl in school. She has long brown hair and kind eyes. She sits with her friends at lunch and I watch her. She has a beautiful smile. I watch her whenever I can, in class, at recess and lunch. Every time I look at her, it feels as if my blood has turned to boiling mercury or icy-cold mineral water. I'm heavy and weightless and hot and cold and fizzy all at once. And I have to look away for a moment. Then I want to run and run and run until I fall down dead. It's always been like this with me. Sometimes I just *feel* so much, I can't believe that the world can contain all of me. I'm afraid that if she ever did love me back, I'd pour so much of myself into her that she'd break apart.

I know what bus she catches and sometimes I can't help catching it too, even though it goes in the opposite direction from my house. I sit behind her and smell the scent of her hair, like sunshine. I imagine walking her home, holding hands. Talking sometimes, and sometimes just being quiet. Smiling.

I didn't have any more luck on Thursday. We had a mock-exam in English in the morning (which was so easy it was insulting), so I didn't get a chance to interview anyone during class. At recess I talked to a few boys playing downball against a wall near the boys' toilets, but they weren't shy about telling me what I could do with my dictaphone. In Physics, I discovered new evidence to suggest that all boys are witless morons.

ZACH HAUSEN

Eye contact: Yes.

Overt signs of shyness: No.

ME: Hey, Zach!

ZACH: Henny Penny Lane, how are things?

ME: Fine. Do you have a girlfriend?

ZACH: No, but just say the word and the position's *yours*.

ME: I don't want to be your girlfriend. Do you have trouble talking to girls?

ZACH: Talking, kissing, *loving*. All systems go. No problems here.

ME: You're standing a little close.

ZACH: Smell my pheromones, baby.

ME: I can. It's not very pleasant. Have you considered deodorant?

ZACH: You love it.

ME: I don't. Really.

ZACH: Are you recording this? Are you going to take it home and listen to my voice while you play with a washcloth in the bath?

ME: I don't have a bath. I shower.

ZACH: Bubble bath, yeah? With candles and stuff. And you just listen to my voice softly caressing

your ears and mind, while you're softly caressing—
(INTERVIEW TERMINATED)

Verdict: Not love-shy.

As I made my way to swim training at lunchtime, I got trapped in a throng of giggling, Impulse-drenched, hair-sprayed girls. They were discussing outfits and boys and how to sneak alcohol into the school social, and boys and boys and boys. Having spent the last two days talking to the boys of this school, I wanted to tell them they were wasting their time. But taking a good look at each of them, I realised that these vacuous excuses for young women were perfectly matched to those Cro-Magnon, meathead boys. I wondered if one of these girls was PEZZimist's crush. I doubted it. Surely he'd have better taste.

'Do you know if Nick Rammage is going to the social?' said one of the girls. 'He's so hot. I'm going to ask if he'll go with me.' I could smell her cigarette-and-chewing-gum breath from a metre away.

Another girl flicked her hair. 'Don't be stupid,' she said in a stunning example of pot–kettle hypocrisy. 'He's got a girlfriend. From his old school.'

I clawed my way out of the pack, gulping down fresh air. The pong of Teenage Girl irritated me all through swimming, and lingered even after I'd showered and changed.

Hugh Forward and I were both class captains as well as Year Ten captains, and there were four other Year Ten class-captains at our meeting. Three of them were girls, so that left Nedislav Radnik.

He was a definite possibility. He'd only been voted in as a class captain because of his Nordic good looks (did I mention that almost all teenage girls are totally shallow?), and never contributed to our meetings. I watched Nedislav carefully as we talked about the catering and decorations budget for the social, and then discussed the possibility of building a new weatherproof bike-shed. He didn't say anything, just doodled aimlessly on the cover of his school diary.

I tried to corner him at the end of the meeting, but Hugh was hanging around as though he wanted something.

'Are you going to Debating straight after school, Penny?' he asked, tidying up his notes at a glacial pace.

I made up some excuse about having an oboe lesson. I could easily tackle six or seven more boys in the hour between school and the Debating semifinal.

'Oh, okay,' said Hugh. 'I guess I'll see you there, then.'

Of course he'd see me there. We were on the same team, after all.

I sprinted down the corridor, and found Nedislav outside his locker. He looked startled. I stood squarely in front of him so he couldn't run away. Perhaps I needed to be more subtle this time so as not to scare him off.

NEDISLAV RADNIK

Eye contact: Sporadic.

Overt signs of shyness: Darting eyes, uncommunicativeness.

ME: Hey, I just wanted to ask you something about the meeting.

NEDISLAV: Um.

ME: Can you remember if Hugh said we had $1735 left in our budget? Or was it $1375?

NEDISLAV: Um. I don't remember.

ME: You don't remember? It was five minutes ago. I don't think you really understand the responsibility you have, as a democratically elected representative of the student body.

NEDISLAV: D-don't *you* remember?

ME: Not that I think the majority electoral system we have in this school is particularly democratic. I've been telling Mr Copeland that we need to move to an instant runoff preferential system to elect the class captains, and either the Sainte-Laguë method or Hare-Clark proportional system for the prefects and school captains. But as usual, everyone is resistant to electoral change. It's probably because Mr Copeland is British. (SUBJECT APPEARS AGITATED…AN EXCELLENT SIGN! TIME TO CHANGE TACTICS.)

ME: Are you planning on going to the social?

NEDISLAV: (DISTRACTED) What? No.

ME: Why not? It'll be fun.

NEDISLAV: I don't really go out very much.

ME: Why? Do you find it difficult to socialise?

NEDISLAV: (LOOKS BEYOND THE INTERVIEWER AND SHOWS SIGNS OF RELIEF)

KATE PITTMAN: Hey, baby.

NEDISLAV: Heyyy.

(KATE PITTMAN, IGNORING INTERVIEWER, PROCEEDS TO WRAP HER LEGS AROUND SUBJECT'S WAIST, WHILE LICKING HIS EAR. SUBJECT SHOWS NO SIGN OF CONCERN.)

ME: Right then.

KATE PITTMAN: (MOANS)

Verdict: Not love-shy.

In Media Studies, Sarah Parsons handed me a pale pink envelope. It was an invitation to her sixteenth birthday party. I guessed she had invited the whole swim team. I thanked her and let her know I'd definitely be there.

I couldn't say I loved attending parties. To be honest, I wished there were still structured games and activities, like when we were little. At least then there were prizes to be won. Now it was all just sitting around, making inane small talk, gossiping and (depending on the level of parental supervision) drinking.

I understood that people enjoyed drinking, and that it made me seem like a wowser when I didn't. But drinking made people *stupid*. And it was also dangerous. Never mind the fact that one teenager died every week from drinking in Australia. Never mind the increased chances of having employment problems, other substance-abuse problems, and engaging in violent or criminal behaviour. It was my *brain* I was worried about. My brain was my favourite part of me, and I was hardly going to interrupt its vital adolescent maturation phase with a neurotoxin such as alcohol.

So I just didn't see the point of parties. I quite liked it when there was dancing, but that usually didn't happen until after midnight, by which time I was totally ready to go home. But I knew going to parties was part of The High School Experience, and that apparently I'd Look Back on My High

41

School Years as the Best of My Life. Which I totally doubted. I suspected I'd look back on my years as an award-winning, history-making, internationally-acclaimed journalist as the Best Years of My Life. High school wouldn't rate a mention.

However, apart from the whole High School Experience thing, parties were a great way to soften people up, get to know my fellow students, make them comfortable with me and sniff out potential stories. I was half considering starting an anonymous gossip column in the *East Glendale Gazette*. Or maybe a blog. Everyone was saying that blogging was the future of journalism, and while I was obviously going to end up as one of the media elite, I supposed it wouldn't hurt to dabble in the less reputable forms of reportage. As long as I didn't get sucked into that black narcissistic hole of endlessly reporting daily minutiae. As if anyone cared what you had for breakfast. Get a real job. Not that I would get sucked in, of course. I'd be one of those hard-hitting, behind-the-scenes bloggers who expose corruption and scandal in the mainstream media and government. Like Julian Assange, but without the getting-arrested-for-sex-crimes part. It might actually be a good back-door entry into real journalism. But an East Glendale gossip column probably wasn't the back door I was searching for. And anyway, I had more important things on my mind.

I was only two days into my interviews, and I was already

seeing potential for a whole series of articles about teenage boys, of which the love-shy article would be only one. Why did Nedislav Radnik struggle to communicate verbally, but had no trouble with explicit public displays of intimacy? What exactly made Zach Hausen such an over-confident sleaze? Maybe one day all my articles would be collected in a book.

I eyed off my next subject. Bradley Wu. He'd won some short-film competition last year, and we'd done a piece on him for the paper. He was skinny and didn't have any friends because he spent all his time in front of a computer, painstakingly editing his videos frame by frame until they were perfect. I hadn't done the interview myself (it wasn't much of a challenge, after all: STUDENT WINS FILM GLORY blah blah yawn), but I vaguely remembered the article. It had contained an inappropriate apostrophe and two spelling mistakes because people just don't care about attention to detail. But I couldn't remember if Bradley had come across as being particularly shy or anxious.

I squinted at him. Actually, I *had* interviewed Bradley for something. I remembered he had a slight lisp and said *adverTISEments* instead of *adVERtisements*. I just couldn't remember what the article was about.

I slid into the chair next to his. He was editing another short film – something involving cars and a guy wearing only one gumboot. He was wearing headphones and peering intently at the screen. I tapped him on the shoulder and he started. I touched the record button on my Dictaphone app and smiled in a friendly and encouraging way.

BRADLEY WU
Eye contact: Yes.
Overt signs of shyness: Some reticence in answering questions.

ME: Bradley, I was wondering if I could have a word.

BRADLEY: I'm actually in the middle of something.

ME: It'll only take a minute. I just have a few questions.

BRADLEY: Yeah, thanks all the same, Penny, but I remember what happened last time you just had a few questions.

ME: Yes. What was that again?

BRADLEY: Your little article on gay students at East Glendale?

ME: Oh, of course. I remember. It was a lead feature, not a little article. It was on the front page.

BRADLEY: I know it was on the front page. Do you know how I know? Because my girlfriend, my sister and my mother all read it.

ME: That's great! It's awesome to see that people are reading my work. Very gratifying. Tell them thanks from me, and that I'm glad they liked it.

BRADLEY: They didn't like it.

ME: What? Why? Was it the layout? Because I don't have final sign-off on that. Tragically. I seriously can't believe how frustrating it is working with these morons. They think just because it's only a school paper, we don't need to have any journalistic integrity. Or proofreaders. Don't they remember that Thomas Jefferson once said, 'Were it left to me to decide whether we should have a government without newspapers, or newspapers without a government, I should not hesitate a moment to prefer the latter'? Newspapers are the most fundamental expression of democracy! The voice of truth!

BRADLEY: Except it wasn't.

ME: Wasn't what?

BRADLEY: The truth.

ME: What? Of course it was the truth. The layout doesn't change that.

BRADLEY: I don't care about the layout. You said I was gay!

ME: So?

BRADLEY: I'm not!

ME: Are you sure?

BRADLEY: Yes! I have a girlfriend!

ME: So? Freddie Mercury had plenty of girlfriends.
And Anthony Callea.

BRADLEY: I'm. Not. Gay.

ME: Why do you have such a problem with gay
people?

BRADLEY: I don't. But I'm not one of them.
And I had to explain that to my girlfriend. And
my mother. So if you don't mind, I'm going to
politely decline this opportunity for another fifteen
minutes of Penny Drummond fame.

Verdict: Not love-shy.

I spoke to another six boys after school, bringing my total
number of interview subjects to eighteen, before sprinting
to the local town hall for the Debating semifinal. Our topic
was *Should the Arts be Government Funded?* and we were
Negative. We won, of course, mostly because the other team
didn't seem to know what 'the Arts' actually meant, and
kept talking about libraries and swimming pools.

Hugh Forward asked me if I wanted to get an ice-cream

afterwards and talk strategy for the final. I pointed out that the final was two weeks away and was a secret debate, and as we wouldn't know the topic until an hour beforehand, there wasn't much strategising that could be done at this stage. Anyway, I wanted to get home and check for new blog posts.

As the train rattled its way homewards, I reviewed my findings. There were seventy-seven boys in the yearbook, and I knew that four had left at the end of last year, bringing it down to seventy-three. I had fifty-five left to interview. I was making good time, but felt a little concerned that I had not yet met a single boy who even warranted a yellow highlighter, let alone a green one. Still. There were plenty more to go.

17:43

- The other day, my French teacher asked me to conjugate the verb *être*. When she spoke to me I could feel my face getting red. But I could do it, as long as I didn't look at her while I was speaking. Teachers don't call on me very often. I think I made her uncomfortable today. I do that to people. People don't like it when you don't make eye contact or smile when you talk. Usually a teacher only does it once, and then they leave me alone. Hopefully this one will have learned that now.

Afterwards, I bought a lemonade from the vending
machine and went and sat in an empty classroom.
I realised that those words had been the first time I'd
spoken aloud in four days. *Je suis, tu es, elle est, ils sont*.
I am, you are, she is, they are. I was exhausted after that
class. You get used to not speaking, your tongue becomes
lazy. Then it becomes draining to just say a single word.

I blinked. French. PEZZimist took French. French was an elective, and there was only one class this year. I'd written an article for the *Gazette* a few months ago about the dwindling popularity of language classes in our school, and called for the addition of Indonesian, Arabic and Japanese to the current offering of French, Italian and German. French was hardly an international language anymore, and what good would German be to someone hoping to work in international business in the Asia-Pacific region? I'd clipped out the article and slipped it under the principal's door, just in case he hadn't read it already, so probably next year things'd change.

But that was all beside the point. The point was, PEZZimist took French.

I pulled up the East Glendale website and clicked through to the Student Portal where all the timetables were. Fifth period tomorrow. I could just walk right in and find him.

4

EVEN THOUGH I'D AS GOOD as found PEZZimist, and I'd already discounted everyone in my English class, I interviewed them all anyway. After all, I needed a control group to compare PEZZimist to. And if nothing else, it was an interesting sociological insight into the mind of the Average Adolescent Male, which would be useful background information for my article.

Rory Singh answered my questions in sleepy monosyllables, and James O'Keefe confirmed that rumour about him and Caitlin Reece in the photography lab. Andrew Rogers, Con Stingas and Luke Smith sniggered and stared at my breasts the whole time, but didn't show any signs of actual love-shyness, just idiocy. I'd already interviewed Perry Chau, and Max Wendt showed me a photo on his phone of him and Arabella Sampson dancing at Arabella's cousin's eighteenth. Clayton Bell insisted that I interview him to prove I wasn't homophobic, then badgered me to allocate more money from the SRC budget to the Gay–Straight Alliance. Peter Lange showed me a text message from the St Aloysius girl that combined fractal geometry, some filthy language and the first sixty-nine digits of pi.

I turned my attention to the dorks in the front row. We were supposed to be working on our essays, but Mr Gerakis had slipped out of the classroom to do some photocopying, so I was free to talk to them.

Youssef Saad was quite charming, making constant eye contact and smiling the whole time. He answered each question thoughtfully, with his head cocked on one side. Pink highlighter for him. Patrick Ryan had what appeared to be Weetbix stuck in his braces. I prayed he would be a pink highlighter, and luckily he told me that a girl from his Christian Youth Group had just accepted his invitation to go to the social. Florian Lehner was a bit twitchy, but informed me he had a girlfriend in Austria who he missed very much, but that they Skyped every day and that she would wait for him until he was old enough to move back to Austria without his parents. I looked at his wispy blond hair and nonexistent chin, and predicted that the Austrian girlfriend was probably as shallow as all the other girls in the world, and would not wait. Nonetheless, he was a pink highlighter.

That only left one dork. Logan Esposito. He was somewhat of a puzzle, as he looked like a stoner, but got abnormally high marks and always sat up the front of the class. His T-shirt implied he was a fan of something called Mastodon which, if the horse skeletons and gothic font were anything to go by, was some kind of metal band. This didn't really fit the love-shy mould of loving classical music and light opera.

But as I was approaching Logan, Mr Gerakis returned and levelled a stern look in my direction. I went back to my seat and updated the yearbook. There were an awful lot of pink not-love-shy crosses. No green or yellow. This investigation wasn't proceeding as I had planned.

When the bell went for recess, Logan scurried away quickly, without speaking to the other dorks. I gathered my books and followed him. He put his books in his locker and rummaged in his bag until he produced a Kit-Kat. Ah. I'd read that low testosterone levels made love-shy boys more likely to crave sweets. This could be promising. Logan was not really bad-looking, now that I thought about it. He was tall and thin, with dark brown hair hanging just below his ears that would look quite nice if he bothered to wash it. He had bad skin, but he was a sixteen-year-old boy, so who could blame him? Although that Kit-Kat wasn't going to help.

LOGAN ESPOSITO

Eye contact: Yes, but in a creepy, starey way.

Overt signs of shyness: Extreme agitation.

ME: So, Logan. Do you have a girlfriend?

LOGAN: (STARES AT INTERVIEWER)

ME: Logan? Are you okay?

LOGAN: (SHAKES HEAD)

ME: Do girls make you uncomfortable, Logan? Do you find talking to me difficult?

LOGAN: (SHAKES HEAD)

ME: In your own time, Logan. Just breathe.

LOGAN: She...She...

ME: She? Who? Are you wearing eyeliner?

LOGAN: (DARK LOOK) She was my everything. She said she loved me. She made everything different. She held my hand and took me to places I'd only dreamed about. The scent of her skin, her hair, aroused me like—

ME: Is this going somewhere?

LOGAN: She said we'd be together forever. She said I was her One and Only. She said she'd never leave me. She whispered it into my ear when we lay naked together under the stars. And then...

ME: And then?

LOGAN: And then I found her making out with Jamal Zayd around the side of the canteen.

ME: I'm very sorry for your loss.

LOGAN: Everything is turned to ashes.

ME: You seem to be enjoying that Kit-Kat.

LOGAN: My soul's fire is extinguished. I will never love again.

ME: I'm sure you'll perk up in a day or two.

LOGAN: Do you think...Would you...

ME: What is it?

LOGAN: Would you mind if I smelled your hair?

ME: Yes. I would mind.

(INTERVIEW TERMINATED)

Verdict: Not love-shy.

Our SRC meeting was cancelled due to an outbreak of glandular fever, which meant we wouldn't be able to reach quorum. I thought about writing an article about how the poor hygiene standards of secondary schools contribute to the spread of disease among the students – it could make a fascinating exposé for the *Gazette*. But I couldn't stop thinking about PEZZimist, with only one hour to go until I got to meet him! I decided instead to kill time visiting the numerous other clubs and societies that met on a Friday

lunchtime and tick some more names off the love-shy list –
to be thorough.

The Foreign Film Society was in the middle of watching
Les Quatre Cents Coups, so I couldn't interview any of them.
I checked out the Fencing Ring, but things were looking
a bit violent and I wanted to keep both my eyes. So I let
myself into the Medical Ethics Society room and sat down
next to a likely candidate.

He was wearing a too-small brown argyle jumper that
was pilling around the middle, and high-waisted jeans. On
the right sort of person, his outfit would have screamed
hipster-irony. But this was not the right kind of person. His
hair looked like his mum cut it, his eyes were squinty, and
his skin was riddled with acne. This was no hipster. This
guy was a *dork*.

SHAUN DAVIES
Eye contact: Little.
Overt signs of shyness: Fidgety,
non-communicative.

ME: What's your name?
SHAUN: (QUIETLY) Shaun. Davies.
ME: So, Shaun. Do you think neonatal circum-
cision is a breach of children's rights – namely

the right to be free from physical intrusion and the right to choose in the future – therefore amounting to child abuse?

SHAUN: (MUMBLES)

ME: I can't hear you.

SHAUN: We're supposed to be talking about medical futility.

ME: I don't care. Have you ever kissed a girl?

SHAUN: (AGITATED) What? That's none of your business. Jesus.

ME: Does it make you feel uncomfortable to talk about girls?

SHAUN: (TRIES TO IGNORE INTERVIEWER)

ME: Does talking to *me* make you uncomfortable?

SHAUN: Yes. Are you even a member of this club?

ME: Are you uncomfortable because I'm a girl?

SHAUN: Because you're *nosy*. My love-life is none of your business.

ME: I'm just trying to help you, Shaun. I can bring your condition to the attention of the world.

SHAUN: I don't *want* your help. I don't *need* your help. Leave me alone.

Verdict: Possibly love-shy.

My first yellow-highlighter candidate! As I left the Medical Ethics Society meeting, I considered the possibility that Shaun Davies might be PEZZimist. He was certainly cagey. And he clearly didn't want to talk to me. He *could* be PEZZimist. Maybe. But there were two girls in the Medical Ethics Society, and it wasn't exactly a big group. So he must have to interact with them sometimes. Maybe I could talk to one of them. Ooh! Maybe one of them was the girl he liked, and that's why he *joined* the Medical Ethics Society (because really, why else would you? What was the point of sitting around for an hour once a week discussing the pros and cons of euthanasia? It's not as if any of those people were smart enough to ever become a real doctor, let alone sit on a real medical ethics committee, so it was all totally hypothetical). But neither of the girls had long hair, or were what I would call pretty, so that ruled out that theory.

But still, Shaun Davies was my only lead so far. Until I went to check out PEZZimist's French class, of course. I suppose that was the thing really. I had read PEZZimist's blog posts. I knew he was smart. I knew he was...I don't know...poetic (or melodramatic). And Shaun Davies just seemed too...ordinary. I mean, I knew PEZZimist was going to be a bit weird, but Shaun Davies didn't seem weird *enough*. He was just a dork. He was my only lead, but I kind of hoped it wasn't him.

I found myself with fifteen minutes to kill before the bell rang for the end of lunch. I considered heading back to the library to stake out the love-shy computer again, but decided against it. Whoever PEZZimist was, he was pretty good at keeping his identity a secret. I'd nearly busted him the other day, and he was way too smart to return to the scene of his almost-outing. Instead I headed to the canteen to knock off another couple of interviews.

Our school canteen smelled like tomato sauce, hot dogs, deodorant and Teenage Boy. The floor was sticky underfoot from spilled cans of soft drink, and that late into the lunch hour, I had to wade through piles of chip packets, sandwich crusts and empty bottles in order to find my way to a table. Not that there were any free tables today. They were all crammed with teenagers eating, talking, making out, fighting and throwing processed meat at the ceiling.

I scanned the room. Trendy people, beautiful people, scary pierced people, stoned people, music geeks, theatre geeks, maths geeks and chess geeks. Cricket jocks, soccer jocks, basketball jocks, volleyball jocks and rowing jocks. White kids, Asian kids, Aboriginal kids, Indian kids and African kids.

But no one looked love-shy. I didn't even know where to start. If *I* were love-shy, I'd stay away from the canteen altogether. It was nerve-racking even for *me* to be standing in the doorway, and I was an extremely well adjusted, socially able person.

'Penny!'

It was amazing that someone with such a tiny voice could make herself heard over the hormone-induced roar.

Rin was sitting near the vending machines with a bunch of other Asian girls and guys. She grinned and beckoned me over.

'Hi,' I said.

'Sit with us,' said Rin. The other girls looked surprised, but generally amenable to the idea. I pulled up a chair that had been kicked over at the next table, and sat down. I felt sort of luminous, among all that black hair and olive skin. I also felt the size of a house.

Rin introduced me to everyone around the table. Cherry, Rebecca, Pieng, Stephanie...I did my best to remember each one by mentally applying mnemonics. Cherry was eating an apple, which was helpful. Rebecca, who had a sassy black bob and pink-framed glasses, was carefully poking holes in her rice with a pair of chopsticks. *Rebecca-the-wrecker*, I thought. *Pieng-never-eats-a-thing. Stephanie-to-the-left-of-me*. The boys were Lee (*taller-than-a-tree*), Charlie (he wore a brown shirt – so *Charlie Brown*) and Jie (*Jie-Whiz*).

The girls each had a cute plastic lunchbox with compartments and a neat little groove for holding chopsticks, each decorated with Japanese cartoon characters. What remained of their lunches looked about a million times tastier than every cheese and vegemite sandwich I'd ever eaten. Rin offered me a red box of something called Pocky, which turned out to be a long, skinny pretzel dipped in chocolate. It was awesome.

I eyed the three boys, and made a mental note to cross them off my list, due to the fact that they were engaged in various stages of foreplay with their respective girlfriends. The way this was going, I was going to need a new pink highlighter.

'So what are you doing this weekend?' Rin asked me.

I shrugged and said something about homework. My mind was in another place altogether, thinking about Shaun Davies and pezzimist and wondering if he was here, right now, in this room. Perhaps I should comment on his blog, instead of trapping him in French? But I didn't want him to think I was stalking him. Our meeting had to seem more casual than that.

The bell rang for fifth period, and the canteen erupted into a storm of pushed-back chairs and groans and more rubbish. I stood up, feeling a little tingly. This was it. I was about to meet pezzimist.

'See you in the lift,' said Rin, smiling.

'Yeah,' I said, not really listening. 'See you.'

I let myself into Ms Leroy's French class about five minutes after the bell. I was supposed to be in Maths, but I could just lie and say that SRC had gone overtime.

'It's Penny, right?' Ms Leroy gazed at me from the whiteboard. 'What can I do for you?'

'*Bonjour, madame,*' I said, using my entire French vocabulary all at once, and glanced at the class.

Shaun Davies was there. Front row.

My heart sank. PEZZimist was Shaun Davies.

'Penny?'

'Um,' I turned back to Ms Leroy. 'I was wondering if I could do a quick survey of your class, for the *Gazette.*' Maybe there was another potential love-shy in the class. I looked around. There was Youssef Saad. And Bradley Wu. And Zach Hausen.

'What kind of survey?' asked Ms Leroy.

'Er,' I said. 'About...' I scanned the walls for inspiration and saw a poster of the Eiffel Tower. Such a ridiculously phallic piece of architecture. 'Condoms,' I said. 'Condom vending machines in the school toilets.'

Ms Leroy frowned. 'I'm sorry, Penny,' she said. 'But this is French class, not Human Biology.'

'What if they gave their answers in French?'

'I'm afraid not,' she said, shaking her head. 'We have important vocab to learn today.'

'Okay then,' I said, with one last desperate glance around the room. 'Thanks.'

I shut the classroom door behind me and stood in the empty corridor. Shaun Davies.

I'd been checking PEZZimist's blog all day to see if he made any mention of talking to me. If he *was* Shaun Davies, surely he'd mention it. As soon as I got home, I opened my laptop. As I waited for it to start up, I pulled out my pink highlighter and crossed off the two boys – Jacob Printz and Tigger Paulson – I'd spoken to at the basketball game I'd crashed, and Jack Horwicz, who I'd run into at the train station. Jack had thought I was trying ask him to the school social, and told me he had his sights set on Anya Pederson, and then tried to read me a poem he'd written her. Luckily I had a red pen with me so I could make some helpful suggestions about it, and point him in the direction of resources where he could expand his woefully limited vocabulary and brush up on iambic pentameter.

I frowned and flipped through the pages of the yearbook. Jack Horwicz had been my thirty-seventh interview. I only had one possible candidate for love-shyness so far, but then I was only halfway through the Year Ten boys. There were still heaps of opportunities to find PEZZimist. It didn't have to be Shaun Davies. I wondered absently why the idea of it being him bothered me so much. Was it because I knew that, if it *was* him and I had to save him there wasn't much I could do? He was short and unfortunate-looking and had terrible posture and absolutely no charm or personality. I *knew* PEZZimist had more in him than that. He was an ugly duckling, just *waiting* for me to help him transform into a swan.

I opened Firefox and a new post from PEZZimist appeared in front of me.

15:18

Some mornings I wake up and I know that getting out of bed is just going to make it all worse. I'm so tired. This morning I told my mother that I wasn't going to school. She wasn't happy, but she couldn't force me. I stayed in my room all day, because I knew she was in the house and I didn't want to talk to her. I waited until she'd gone out before I went to the toilet. Then I watched TV before going back to bed. She's back now. I can hear her in the kitchen. She makes me sick. Maybe if she'd ever done anything to help me meet a girl then I wouldn't have to hide here at home, pretending that the girl is here with me, winding her hair around her finger and smiling, her eyes dancing. We could just lie here together, on my bed. Just touching a little bit, nothing crude. Just being together. Me and her. Safe from the world.

Instead I'll just lie here all day, staring out the window at our back garden, which I hate. My mother had an astroturf lawn installed a few years ago, so she'd only have to look after the front garden – after all, that's the one other people can see. The backyard is just a big square of ugly green plastic, utterly devoid of life. A fake garden to go with our fake lives. One day I'm going to have the most beautiful living garden, full of secret green places.

He hadn't gone to school. He hadn't been in his French class.

PEZZimist wasn't Shaun Davies. Thank *goodness*.

I read PEZZimist's post three more times. He obviously didn't have a great relationship with his mother, but why not? Was she cruel and unloving? Or maybe it was him. Maybe he shut her out and she was hurt. And what about his father? Were his parents still together? Did he have any siblings?

Maybe if she'd ever done anything to help me meet a girl then I wouldn't have to hide here at home.

What kind of teenager actually *wants* their parents to intervene in their love-lives? Was he really so desperate that he wanted his mum to set him up with a girl? And he went to our school! Our school, which contained nearly five hundred totally eligible girls. *Finding* girls clearly wasn't his problem. *Talking* to them was. And I couldn't see how having your *mother* hovering over your shoulder would help with that particular situation. It was all starting to feel very Norman-Bates-in-*Psycho*, so I shut down my laptop and went into the living room.

Dad and Josh were sitting at the dining table, drinking gin and tonic and bending over a large jigsaw puzzle. The picture on the box was a science-fictiony sort of thing: a bronzed man wearing a *very* short toga and sandals, face to face with a unicorn, with the Death Star in the background, all surrounded by pink hazy clouds. It was seriously the ugliest image in existence.

'Is everything okay?' I asked, frowning at the picture over Dad's shoulder.

Dad looked up and gave me a hug. 'Isn't it fabulous?' he said, gazing back at the puzzle as if it were a work of art.

'It is many things,' I replied. 'But fabulous is definitely not one of them. It's hideous.'

'That's the point,' explained Josh. 'We've decided to try and find the ugliest jigsaw in the world. It's going to be like a quest.'

I raised my eyebrows. Perhaps Josh *was* a bad influence on Dad. 'I think the quest is over. Also...why?'

'Something to do on a Friday night.'

'We're inventing a scoring system,' said Dad. 'Puppies, kittens or any sort of baby animal scores five points. If the baby animal is in a bucket or flowerpot, or wearing a hat – that's an extra ten points. Windmills and bicycles are worth fifteen points, and little girls with oversized heads get twenty. A unicorn is the holy grail of ugly-puzzledom, worth a full thirty points.'

I shook my head. 'I still don't get it. You're doing a jigsaw. On a Friday night. For *fun*.'

Dad and I used to play Scrabble on Friday nights. But Josh can't spell, so we stopped.

'Do you want to help?'

'Isn't there some kind of *nightclub* or something you can go to?' I asked. 'Don't you want to engage in any kind of morally dysfunctional, risk-taking behaviour?'

'Not really,' said Dad. 'Why, is this setting a bad example for you?'

I looked back at the jigsaw. The man's toga really was *very* short.

'We ordered pizza,' said Dad, leaning away from the jigsaw to give me another squeeze around the shoulders.

'The really spicy Mexican one?'

'With extra jalapenos.'

I poured myself an orange juice and clicked a few pieces of pink cloud into place before I realised what I was doing.

'Do you have any plans for the weekend?' Dad asked.

'Any hot dates?' added Josh with a grin.

I put down the piece of Death Star that was in my hand. Josh was nice, but I didn't like it when he joked around as if he were part of the family.

'No.'

'It's a tragic thing,' said Josh, 'to see such a pretty girl stay home on a Friday night.'

I scowled at him. 'Says the man doing a jigsaw puzzle.'

'Touché.' Josh sipped his gin and tonic. 'But seriously, Penny. The boys must be falling over themselves to ask you out.'

I picked up another puzzle piece, half pink cloud, half unicorn tail. The truth was, no one had ever asked me out. Not that I *wanted* to date any of the boys at my school – especially not after having spent the week *talking* to them. Going on a date with a boy was absolutely the most boring thing I could imagine. If they weren't crying about how their girlfriend had dumped them, or trying to smell my hair, they'd be talking about cars or football, or making fart-noises under their arms.

And the whole idea of *dating* was so antiquated anyway. Who went on *dates* anymore? As far as I could tell, teenagers nowadays just got drunk at parties and hooked up with whoever was closest. And I certainly wasn't doing *that*, not with the current epidemic of infectious mononucleosis sweeping our school. Ew.

Still. It would be nice to be asked occasionally.

'There's no rush, is there, sweetheart?' said Dad. 'You've got all the time in the world.'

The doorbell rang and he fished his wallet out of his pocket.

Dad was right. I did have all the time in the world. And there were much more important things to focus on now, such as my love-shyness story. And pizza.

By Wednesday evening, I'd been searching for PEZZimist for a week and a half. My yearbook was covered in pink highlighter, with the occasional hopeful splodge of green crossed out later.

I'd been to Maths Club, Chess Group, the Beekeeping Society, the Biodiversity League, the Code-breaking Circle, Art Club, Drama Club, the School Choir, Madrigal and Barbershop Quartet; the Swing Band, Orchestra, the Christian Circle, Economics Society, Fencing Ring, Foreign Film Society, History Club, Jewish Union, Medical Ethics Society, Philosophy Alliance, the Gay–Straight Alliance, Photography Club, Stage Crew, Swim Team, Table Tennis League and the Ultimate Frisbee Society.

I was exhausted.

And I had no suspects. There were two or three green highlighters, but they were total long shots. And not a speck of yellow.

I'd even gone back to Ms Leroy's French class – or at least I'd tried to. Ms Leroy had frowned at me and shut the door in my face. I'd had a glance around, though, and couldn't see anyone I hadn't already crossed off my yearbook list. Maybe PEZZimist didn't take French at all. Maybe whoever I'd spooked in the library had just been curious. Maybe he (or she!) had a friend who was love-shy. Or a sibling?

What if he was lying about his age? If he wasn't in my year level... there were approximately five hundred boys at my school who I *hadn't* interviewed. Five hundred and fifty stinky, scratching, grunting boys. And I didn't know most of the other year levels. I mean, I knew the Year Elevens and Twelves, but who knew anything about Year Sevens? Surely they were too young to be love-shy.

I sighed and opened the yearbook again. I must have missed someone. Or maybe PEZZimist was just an accomplished liar. Maybe he had fooled me.

No. My journalistic instinct was better than that. I *know* I would have recognised him if we'd spoken face to face.

'Penny?' It was Dad, with the phone in his hand. 'It's your mother.'

I felt something bunch up inside me. 'Tell her I'm busy.'

Dad raised his eyebrows. 'But you're not busy.'

'Tell her I'm not in.'

'But you *are* in.' He put on his most serious face. 'Penny. You can't lie to your mother.'

I wanted to say *Why not? You did. For fifteen years.* But that wouldn't be fair. Dad tossed the phone to me and I glowered at him. He gave me a sad sort of smile and headed back into the living room. I looked at the phone. Stupid phone. I sighed and picked it up.

'Hello?'

'Hi, sweetheart.'

'Hi.'

'How are you?'

'Fine. Good. Great.'

I hated talking to my mother. I hated the way she always tried to sound bright and chirpy, as if everything were wonderful. I hated the way she made it sound as if she *had* to move to Perth for work. I hated the way she sounded as if she didn't have a choice, that there was no way she could have possibly stayed in the same city as us.

And I hated the way she never asked about Dad.

It wasn't like he *chose* to be gay. What would she rather, that he'd just kept it a secret? And been miserable for the rest of his life?

I'd always thought she was open-minded. She had a climate-change bumper sticker and listened to ABC radio. She bought recycled toilet paper and worried about the state of public education. I never would have imagined she was homophobic.

Dad said that she was just upset. That she had every right to be angry with him. That it was understandable that she needed space. But it'd been two years. She wouldn't speak to him, except to ask for me when he answered the phone. She wouldn't come here to see me – I'd have to go to Perth. That song on Dad's Sting album said if you loved somebody, you should set them free. I never understood that when I was little – why would you dump someone if you loved them? But now I thought I got it. Surely if Mum loved Dad, she'd want him to be happy?

'So I thought maybe you could come and visit me during these school holidays,' said Mum.

Fat chance.

'Penny?'

I closed my eyes. 'Maybe,' I said. 'It depends on what's happening with the paper. And my swimming. I can't miss any training sessions. I'll get out of shape.'

'We have swimming pools here, you know,' said my mother, jokingly. 'And an *ocean* as well. Very nice for swimming.'

I scowled at the phone. 'I'll talk to Dad about it.' I knew that would shut her up.

Her voice went wobbly as I said goodbye, just like it always did.

I felt tears pricking my eyes as I put the phone down on my desk, which just made me more irritated. How dare she emotionally manipulate me?

The yearbook stared at me, screaming my failure in great fluorescent slashes of pink highlighter. I shoved it into a drawer and turned off my computer.

Dad was hovering in the kitchen, waiting for me to return the phone to its cradle.

'How is she?'

'Fine.'

I examined the contents of the fridge. Leftover Chinese food, a shrivelled avocado, half a watermelon, some yoghurt. We were totally overdue ordering groceries.

'And...?'

I found some marinated olives up the back and ate one straight from the jar, licking the oil from my fingers. Dad continued to look expectant. I spat the pit into the bin.

'I don't know, Dad. The usual. Everything's fantastic. She loves the climate in Perth so much. She's really busy at work. Who cares?'

'I care.'

I ate another olive. 'I don't know *why*. She doesn't seem to care at all about *you*. She certainly never *asks* about you. I don't understand where she gets off on being so wounded and hurt and moral-high-groundy when she doesn't seem to miss you at all!'

Dad leaned on the breakfast counter. 'Well, I miss her.'

'Why?'

He shrugged. 'She was my best friend for fifteen years, Penny. Just because I don't want to be married to her any-more doesn't mean I don't still care about her.'

'So don't you think she should feel the same way about you?'

Dad shook his head. 'She's allowed to be upset. I betrayed her.'

'It's not like you *cheated* on her,' I said, putting the olives back and closing the fridge door with a little more force than was necessary. 'You didn't meet Josh until over a year after Mum left. And it wasn't like you *knew* you were gay when you married her.'

'It's complicated, Pen,' said Dad. 'And I understand that she needs time. I wish you'd cut her a little more slack.'

'Well, I wish she'd cut *you* a little more slack.'

'Just promise me you'll give her a chance, okay?'

I stuck my tongue out at him and flopped onto the couch. The chances of there being something acceptable on

72

television were slim, but right then I'd have watched just about anything in order to escape that conversation, and the book filled with pink highlighter in my room.

I went to bed without checking PEZZimist's blog. I was giving up. No, not *giving up*. I was *freeing up my time to pursue different goals*. Yes. That was better. I hadn't *failed*. Who wanted to read about some loser who couldn't get a girl anyway?

I read a few chapters of *Catcher in the Rye* for English. Who needed stupid old PEZZimist? There were other stories out there. Surely Nellie Bly started plenty of stories she didn't finish because it turned out they were boring.

I switched off the light, but I couldn't sleep. Dad had gone to bed and the apartment felt very quiet.

For some reason – probably because of Mum's phone call and that stupid conversation with Dad afterwards – I was reminded of the first few nights after Mum left. Dad had just wandered around the house staring at strange things like the orange lampshade on my bedside table, a half-empty packet of basmati rice and the floral-covered ironing board. He'd looked as though he'd finished a marathon and didn't know whether to laugh with relief, or collapse in a heap because it was over. I think most of the time he'd come down on the side of collapsing.

The only problem with living in the city was that it was never truly dark. The wooden venetians blocked out a lot of the city light, but my room was always illuminated with an artificial orange glow, no matter how late it was.

I turned onto my side. The sleep light on my laptop was pulsing on and off. Had PEZZIMIST posted anything new? How was he feeling? Had he managed to talk to the brown-haired girl?

I wasn't going to check. I was abandoning that story. It was never going to go anywhere.

But what if he'd said something that would help me figure it out? The missing piece of the puzzle?

He was still out there. Still full of loneliness and suffering. He needed me.

I rolled out of bed and woke my laptop.

23:02

Today was bad. I was nervous and jittery all day, like I'd drunk too much coffee.

The only time I felt calm was at lunch, when I could watch my girl.

She sat in her usual place with her usual group of friends.

They were all looking at something on a mobile phone,

passing it around and laughing. I hate mobile phones. The telephone's the most stupid invention ever. I hate the way you can't see the face of the person you're talking to, so you have no clue whether they're making fun of you, or listening at all. It's hard enough talking to people in person. Although I suppose text messages might be okay. I like writing things down. I think I could say more in a text message to my girl than I could to her face. But I never will, because I don't have her number. Or a mobile phone. Maybe I could email something to her school email address. But then what if she laughed at me?

I can't remember the last time I laughed.

He really was a massive drama queen. I was just about to re-read it to see if it could really be as soppy as my initial impression, when I noticed a little green *online* spot next to PEZZimist's name. He was online. He was there, in his own bedroom, sitting in front of his own computer, looking at the very same page on the very same website that I was.

Without realising I was doing it, I brought my cursor up to his name and clicked. A window popped open: *private chat between GUEST and PEZZimist*.

I could just *ask* him, right now, and get an answer to the whole thing. I placed my hands on the keyboard and noticed they were trembling. I swallowed.

GUEST: hello?

GUEST: are you there?

GUEST: i need to talk to you. i think i can help.

GUEST: please.

I waited. There was no reply. Maybe he was typing out an essay-length response. Or maybe he'd gone to the toilet. Or maybe he was too shy to say anything at all.

But then the little green spot disappeared. I'd scared him away.

I climbed back into bed, my mind full of mysteries and hidden faces.

5

On Friday, I forgot the name of Othello's wife in English, didn't hear anything Ms Wilding said in Biology about the Linnean system of binomial nomenclature, argued with Hugh Forward about the price of helium balloons for the social *and* bombed my Maths quiz (I was facing a *B*, a letter I was totally unfamiliar with). It was a total write-off of a day. Of a week, really. Stupid PEZZimist.

The only good part of the day was lunchtime swimming practice, where I beat my personal freestyle record. But my good mood was short-lived – I spent too long in the pool and didn't have time for a shower before class.

When the bell rang at the end of a somewhat chlorine-scented final period, I inwardly groaned with relief for probably the first time in my life. I felt as if I were in one of those '80s High-School-Sucks teen films and would spill out the front door in a wild joyful rush with the rest of the student body.

Instead I traipsed to the train station.

It was one of those afternoons that seemed warm and sunny, but where the wind was so icy it chilled your bones. I shuffled from foot to foot on the platform and wished I'd worn a thicker jumper. A voice sounded over the PA, announcing that city-bound trains were delayed approximately fifteen minutes, due to a fallen tree on the tracks. This was hardly a promising way to begin my weekend.

I trudged up the platform against the wind, and queued at the coffee cart, hoping that the warmth of the cup on my hands and the liquid in my mouth would override the disappointment of what I was sure would be a decidedly average cup of coffee. The guy in front of me ordered a skinny mochacino with whipped cream and extra chocolate sprinkles, and I wanted to smack him in the head. Had he no sense of culture?

The coffee-cart woman handed his coffee to him with a sneer (you know you've ordered the wrong thing when you get attitude from someone wearing a magenta-and-lime floral apron), and as he turned away I felt a jolt of recognition. I watched him shuffle away.

'Yes, love?' Floral Apron was staring at me in a bored sort of way.

'Flat white, please,' I said, still watching the guy. 'Extra strong.'

He went to my school. He was short and pudgy, with metal-rimmed glasses that kept slipping down his nose. He was wearing grey slacks (slacks!) and a white collared shirt with a black knitted vest. I remembered Shaun Davies' horrible brown jumper, and considered starting a new internet meme called Hipster or Geek. This boy was definitely Geek. He had rather dirty earbuds in, and was clutching a thick fantasy novel in one hand and his disgusting creamy sugary beverage in the other. His face looked as if it had been cobbled together from leftover bits – he had heavy eyebrows and a wide jaw, but a small, freckled nose and quite feminine blue eyes. His cheeks were mottled red from the cold wind, and he bobbed his head up and down a little to his music, which made him resemble one of those bobblehead dolls.

Why hadn't I interviewed him? I studied the guy more carefully and realised he was in the year above me. But he did look very young. Maybe he skipped a year.

It was a long shot. It probably wouldn't lead anywhere.

But what was the harm? It wasn't as if I was going anywhere in the next ten minutes. It'd take my mind off the sour, watery burnt-milk taste that this *alleged* coffee beverage was coating my tastebuds with.

SUBJECT UNKNOWN

Eye contact: None.

Overt signs of love-shyness: LOTS.

ME: Hey, um, excuse me?

HIM: (NO RESPONSE)

ME: Hey! There's a couple of things I want to ask you.

(SUBJECT REMOVES EARBUDS WITH A DEGREE OF TREPIDATION.)

ME: Thanks. Hi, I'm Penny. I go to East Glendale too. You're in Year Eleven, right?

HIM: (NODS. FROWNS.)

ME: What's your name?

HIM: (MUMBLES)

ME: Speak up.

HIM: Hamish Berry. What do you want?

ME: Hamish, do you have a girlfriend?

(SUBJECT SHAKES HEAD AND GOES A FUNNY COLOUR.)

ME: Have you ever kissed a girl?

HAMISH: Screw you.

(SUBJECT RETREATS TO THE OTHER END OF THE PLATFORM.)

ME: Wait! I wasn't finished.

(INTERVIEWER CATCHES UP.)

ME: Do you feel uncomfortable talking to girls?

HAMISH: (VEHEMENT) I'm not *gay*, you know.

ME: I never thought you were. I think you're shy.

HAMISH: Get lost.

ME: *Love-shy.*

HAMISH: (FREEZES)

ME: You are, aren't you? You're love-shy. I know all about your condition. I want to help you.

(SUBJECT'S FACE GOES ALL CRINKLY.)

Verdict: LIKELY LOVE-SHY.

I'd found him.

'Just leave me alone, okay?' He still wasn't making eye contact.

'I'm afraid I can't do that.'

I made a mental list of things I'd need to fix about him. Some elocution lessons, to start with, because he had a slight lisp and his diction was dreadful. A haircut. Facial wash to clear up his skin. New clothes. I'd be the Henry Higgins to his Eliza Doolittle. Except for the part where they fall in love.

Hamish's eyes darted around, searching for someone to rescue him. I seriously doubted he'd have a Kate Pittman to come and maul him like Nedislav had. Hamish clearly realised this too, because his face fell.

'What do you *want*?'

'I want to help you. I want to *fix* you.'

'I'm not broken!'

'Oh,' I said, 'I think you are. You totally fit the profile. I can tell you so much about yourself.'

'Go on, then.'

I'd been reading about love-shyness for two weeks now, and was close to being an expert.

'You listen to classical music and old school Broadway showtunes. You prefer citrus fruits to other kinds. You like sweet things. You like romantic films, but not romantic *comedies*. You're spiritual, but not religious. You have a weird relationship with your mother. You don't have any sisters. You've never felt comfortable around other boys. You hate sport. You want a girlfriend with long brown hair and a pretty face. You're probably allergic to milk or wool.'

Hamish was shaking his head as though I were crazy.

'Tell me I'm wrong,' I said.

'You're wrong.' He pulled his iPod out of his pocket and showed me the song he'd been listening to: 'Hurt', by Nine Inch Nails. 'I don't like fruit at all. I like science-fiction films. I'm an atheist. My mother is fine, and I have three sisters.'

I took a half-step back. How could that be? He didn't fit the profile *at all*. 'What about the rest?'

'So I don't have a girlfriend and I can't catch a ball,' he said. 'Big deal. It makes me a loser, not a *psycho*. And what the hell does having a milk allergy have to do with it?'

'*Do* you have a milk allergy?'

'No! I'm not allergic to anything, apart from weird bossy girls who ask intensely personal questions. What is *wrong* with you?'

This wasn't going at all the way I'd planned. 'But you visit loveshyforum.com, right?'

Hamish looked around to make sure no one else was listening. 'Once or twice,' he said through clenched teeth. 'But I'm not *like* them. I just want to meet a nice girl, that's all. I'm not a *freak*.'

'But you post on there all the time.'

'I've never posted anything on loveshyforum.com.'

'But I've *read* it!' Why was he still lying to me? 'You're PEZZimist!'

Hamish froze for a moment, his face as shocked as if I'd said he was Superman. Then he began to laugh.

'What?'

'I'm not PEZZimist,' he said. 'No way. I *wish*.'

What? There was *another* student on loveshyforum.com? Was it possible?

'What do you mean, *you wish*? Do you know who he is?'

Hamish looked a little more confident, now he knew something that I didn't. 'Yeah,' he said. 'I know who he is. But why should I tell you? You'll just go and pester him like you're pestering me.'

'I'm not *pestering* you,' I said. 'I'm *researching*. I want to write a piece on love-shyness. I want to *help* PEZZimist and document the whole process. It'll be huge! It'll bring the whole condition out into the open, get love-shys the support you need.'

'*They* need,' said Hamish. 'I'm not one of them.'

'Then why did you go to the website?'

'I told you, I want to meet girls. I thought someone on there might have some advice.'

'And did they?'

'No. They're all a bunch of self-obsessed psychos. It makes me feel better though, knowing I'm not as crazy as them. I'm just ordinary shy.'

He didn't seem shy to me. I was finding him quite rude and obstructive.

'Tell me who PEZZimist is,' I said.

'Why did you think he was me?' asked Hamish, ignoring my question.

I told him about the yearbook and the coloured high-lighters, and how I'd run out of Year Tens. He started to

84

laugh again. I noticed he still hadn't managed to look me in the eye. He might not think he had a problem, but he clearly needed help.

'How do you know who he is?' I asked.

Hamish shrugged. 'When you're as much of a loser as I am, you spend a lot of time watching other guys for clues on how to be less lame. It wasn't that hard to figure it out.'

'Tell me who he *is*!' I said. 'Or else I'll never leave you alone.'

Hamish seemed genuinely frightened by that, but he shook his head. 'Look,' he said. 'All I can tell you is...the yearbook was a good idea, but it's a bit out of date.'

Out of date? What did that even *mean*? While I was puzzling over it, Hamish's train pulled up and he took his opportunity to escape.

My train arrived on the opposite platform, and I got on, still confused.

The yearbook was a good idea, but it's a bit out of date.

It was last year's yearbook. There wasn't a more recent one. This year's wouldn't come out until December.

Hamish had said something else, too, when I'd said he was PEZZimist.

No way. I wish.

But he'd spent the rest of our conversation (interrogation, I suppose I should call it) saying how much he despised the

85

love-shys, because they were all freaks and psychos. So why would he *wish* he were PEZZimist?

Something was niggling at the back of my brain, but I couldn't quite snag it.

It's a bit out of date.

Maybe I'd give up on PEZZimist. Hamish clearly had plenty of problems. I could focus on him.

But it was PEZZimist who'd got me into this whole thing, and I wouldn't be satisfied until I'd solved the mystery.

When I arrived home, I threw my swimming towel into the washing machine and rinsed out my bathers.

I heard Dad's key in the front door. 'Penny? Are you home? Josh found us the best jigsaw ever. It's a chimpanzee. Wearing a baseball cap. Riding a bicycle. Can you imagine anything more perfect?'

Josh followed him into the living room. 'Only if there'd been a cricket sitting on the baseball cap, waving a tiny flag. Are you going to help, Penny? Your dad ordered quesadillas.'

I shook my head. 'I've got homework.'

I went to my room, but could still hear Josh and Dad talking as they clicked puzzle pieces into place. Dad was in a good mood, which meant an airing of his seemingly end-less collection of dreadful plumber jokes.

'Did you hear,' I heard him say, 'that someone broke into the local police station and stole all the toilets? Now the cops have nothing to go on.'

'That's terrible.' Josh's voice was muffled, as if he had his head in his hands.

'You know a good flush beats a full house every time.'

'Stop!' groaned Josh. 'Please! I'm dying. My brains are leaking out my ears. Quick, pass me a napkin so I can catch my occipital lobe.'

There was a tap at the door.

'That's weird,' said Dad. 'I didn't hear the buzzer. I wonder if someone let him in downstairs.'

'Who *cares*,' said Josh. 'I have never been so thankful to hear the courteous and melodious knock of the quesadilla man. Plumber! Fetch me my guacamole!'

I heard Dad open the door, and distant voices.

'Penny,' he yelled. 'Someone to see you.'

I felt a flicker of excitement. Was it Hamish? Had he had a crisis of conscience and come to tell me who PEZZimist was?

It was Rin. She stood shyly in the doorway, smiling at her shoes. Of course it wasn't Hamish. He wouldn't know where I lived. Nobody knew where I lived. Except Rin.

'Hi,' I said. 'Is everything okay?'

'Oh,' said Rin. 'Yeah, everything's fine! I just wanted to

give you this.' She proffered a red box of Pocky. 'I know you liked it the other day at lunch.'

'Thanks,' I said, taking the Pocky. Rin flashed her shy grin. We stood there awkwardly for a moment.

'Penny?' called Dad. 'Is your friend coming in?'

'Um,' I said. 'Do you want to come in?'

Rin beamed as if I'd offered her a million dollars, and ducked her head in a nod. I led her into the living room.

'This is my dad, Allen, and his boyfriend, Josh.'

I quite liked introducing Josh as Dad's boyfriend and seeing how people reacted. Rin didn't bat an eyelid. She gave a little bow.

'I'm very pleased to meet you,' she said. 'My name is Rin Tamaki. I live in the apartment next door.'

I poured Rin a glass of lemonade. Dad examined the Pocky box with interest, and Josh had to take it away to stop him sampling one.

'Not until after dinner,' he said, sternly.

Dad stuck his tongue out at Josh.

'So, Rin, are you going to help us with our jigsaw?' asked Josh. 'This one is a real find, worth forty points.'

'I don't think Rin wants to join in your lame Friday-night debauchery,' I said.

Rin approached the table, and Josh explained the ugly puzzle scoring system. She giggled and snapped a piece of chimpanzee backpack into place. I felt a prickle of annoyance. Now I was going to have to join in on this jigsaw nonsense as well, to be polite. I thought longingly back to the days when it was just me and Dad and the Scrabble board.

'Tamaki,' said Dad. 'Is that Japanese?'

Rin nodded. 'My parents moved here in the '80s.'

'I've never been to Japan,' said Dad. 'I'd love to, though.'

'I've never been there either,' said Rin.

'I have,' said Josh. 'I went on a school exchange in Year Ten. It was awesome. Best food I ever had.'

Rin beamed.

The buzzer rang, and this time it was dinner.

'Have you eaten, Rin?' asked Dad. 'We ordered plenty.'

'Oh, no,' said Rin. 'I couldn't. I can't just turn up to your house and eat your food. I wasn't even invited.' She glanced at me.

'No,' I said. 'You should stay. We're going to watch *Back to the Future* later.'

'And eat Pocky,' said Dad, eyeing the red box.

So Rin stayed. I couldn't remember the last time I'd had a friend over. I generally only socialised in groups – at parties and other organised events. I didn't really *hang out* with anyone. Too much one-on-one small talk made me uncomfortable, and anyway, I was always busy with SRC and the paper and swimming and debating.

I was surprised to learn that it was actually kind of fun. Even the puzzle.

Rin didn't seem embarrassed by Dad and Josh's daggy Friday night antics, and she was pleasantly surprised with her quesadilla. Dad nearly cried when she said she'd never had Mexican food before (except for nachos, which doesn't count). She tried to eat it with her usual precise neatness, but quickly learned that it was physically impossible to eat a quesadilla without ending up with salsa and sour cream all over your face. She dabbed at her chin with a serviette, giggling.

We finished the puzzle in record time, largely due to Rin's wholehearted support for my sorting-into-types jigsaw strategy (separate out the corners, then edges, then all the pieces of backpack, all the pieces of chimp fur, all the pieces of blue background, and so on). Dad and Josh were more ad hoc, randomly pulling pieces and trying to see where they might fit. Very inefficient.

But Rin and I made a great team. I liked working with her. We chatted about school, and teachers, and Rin told me about how one of her friends had pretended to faint in Ms Leroy's French class in the hope that Nick Rammage might catch her and ask her to the social, but that he'd been staring out the window, totally absorbed in his music.

Rin even stayed for the movie, which she'd never seen. She laughed at all the right moments and applauded Josh's

Michael J Fox impression, and I chewed on my Pocky and decided that George McFly was *totally* love-shy.

After the movie, Rin thanked Dad for dinner, and I walked her to the door. She paused shyly.

'Penny?'

'Yeah?'

'I'm glad we're friends. I'm so glad I moved here.'

22:57

I had the most vivid dream last night. I was at this church camp, the one my parents sent me to when I was eleven, except I was sixteen and all the other kids were still eleven. The camp director explained that I hadn't done it right the first time, and I was going to have to stay at the camp until I could learn to behave like a real boy. He handed me a football and took me to the edge of the lake, where there was a boating ramp. And he pushed me off the ramp into the cold water.

It was so cold, the coldest water I've ever felt. I sank down, down, lower and lower. I couldn't move my arms or legs to swim to the surface. I just kept sinking, for what felt like hours. Then at the bottom of the lake there were all these girls, with long floaty hair and eyes the colour of the sea. They swam around me, gently tangling me up with seaweed.

And I laughed and laughed, because they were so beautiful,
and I felt so happy.

I sat there, staring at the screen until my eyes hurt. Who *was* he? With a sigh, I switched off my computer and went to bed.

I woke up at three in the morning, with Rin's voice in my head.

I'm so glad I moved here.

I was a total and complete idiot. Of *course* the yearbook was out of date. I'd crossed off the boys who had *left* East Glendale at the end of last year. But I hadn't taken into consideration the *new* boys who had only arrived this year.

Well, new *boy*, actually. There was only one. The one who stared out the window in Ms Leroy's French class as girls pretended to faint in order to catch his eye.

Nick Rammage.

> *I was too impatient to work at the usual duties assigned women on newspapers.*
>
> NELLIE BLY

6

Nick rammage?

Really?

Nick Rammage, the boy who was too cool to speak to anyone? Nick Rammage, who dressed like an indie model and wore oversized headphones all day long? Nick Rammage, who every girl at East Glendale had a planet-sized crush on?

Maybe there was another new guy in Year Ten. Surely.

Although now I thought about it, Nick didn't seem to have any real *friends*. I couldn't remember actually speaking to him. In fact, I couldn't remember him speaking at all.

I'd never seen him hanging out with anyone at recess or lunchtime; it was as though he just disappeared. I was pretty sure he didn't play any sports.

I'd made one of the worst mistakes a journalist can make. I'd listened to those rumours about him kissing Olivia

Fischer, and the mysterious girlfriend at another school, and believed them. I hadn't verified my sources. Nellie Bly would be disgusted with me.

After I got over my initial disbelief, it started to make sense. He *looked* cool, sure. But it was all an elaborate smokescreen. That was how he got away with it. With his oversized headphones and floppy emo hair and tight black jeans, everyone just *assumed* he was aloof and cool. It was an utterly brilliant disguise.

Except surely it could unravel at any moment. What did he do when those simpering blonde girls approached him? He was one of the most desirable boys at school...why wasn't there a cluster of girls around him at all times? And if he did talk to them, and they realised how *strange* he was (because he must be strange if he was love-shy), how come they didn't immediately run and tell everyone about it?

It was such a puzzle.

Also, why had he left his old school? Had something happened? Or was it just a moving-house thing?

I'd be careful, this time. I didn't want to spook my subject. I'd watch him closely first. Get to know him better before I confronted him. Although I felt as if I knew him well already, from reading his blog posts.

This was so much more than an exercise in journalism. Reading PEZZimist's – Nick's – posts had me convinced that he needed help, and that I was the one to help him. He was obviously a smart, sensitive guy, and all he wanted was to be loved. It seemed so unfair that he couldn't have that. Especially since his *looks* certainly weren't a barrier.

Nick Rammage. I still couldn't quite believe it.

The weekend seemed to go on forever, yet I didn't achieve anything. I went over every single post PEZZimist had ever written, reading each word in a new light now I knew his true identity. I spent hours staring at my Biology textbook, or at a blank Word document that was supposed to become my *Othello* essay for English. Dad tried to get me to go out with him and Josh to see a new exhibition at the National Gallery, but I declined. Instead I did laps in the pool until I nearly passed out, the rushing of water in my ears and across my face reminding me of PEZZimist's dream about the bottom of the lake.

What was wrong with me? Should a journalist become this involved in a story? Was I staying objective? Not that subjectivity was strictly forbidden in journalism. Tom Wolfe and Truman Capote and Hunter S Thompson and the other gonzo reporters and New Journalism people got involved in their stories all the time – and mine didn't involve motorcycles, rubbing alcohol or nineteen different kinds of illegal drug. No, this was good. The deeper I got into this story, the better it would be, I was sure of it. I didn't want to write a dispassionate, clinical analysis of love-shyness. I wanted to write a feature article that would make people laugh, cry and award me a Pulitzer Prize.

Monday morning found me staring at my wardrobe, agonising over an outfit. What did you wear when you were secretly observing a very shy person? I didn't want to stand out. Not that I ever did stand out – I was strictly a jeans-and-T-shirt kind of girl – but I felt that this morning's sartorial choices required an extra level of consideration. And there was always the chance that Nick would notice me watching, and that I'd have to bring all my plans forward and interview him then and there. I didn't want to be wearing anything that would spook or intimidate him. I needed to appear friendly and approachable, but not *desirable*, because that would make him anxious.

What was I doing? Fussing over what to *wear*? I was acting as if I were a typical hairspray-and-eyeliner girl, and I didn't like it one bit. I needed to pull myself together and be professional. I threw on my usual: a comfortable pair of jeans, plainish T-shirt, and sensible sneakers. There. That'd do.

I grabbed my notebook and left the house.

Observations on Nick Rammage, aka PEZZimist.

Monday, 8:36 a.m.

Subject arrives at his locker. He's wearing
fitted black jeans, a black T-shirt with white,
weathered lettering on it, his ubiquitous large
headphones, black Converse sneakers and a
chunky black watch. He carries a black backpack.
Subject doesn't make eye contact with other
students in his vicinity. He keeps his head down,
with his long fringe hanging in his eyes. However,
his casual gait and slouched posture make him
seem aloof to his peers, rather than awkward and
antisocial.

I didn't have English on Mondays, so I couldn't observe
Nick up close in class. I scoured the school grounds for him
during morning recess, but he was nowhere to be found.
How was I supposed to observe and analyse my subject if I
couldn't even *find* him?

I fidgeted through the next two periods, and when the
bell rang for lunchtime I sprang from my seat and sprinted
to the Year Ten lockers, where I spotted Nick pulling his
lunch from his backpack before sauntering outside. I followed at a distance, trying to appear nonchalant. I was
skipping my meeting for the *Gazette* – but I was on official

journalistic business and, despite what Thomas Jefferson said, who really cared whether we led with a story about the school rowing team or an interview with an ex-student who had a minor role in *Neighbours*?

I felt quite the gumshoe, watching Nick, waiting, subtly following him. He ended up on an isolated bench by the science building, overshadowed by a concrete stairwell.

The temperature had risen over the weekend, and it was quite hot in the sun. Being totally aware of the dangers of the sun in regards to *dying of cancer*, something many of the tanorexic girls at my school were not, I situated myself beneath a shady tree and watched Nick from across the courtyard.

1:07 p.m.
Subject is sitting on a bench eating a sandwich. I'm too far away to discern exactly what kind of sandwich, but the bread is certainly white. I hope he knows how high white bread is in processed sugars. He's balanced on the backrest of the bench, with his feet on the seat. His eyes are closed and his head is moving up and down slightly, I assume to the beat of the music pumping through his headphones.

I wondered what he was listening to. Love-shys weren't supposed to like rock music or anything loud or discordant. They liked melodic, romantic music. So the chances that Nick was listening to the kind of music everyone thought he was listening to were pretty slim.

He opened his eyes a crack and scanned the courtyard. I pretended to be absorbed with writing in my notebook. When I looked up, he was staring at someone over to my right. I followed his gaze. Was this her? The long-haired girl?

It was.

She was a Year Nine girl. Her name was Amy Butler, and she was a swimmer, like me. She had long brown hair (of course) and was very pretty in a petite pixie way. Her hair hung loose down her back. She was sitting with a group of other girls of mid-tier popularity, mostly blonde but not in a pouty, peroxide kind of way, more a healthy, sporty, tampon-commercial kind of way. Amy tended to smile in a distant manner, and when the other girls laughed, she would join in a few seconds late. I could see why she seemed like the perfect love-shy fantasy girl. Sweet, quiet, pretty, long brown hair.

The thing was, I knew Amy Butler. We'd spoken a few times at swimming, and last year she'd been in the SRC, so I'd had plenty of meetings with her. And Nick had it all wrong.

Amy wasn't the gentle, romantic girl he was looking for. She was quiet, sure. But that wasn't because she was shy and sensitive. It was because she was kind of *boring*. She wasn't smart, or funny, or rude, or irritating. She had excellent backstroke technique, but that was all I could think of in her favour, apart from the fact that she was pretty. She was sort of... nothing.

The only time I'd ever seen her do anything out of the ordinary was at Aylee Kim's birthday party in January, where she drank too much Tia Maria and was sick in the pool. Nick wouldn't be too keen to hear *that*. Hardly the proper behaviour for the ideal nymph-like fairy creature that he thought she was.

I wanted to help Nick, I really did. But I wasn't sure helping him hook up with his dream girl was going to work. He was too smart for her, too sensitive, too romantic. She'd break his heart in five minutes, and he was so fragile he'd never be able to put all the pieces together again.

I looked back at him. The expression on his face nearly broke my heart. Such yearning and longing and loneliness, painted there for all to see. Then he started and looked straight at me, and his usual mask of detached cool resumed its position.

This was going to be trickier than I'd thought.

Nick's shoulders tensed slightly, and I looked around. A

blonde girl was approaching him, blushing furiously. It was like watching a nature documentary. She glanced back at her friends, who shot her encouraging grins, then turned to Nick, gazing at him longingly.

Nick had seen her, I knew he had. How would he respond? Would he talk to her? *Could* he? I saw him start in a casual sort of way, and reach into his back pocket. He pulled out a mobile phone and pressed it to his ear. I couldn't hear him, as he was too far away, but it looked as if he'd just answered a call.

I thought he didn't like talking on the phone?

Actually, I thought he didn't even *have* a phone?

Nick laughed into the phone and stood up, jumping off the bench in one easy movement. The blonde girl froze, unsure how to proceed. Was she going to wait until he finished his call? Or was she planning on interrupting him and hoping her orange skin and perky breasts would convince him to hang up?

Totally absorbed in his phone conversation, Nick walked straight past the girl, seemingly without noticing her.

Smooth, very smooth. I wondered if that was what he did every time, or whether he had different subterfuge tactics. I'd find out.

22:00

There's this girl who's watching me. That's not new, girls are always watching me. They watch and they smile and they toss their hair. But they don't actually **want** me.

But this girl, this new girl. She's different. She's **sneaky**. She's not watching me like I'm a new dress she wants to try on. Or a piece of meat she wants to sink her teeth into. When this girl watches me it's like she's looking right into me. I don't like it. It's as if she **knows**. She doesn't want **me**, she wants to unpick me. Take me apart and see how I work, like an alarm clock. She wants to know what makes me tick. And I don't want her to know. She **can't know.** But it kind of feels like she already does.

Why is she watching me?

What does she want?

WHY?

I wasn't at all sure how to approach Nick. I didn't want to scare him off – so no Dictaphone app – but I also needed to be firm and direct from the outset. Maybe just doing it would be the best tactic. Like ripping off a bandaid. I decided to wait until lunch on Tuesday, so we'd have time to talk. I popped into my Debating meeting to let everyone know I'd have to skip this week, then headed into the courtyard to where Nick sat on his bench, watching Amy Butler.

He was there, looking bored, as if we were all far, far beneath him and not worthy of his interest or attention. I snuck up from behind so he couldn't bolt.

'Nick.'

The muscles in his shoulders tensed. He reached into his pocket and pulled out his phone.

'Hello?' he said. I'd never heard his voice before. It was higher than I'd expected, but quite melodic. There was a faint tremor behind his carefully affected drawl.

'Wow,' I said. 'I guess I'd better wait until you're off the phone. Luckily I've got all day.'

Nick slid off the bench and started to walk away. 'Yeah, mate,' he said into the phone. 'Uh-huh. Yeah.'

I followed him. 'Unless you're not actually *talking* on that phone, of course.'

Nick veered off in a different direction and picked up his pace. I walked faster so I drew up alongside him. I could see a clump of girls nearby watching with interest. I let us pull away from them so nobody could hear us talking, and then I reached out and grabbed Nick's phone.

Nick froze, his hand clasped to his ear where the phone had been.

I pretended to talk into the phone. 'Hi,' I said. 'Do you

think I could talk to Nick for a minute? It's kind of important. You can call him back later.' I mimed listening, and then turned to Nick.

'He says that's fine, he'll call you back this afternoon,' I said, and examined the phone. 'This thing isn't even *on*. You're not trying very hard. '

Nick didn't move. His hands trembled, and he stared at the ground.

'Look,' I said. 'I don't want to make you uncomfortable. But my name's Penny and I *really* want to write a story on you. An article. About your condition.'

At the word *condition*, a shudder seemed to go through Nick. It was as though it unfroze him, because he clenched his fists and started to walk away, very fast.

'Hey!' I said. 'Your phone.'

Nick didn't slow his pace or turn around. I hurried after him, the phone in my hand.

He headed for the science labs and I noticed the blonde girls giggling at me, another spurned groupie. How ridiculous. I wasn't one of them, pathetically chasing after the cute boy. I was on a *mission*.

I tailed Nick through a maze of portables, and round the corner of the soccer oval towards the Drama Centre.

'Stop,' I said. 'I just want to talk to you.'

He ignored me and I followed him around a corner.

'Penny!' It was Rin. She was alone, sitting at the bottom of the concrete stairwell that led up to the Drama Centre. She sprang to her feet, looking very pleased to see me.

'Um, hi,' I said, pausing awkwardly, craning my neck to see which way Nick had gone.

'What are you doing?' she said. 'Do you want to sit with me?'

This was the problem with having friends. It was all very well for us to hang out and do jigsaws and eat Pocky, but I was *busy* now. I didn't want us to be friends *right now*. But how was I supposed to explain that to Rin?

'Actually,' I said, 'there's somewhere I need to be. I'm really sorry.'

'Where?'

Nick had totally disappeared from view. I'd lost him. 'Huh?'

'Where do you need to be?'

'Oh, um...' I looked wildly around for an excuse.

'It's Nick Rammage, isn't it?'

I stared at her. 'What?'

Rin nodded. 'You looked like you were following him.'

'No,' I said. 'I wasn't—'

'It's okay. Everyone loves Nick Rammage. He's hot. I totally understand.'

I wasn't sure what to say. I couldn't exactly deny that I'd

been chasing him. There was only one thing for it. I swallowed and told myself it was all in the name of journalism. It was like when Nellie Bly pretended to be crazy so she could report on a mental asylum from within. I was going to have to pretend to be crazy too.

'Yeah,' I said. 'I do like him. He's a...' I took a deep breath and tried to sell it, '...hottie.'

'You'd be good together,' Rin said to her shoes. 'Have you spoken to him?'

'I tried to,' I said. 'But he didn't want to talk to me.'

She shook her head. 'I hear he's totally uninterested in high-school girls. Emma Lee told me he's got a girlfriend who's twenty-one and goes to university.'

I found this difficult to believe, so I didn't reply.

'Oh!' said Rin. 'I'm sorry. I didn't mean to hurt your feelings.'

'It's okay,' I said. 'I know I don't have a chance with him anyway.'

Not that I wanted him. And even if I did, my short hair and big boobs meant I was hardly the love-shy ideal.

'Well.' I shifted from one foot to the other. 'I'd better go.'

Rin seemed to grow smaller. 'Okay,' she said, in a tiny voice. She looked as though she was going to cry.

This was ridiculous. I just wanted to leave and find Nick. But he was long gone now. He'd have gone underground, like a rabbit. Probably hiding in the boys' toilets, and nothing short of a Hazchem suit and oxygen tank could make me follow him in there. And Rin seemed sad, and I didn't like the thought that *I* had made her sad. Why was she sitting here alone anyway? Where were her friends?

My watch told me there were only ten minutes until the end of lunch.

'Actually, I might stay for a bit,' I said. 'If that's okay.'

Rin brightened. 'Of course!'

I sat down on the concrete step next to her. 'So how come you're not at the canteen?'

'Cherry's got glandular fever,' she said. 'And Rebecca is at her Economics Society meeting. And Pieng and Stephanie are…a bit hard to talk to at the moment.'

'Why?' I asked absently, running over my confrontation with Nick in my head. What had I done wrong? How could I do it differently next time? More direct? Less direct? Maybe I could write him a letter?

Rin sighed. 'They're kind of *attached* to their boyfriends,' she said. 'At the lips.'

I rolled my eyes. 'Right,' I said. 'Annoying, huh?'

'Yep. It just makes lunchtime awkward and boring.'

'Because you don't want a boyfriend.'

Rin looked at me. 'What?' she said. 'No, I *totally* want a boyfriend. I just don't think I'll ever *have* one.'

'Why not?'

'You know,' said Rin, shrugging. 'I'm not very pretty. And I'm shy. And...well, I like boys with freckles and blue eyes, but I'm Asian.'

'Nonsense,' I said. 'You're *totally* pretty, and there are plenty of non-Asian guys at this school dating Asian girls. What about Heidi Lim and Steven Pappas?'

'Yeah,' said Rin, 'but Heidi acts like a slut.' She giggled and covered her mouth, as if the word had slipped out without her permission.

I frowned. 'So does Steven Pappas,' I said. 'But he never gets judged for it. And anyway, I don't think that makes a difference.'

'At least people notice Heidi. And my parents are strict, so I wouldn't be able to hang out with a boyfriend much outside of school. It's hopeless. Who would ever want to date a mousy timid Asian girl like me?'

I could think of a couple of candidates. One in particular. A twinkling of an idea flared in my brain.

18:15

The stalker-girl tried to talk to me today. It was as if she could read my thoughts. She knew I was faking it on my mobile phone – it doesn't even have a sim card. It was awful. I felt completely naked, and she mocked me and stole my phone. Bitch. I wish they'd all just leave me alone. I can't ever speak to any of them. I'm too shy and anxious and useless. Nothing would ever come out and I'd stand there like a gaping fish while they pointed and laughed. Or worse, something bad might happen again. I've got a good thing going at this school. People leave me alone, mostly. The clothes help. I don't want to have to change schools again.

LEAVE ME ALONE.

I wanted to slap him. He was just so *melodramatic*. Didn't he see how ridiculous and self-indulgent he was being? Couldn't he just snap out of it?

And what did he mean by *something bad might happen again*? Why *had* he left his old school?

I COULDN'T FIND NICK ANYWHERE AT school on Wednesday. I guessed I'd scared him off. I spent the day checking his blog and loveshyforum.com every five minutes to see if he'd posted anything. In the end Ms Tidy took my phone off me, with an apologetic look.

'You can have it back after school.'

Traitor. And after I'd helped her out by pointing out the spelling mistakes in the study notes she'd prepared.

I went home in a bad mood, and was surprised to find Josh sitting at the kitchen bench, frowning over a notepad.

'Oh,' he said, rubbing his head in a tired sort of way. 'Hi, Penny.'

'Where's Dad?'

'He's on his way home,' said Josh. 'We've got tickets to Roller Derby tonight, and he said I should meet him here, so I let myself in. I hope that's okay.'

Dad should have told me he was planning to give Josh a key. That's a big thing. I wondered if Josh had a drawer in Dad's room too. Oh! Was that spare toothbrush in the bathroom cabinet not a spare at all, and actually Josh's? I'd just assumed it was a spare. I'd actually used it once, when I'd already packed mine away for our SRC camp last year. Ew.

'Of course it's okay,' I said, although I wasn't sure it was.

'How was your day?' asked Josh. 'Would you like me to make you a cup of tea or something?'

I shook my head, and realised that Josh and I had never been together without Dad before. 'No thanks. My day was pretty crappy. I'm trying to talk to someone for a story I'm writing. But he doesn't want to talk.'

'Why not?'

I shrugged. 'I don't know. He keeps avoiding me.'

'Maybe he's just shy.'

I snorted. 'Maybe. How was your day?'

'Pretty crappy too,' said Josh.

'Why?'

'Oh.' Josh sighed. 'Just money stuff. You know. Bills. Debt. The usual.'

I frowned. Josh wouldn't...he wouldn't use my dad for his money, would he? A million dreadful scenarios ran through my head, ending with a particularly lurid one where Josh fell in love with a tattooed drug dealer and used his key to get into our flat when we weren't here and sold our TV and Blu-ray player for crack.

'Don't look so worried,' said Josh with a smile. 'I'm fine. It's fine. It's just boring having to go through it all.'

I nodded.

'Hey, Penny? I just wanted to thank you.'

'What for?'

Josh smiled again, and there was a kind of understanding frown that went with it. 'I know it must have been really hard, finding out about your dad. And your mum leaving, and everything. That's a lot of change for anyone to go through. And I know you could have totally resented your dad, and you would have had every right to be mad at him. And you also had every right to hate me. So I'm glad you didn't. Glad you don't. I think we get on well, and it makes me happy, because you're a pretty awesome person. And I know it makes your dad happy too.'

I immediately felt guilty for imagining Josh falling in love with a tattooed drug dealer. Of course Josh loved my dad. You wouldn't do stupid jigsaws with someone on Friday nights unless you loved them. And I'd seen the way they looked at each other, the way when we were watching TV, Josh would reach out and touch Dad's hand, and Dad would smile over at him. That wasn't fake.

'You needn't thank me,' I said. 'I should be thanking *you*

for making Dad happy. You've been really good for him.'

And I meant it. Even though sometimes I missed being able to spend Friday nights with just Dad, I was glad Josh was around.

'I think we're both good for him.'

I grinned. 'Agreed.'

I heard Dad's key in the lock, and Josh winked at me as Dad came in, full of stories of exploding toilets and blocked gutters from his staff meeting that afternoon.

I retreated to my bedroom with a smile still on my face, as Dad and Josh left for Roller Derby. My bad mood had vanished. I *was* a good person. Josh was right. And I *would* get Nick to talk to me.

I was waiting in front of Nick's locker before the first bell went on Thursday, all ready to ambush him. But the moment he came around the corner and saw me there, his face clammed up and he turned and left the building. He'd probably run straight home again. My bad mood returned, descending like a thundercloud.

This was too *hard*. How was I ever going to get him to talk to me?

I slumped against his locker and slid down it until I was sitting on the floor. There were plenty of people around, putting bags in lockers, pulling out books, and avoiding going to class assembly. Jack Horwicz walked down the corridor holding hands with Anya Pederson, looking as though he might burst with joy. Clearly his poem had done the trick, almost certainly due to my notes. James O'Keefe and Caitlin Reece emerged from the photography lab looking rumpled. Clayton Bell marched past, his arms full of rainbow-coloured bunting for the Gay–Straight Alliance Lamington Drive. I'd spoken to all of these boys without a problem. What did I have to do to get Nick to open up? All my journalistic tactics were useless if I couldn't get him to speak to me at all.

There had to be a way.

'You're looking rather *PEZZimistic*.'

It was Hamish. I was surprised *he* was speaking to me at all.

'I'm having a bad day,' I said.

'I'm having a bad life,' he replied. 'Wanna swap?'

I looked up at him. He wasn't love-shy at all. He was just a dork. But maybe he could help me get to Nick. And he might also be able to help me with my plans regarding Rin.

'Can I buy you a coffee?' I said. 'Or whatever concoction of cream and sugar you would like to pretend is coffee?'

Hamish looked wary. 'Why?'

I thought of what Rin had said, about her being invisible.

115

'I have a proposal,' I said, standing up. 'I think I can help you, if you promise to help me. Meet me after school.'

We went to Scuttlebutt, a café near school that I liked because it was dingy and atmospheric, and made me think of newspaper reporters leaking exclusives to each other. And also pirates.

The bearded hipster behind the counter gave me a reproachful look when Hamish ordered a peppermint-mocha whip with chocolate sprinkles. I had a flat white.

Away from the bustle of school halls, Hamish seemed all nervous again. I supposed he wasn't used to one-on-one encounters with girls. I decided to skip any small talk, as I knew he'd be rubbish at it and it'd just make him more anxious.

'I need your help,' I said. 'Nick won't talk to me.'

Hamish raised his eyebrows. 'So you figured it out.'

'That PEZZimist is Nick? Of course I figured it out. But now he won't talk to me.'

'You frighten him.'

'But I'm trying to *help* him,' I said. 'I'm not like those other girls. I'm not trying to get into his pants.'

Hamish spooned sugar into his coffee. 'Are you sure about that?'

'Are you kidding? Nick's totally neurotic.'

Hamish just raised his eyebrows and said nothing.

I observed him carefully. He was a good few inches shorter than me, and slightly plump. His dark brown hair was whisper-fine, the kind of hair that would all fall out once he turned thirty. But he had nice eyes behind his glasses. His skin wasn't *too* bad, and the freckles on the bridge of his nose were kind of cute, if you went for that sort of thing. He wasn't a total lost cause. It was just the angry attitude that was going to repel the ladies.

'Why did you say *I wish*, when I asked if you were PEZzimist?' I asked.

Hamish licked sugary foam from his spoon. 'He's got a lot more to work with than I do,' he said. 'He's tall, he's good-looking. All he needs to do is get over himself.'

I considered mentioning something about pots and kettles exchanging words, but decided against it. 'What do you want, Hamish?' I asked instead. 'If you had one wish.'

He answered immediately, without thinking, 'A girlfriend.'

'But why? Why is having a girlfriend so important? Heaps of people don't date at school.'

'And look what happens to them,' he said darkly.

'They study more? Get better grades?'

'You don't understand.' Hamish threw down his spoon with an angry clatter. 'Having a girlfriend means *everything*.'

'That's nonsense,' I said. 'That's just what romantic comedies and pop songs have brainwashed you into believing.'

'You'd like to think that, wouldn't you? Well, you're wrong. A Harvard University paper studied a bunch of high-school leavers for ten years, until they were twenty-eight. And the ones who hadn't dated in school had an initial advantage, because they stayed home and studied more. But it didn't last. The ones who *had* dated ended up richer, happier and with better jobs.'

'I find that hard to believe.'

'Did you know that 70 per cent of the best white-collar jobs are obtained via informal social networks? And that 90 per cent of job terminations are because of a lack of interpersonal skills, not a lack of knowledge or technical ability?'

I blinked. Well, at least it wasn't small talk. 'But—'

Hamish continued, his voice getting louder and louder so that other people in the café turned to stare at him. 'If you're in a couple, you're more likely to recuperate faster when in hospital. You're less likely to be vulnerable to psychiatric disorders. You'll live longer and be healthier. If you're a woman you're less likely to suffer complications when giving birth, and if you're an alcoholic you're more likely to stop drinking. It's a fact, Penny. Couples have it better than single people.'

I thought about my parents. Did they have it better when

they were still together? My mum certainly did. She doesn't sound happy when I talk to her on the phone. But what about Dad? I thought about the way he was when he was with Josh – comfortable, happy, relaxed. I remembered the lines that developed on his face in the weeks before Mum had left, and the grey patches of hair that appeared above his ears. He hadn't been happier then. And neither had I.

But Dad had Josh now. I wondered absently if Dad would like Josh to live with us. Would they be living together already if it weren't for me? They'd only been together for six months.

Dad *had* someone. And he was happy. Mum didn't have anyone, and she wasn't happy. Nick didn't have anyone, and he wasn't happy. Hamish didn't have anyone, and he wasn't happy.

And *I* didn't have anyone.

Was I unhappy? I didn't think so. I mean, maybe I'd fall in love one day, but I had so much to *do* before then. I didn't want to mess around with *dating* and *boyfriends* and all that nonsense. What a total waste of time. I wasn't going to date boys who I didn't think I'd last with. So I preferred to wait until I found the right guy, the *one guy*, and then fall in love, once I'd established myself as an internationally successful journalist.

But was Hamish right? Was I jeopardising my career by not dating in high school?

It sounded crazy.

Hamish was nearly in tears. He really wanted this.

'So what do you think is stopping you from getting a girlfriend?' I asked.

He shrugged in a very emo way. 'Everything,' he said. 'My looks. The fact that I'm shy. Not *love-shy*,' he added hurriedly. 'Just ordinary-shy. I don't have many friends. I'm not popular. I don't get invited to parties. I never get to meet any new people, and the girls I have spoken to just don't like me.'

'*I* like you,' I said, trying to sound as if I meant it.

'No, you don't.'

He was probably right. I didn't really know Hamish, but I disliked his defensive angriness, and the way he made me feel as if I might be more like him than I wanted to be. But did that mean that I disliked *him*? I decided to change the subject.

'I think I can help you,' I said.

'How?'

I didn't want to tell him I could get him a date with Rin, because I didn't know if it was true. What if Rin wasn't interested in Hamish? He wasn't exactly the catch of the day.

'I need you to help me first,' I said.

Hamish shook his head. 'You have to put something on the table,' he said. 'Otherwise I'm going home to watch porn on the internet.'

I definitely couldn't subject Rin to Hamish. Not yet, anyway. Not until I'd fixed him up a bit.

I thought about it for a second. 'You can go on a date with me,' I said. 'Like a rehearsal-date.'

Hamish seemed offended. 'I don't want to go out with you.'

'Why not?' I asked. 'What's wrong with me?'

Hamish shrugged. 'You're bossy,' he said. 'And you're not pretty. Even though you have an awesome rack.'

And he wondered why he didn't get anywhere with girls.

'You don't seem very shy *now*,' I observed.

'It's because I'm not attracted to you.'

I'd almost had enough of this. 'Fine,' I said. 'What if I take you to Sarah Parsons' birthday party next week? You can meet new people, hang with the cool crowd.'

Hamish looked like a dog who'd been offered a terrifying yet enticing bone. 'What do you want in return?'

'I want you to help me talk to Nick.'

'How? He doesn't even know who I am. I don't post on the love-shy forum.'

'But you must know how he *thinks*. You'll know how I can get to him.'

'Why do you think I'd know that?' said Hamish, leaning back and folding his arms. 'How many times do I have to tell you I'm not love-shy?'

'I know you're not,' I said. 'But you've been visiting the site for longer than I have. You know more about them. Plus you're a boy. I don't understand boy-brain at all. You can be my translator.'

Hamish gazed at me for a moment. 'Fine,' he said. 'I'll help you.'

'Great,' I said. 'So what do I do?'

'Buy me a doughnut.'

I gave him a flat look, but went to order a doughnut, plus another coffee for myself. I sat back down, staring at Hamish expectantly.

'Well?'

The waitress brought over his doughnut, and he took a bite. 'Well,' he said, his mouth full. 'First you need to be less intimidating.'

'How?'

'Make your boobs look smaller.'

'*What?*'

'You have epic cans, Penny. They're enough to smother a tiny love-shy boy to death.'

I folded my arms across my chest.

'Seriously,' he said. 'You're a very intimidating person.'

'Because I'm smart?'

Hamish shook his head. 'Because you're intimidating. You're loud and bossy, and you talk a lot but don't seem to do much listening. You think you're the best at everything, which is probably true. But that doesn't make you any less intimidating.'

My cheeks grew hot. 'I'm not bossy!' I said. 'I just like things to be done properly. It's not my fault that nobody else pays enough attention.'

'Whatever.' Hamish shrugged.

'And I *do* listen! I'm a journalist – part of my whole *reason for existing* is to listen to people's stories and then share them with the world!'

Hamish nodded in what I felt was a patronising way. I *wasn't* bossy and intimidating. Was I?

'Just tell me what I can do to get Nick to talk to me,' I said, glaring at him.

'Fine,' said Hamish, and leaned forward. 'You have to get into his friend zone.'

'His friend zone? Please explain.'

Hamish's face clouded over, as if I was forcing him to talk about something that distressed him. 'It's when someone stops viewing you as a potential partner, and sees you as just a friend. It's the curse of the shy guy.'

'A curse? Why? What's wrong with being someone's friend?'

'Once you're in the friend zone, you never get out.'

I laughed. 'Are you serious? Heaps of people who are friends end up together. It happens all the time.'

'Nope. Once you're in, you'll never get out.'

'Come on,' I said. 'It's not *The Twilight Zone*. Don't be ridiculous. How are you supposed to get to know someone if you can't become friends first? How are you supposed to judge if they've got a nice personality?'

'That's bullshit,' Hamish said. 'Girls always *say* they want a guy with a nice personality, but they don't. They either want someone who's hot, or someone who's rich.'

I wanted to smack him. 'Do you think maybe you don't have a girlfriend because you run around saying that all girls are shallow?'

'It's a real problem, Penny,' said Hamish. 'Particularly for shy guys. All we want to do is make a girl happy. So we're nice, we're accommodating. We tell her how beautiful she is, and we buy her flowers and send her love letters. But that's not what girls want. They don't want *nice* guys. They want mean, aggressive alpha guys. You act like a caring human being, and she'll end up going shopping with you and taking you to the hairdresser before she runs off on a hot date with some tattooed meathead on a motorbike, leaving you to water her plants and let the cat out.'

I took a deep breath. 'Okay,' I said. 'What you're saying now? It's really offensive.'

'Because *you* know so much about dating.'

'I know more than whatever misogynistic men's magazine

124

you picked up that charming little series of impressions from.'

'Believe me, don't believe me,' said Hamish, finishing his doughnut and licking his fingers. 'I don't care.'

I sighed. 'So what does this have to do with Nick?'

'If you're in his friend zone, he won't be scared of you anymore. He'll know you're not trying to hit on him, so he'll relax.'

'Okay,' I said. 'So how do I get into Nick's friend zone?'

'I don't know,' admitted Hamish. 'I guess you have to find a way to talk to him that completely removes all aspects of romance. A situation where romance and sex are totally, utterly, not options.'

'Right,' I said. 'That shouldn't be hard, given that I have no interest in pursuing either romance or sex with him.'

Hamish nodded. 'You just have to figure out how to let *him* know that.'

I thought about my plans for Hamish and Rin all the way home, and as I got out of the lift on our floor, I was convinced that it would work. It was a win-win situation. Everyone would benefit!

I walked straight past my apartment, and knocked on

Rin's door. I heard a burst of Japanese inside, and the sound of bare feet padding towards the door.

'Penny!' Rin seemed disproportionately happy to see me.

'Hey,' I said. 'I just came by to see what you're doing over the weekend.'

Rin shot a look back into her apartment. 'Hang on,' she hissed. 'We can't talk here.'

She pushed me back into the corridor and followed me out, closing the door behind her. 'My parents,' she said. 'Very strict.'

'Right,' I said. 'Well, Sarah Parsons is having her birthday party on the weekend, and I thought you might like to come along.'

Rin's eyes lit up. 'Really? Sarah said I was invited?'

'She did indeed,' I lied.

Rin looked as though she might burst. 'That's so exciting!' she said. 'I'll have to tell my parents something. I'll figure it out, don't worry. Oh my God, what am I going to wear? Will there be lots of boys there? Who else is going? Should I wear heels or flats? Will there be dancing? Oh, and you *have* to stay for dinner.'

I blinked. That was a lot to take in all at once. Rin opened the door to her apartment and dragged me in after her.

'Take off your shoes,' she said, and pointed to a rack of shoes by the door.

I slipped off my sneakers and put them carefully on the rack.

'*Okaasan!*' she called, and pulled me into the living room.

Rin's apartment was the same as ours, except with different furniture. Their sofa looked much squishier and more comfy than ours, and instead of a proper dining table and chairs, there was a very low square table with cushions around it. A big fat buddha sat on a little red mat on the sideboard near the window, grinning at me.

Rin's mum was in the kitchen doing something involving rice and vegetables. It smelled amazing. I didn't think I'd ever smelled cooking in our apartment. Just the slightly damp smell of freshly arrived takeaway food.

'*Okaasan, kochira wa Penny desu,*' said Rin to her mum. '*Tonari ni sunde iru gakkou no tomodachi desu.*'

Mrs Tamaki smiled. 'It's very nice to meet you, Penny,' she said in accented English, and made a little bow. She seemed very young to be Rin's mum, her black hair pulled up into a neat bun. She wore a pale blue cardigan, a fabric apron over loose cotton pants, and white linen slippers.

'It's nice to meet you too, Mrs Tamaki,' I said, returning the bow.

'Can Penny stay for dinner?' Rin asked her mum.

'It's okay,' I said. 'I don't want to intrude. I'll be fine at home.'

127

'I'd like to meet this new friend Rin tells me about,' said Mrs Tamaki. 'Please stay.'

Rin took me into her bedroom. It was covered with posters of anime and manga characters, and soft toys and figurines. She pointed out each one to me, happily explaining what they were from and what their special abilities were.

'I should lend you some manga,' she said. 'I think you'll really like it.'

I laughed. 'I might have to learn Japanese first.'

'Don't worry,' said Rin. 'I've got some in English too.'

Those big eyes and teeny mouths kind of creeped me out. But I let her press a few comics into my hand, and listened carefully as she explained how to read them, back to front starting from the last page.

Mrs Tamaki called us back into the living room, and I was introduced to Mr Tamaki, who had just arrived home from work. He was tall, with a kind face and silver hair around his temples. He wore a very nice suit that I thought my dad would approve of.

We sat cross-legged at the table, and Rin poured me a glass of Coke. Mr Tamaki had a beer.

'*Itadakimasu*,' said Rin and her parents, bowing their heads.

'We're saying thank you for the food,' Rin explained.

'Like saying grace?'

128

'Sort of. Except we're thanking the chicken for giving us its life, and the farmer for growing the rice and vegetables.'

'And Fumiko for cooking it,' added Mr Tamaki with a wink.

I liked the sound of that. 'How do you say it again? Eat a dirty mouse?'

Rin let out a yelp of laughter. '*Itadakimasu.*'

'Eeta-dacky-muss,' I said slowly. Rin and her parents looked pleased.

'Can you use *hashi*?' asked Mr Tamaki, indicating his chopsticks.

I picked up mine and clicked the ends together to prove it. Mr and Mrs Tamaki seemed impressed.

Dinner was amazing. There was miso soup to start with, then a green bean and spinach dish called *goma-ai*, and something else called *oyako donburi*, which was chicken with egg and mushrooms on rice.

Rin's parents asked me about school, and nodded admiringly when I told them I was a good student, and that I was involved with the SRC and the *Gazette* and Debating and Orchestra. Rin beamed the whole time, clearly delighted to have a friend who her parents approved of.

I asked about Rin's brothers, and Mr and Mrs Tamaki nearly fell over themselves telling me how well their uni studies were going, and which areas of medicine they were planning to specialise in. I wondered if either of the boys had a girlfriend, and remembered what Hamish had told me about people who dated in high school ending up more successful than people who hadn't.

'What do you want to do when you leave school, Penny?' asked Mr Tamaki.

'Study journalism,' I told him. 'I want to be a journalist.'

'A difficult line of work,' he said. 'Very stressful.'

'But rewarding,' I said. 'I want to tell the important stories. The ones that aren't being told.'

I thought of Nick, and hoped that Hamish's friend-zone theory was correct.

I was expecting something exotic for dessert, possibly involving sticky rice or red bean paste. Or more Pocky. But it turned out to be rocky road ice-cream, which was just fine by me.

After dinner I thanked Mr and Mrs Tamaki for their hospitality.

'You must come again,' said Mrs Tamaki. 'Any time.'

I stood up, my knees creaky after sitting cross-legged for so long. Rin walked me to the door.

'Thanks for dinner,' I said. 'It was delicious.'

'That's okay,' said Rin. 'Thanks for inviting me to the...you know.' She winked.

I winked back, and realised that for the first time in my

life I was genuinely looking forward to going to a teenage birthday party.

21:44

I don't like the bright sun, or the shock of cold water.
I've been thinking about that church camp my parents
sent me on when I was eleven. They're not very religious,
but my father thought it would help me be more social.
As soon as I arrived, I hated it. On that first afternoon, we
were all told to change into our bathers (I always wear a
T-shirt because I burn very easily) and headed down to
the lake.
The water was cold. So cold that when it lapped around
my feet, I shivered and my toes ached. But I wanted to
go in. It would just take some time. It always takes time,
because I'm sensitive to the cold. So I eased myself in,
little by little. Inch by inch. But the other boys laughed
at me and called me a pussy and a faggot. I didn't care, I
was used to it. I just ignored them and kept inching in. But
they wouldn't go away. They came closer and splashed me.
Every splash was like sharp blades raking across my body. I
screamed at them to leave me alone. It didn't work. They
got rocks from the lake shore and threw them at me.
Hard. I got out of the water and ran for the cabins.
It was hot for the rest of the camp, but I wore long

sleeves every day to hide the bruises. I didn't go swimming again. I never went swimming again.

I read Nick's post six times. Could it really be true? Could kids be so horrid to each other? I pictured tiny skinny Nick in his board-shorts and T-shirt, cringing and crying from the water and the rocks, while all the other boys laughed at him. No wonder he was messed up.

8

FRIDAY WAS THE SWIMMING CARNIVAL. Everyone dressed in their house colours and stood on the sidelines and cheered. My house was Merri, and our colour was white (white? Who ever heard of a *white* school house?), and it was always difficult to think of a costume theme. There were only so many times you could all dress up as angels, so this year we'd decided to come as doctors and asylum patients in straitjackets. All the non-swimmers wore white face-paint and scary panda-eyes, and our house cheer was *If we don't win, we'll bite off your arms and legs!*, which at least was different.

I won my first few races easily, which was no surprise. I've been swimming competitively since I was eight. Plus I've got a good strong mindset and don't allow myself to be distracted during a competition.

Except for today. All the time I was waiting for my races, I kept an eye out for Nick. The whole school was supposed to attend the carnival, but it would be pretty easy to wag and stay home. But then, Amy Butler was competing, looking very petite and lovely in a sleek black one-piece. Wouldn't he relish this opportunity to watch her compete? Her hair was tucked into a swimming cap, which Nick probably wouldn't like, but there was plenty of figure to look at. Then again, maybe he'd get freaked out by all the near-nudity. He probably *was* wagging.

I felt I should approach Amy and talk to her about Nick, but I honestly wasn't sure what to say. I didn't want to expose his secret to the school – that'd scare him off completely (and be kind of mean). But maybe I could get them both to come to Sarah Parsons' party? I was sure Amy would be going. I hoped there wouldn't be a repeat of last year's Tia Maria incident.

The carnival was finishing with the relay that would decide which of the four houses got the Swimming Cup. I hated relays – the other people in the team rarely had the same level of commitment as I did. Luckily, as with Debating, I swam last, so I'd at least have an opportunity to fix any disasters perpetrated by my team members. As I was standing in line waiting for the starting pistol to fire, I scanned the seats around the pool for Nick.

And there he was.

The new 25-metre pool and aquatic centre had been built last year, and it still smelled of paint under the chlorine. Nick was sitting up the very back of the raked seating, away from everyone else. I could tell he was watching Amy Butler. She was in Fawkner, the blue house, and she was second-last in her relay queue, so she'd be swimming just before me in the butterfly leg. I was the anchor for my team, swimming the freestyle leg.

The starter gun sounded and the backstrokers kicked off. Olivia Fischer was the first swimmer for my house, and she did okay, but didn't manage to get the lead. Sarah Parsons was next, doing breaststroke. She was rubbish, letting the Fawkner and Rushall teams get ahead of her, even though they'd been trailing behind Olivia in the first leg. Amy Butler was diving in for butterfly before Sarah had made it halfway back to us. After what seemed an *age*, Arabella Sampson finally dived in and I stepped up on the starting blocks, cheering her on.

Arabella made good time and almost caught up to Amy Butler. But as I bent my knees, ready to dive, I saw Amy pull herself out of the water and I automatically glanced up to Nick. As if he could feel me watching, his head swung around to me, and with a start, he got to his feet and made his way down the aisle – not towards the crowds, but towards the fire exit. I'd spooked him again. But I couldn't let him get away this time.

Arabella touched the edge of the pool and I dove over her head into the water. I had to finish the race quickly so I could catch up to Nick.

I swam as I'd never swum before, cutting through the water like a knife. My tumble turn was perfect. With every stroke I imagined Nick taking another step towards the door. I practically flew through the water, taking in great gulps of air on alternate sides every three strokes and focusing on my six-beat kick.

As I touched the end of the pool, I stuck my head up out of the water and searched for Nick, ignoring the cheers and yelling around me. He was nearly at the exit.

My teammates whooped and screamed my name. I knew I'd won, but I didn't care. This was my chance. I had to get to Nick. I hauled myself out of the water and ran towards him, stepping as carefully as I could so I wouldn't slip.

'Penny! You have to stay in the pool!' said Sarah Parsons. 'What's wrong? Are you sick? *Penny!*'

I waved at her in an *I'm fine* sort of way, and kept going. Water streamed off my hair and arms, and I left Penny-footprints with every step I took.

I slipped through the fire exit door just as it swung

closed after Nick. He strode across the quadrangle, empty but for a few chip packets and aluminium cans.

'Nick!' I made sure I didn't call out until I was close enough that he couldn't bolt. He was trapped between the stairs to the library and the bike sheds. He looked down, clenching and unclenching his fists.

'Hey,' I said. 'Calm down. I only want to talk to you. I think we got off on the wrong foot the other day. I want to apologise.'

Apologies weren't easy for me at the best of times, and this time it wasn't even true, because I hadn't done anything wrong! But Nick continued to stare at the ground and do that weird thing with his fists.

'J-j-just leave m-me alone.'

Well, at least he'd spoken to me. That was a step in the right direction.

'Hey,' I said. 'Chill out. You don't have to be shy with me. And there's no one else around, they're all inside.'

I put my hand on his shoulder and felt him convulse slightly. I snatched my hand back. Of course he'd freak out when I touched him. He'd barely ever *spoken* to a girl before, and I was practically naked.

Nick stared at me, his face a mask of horror. All the cool aloofness fell away and I saw how utterly terrified he was.

The look of horror got worse, and his trembling more

intense, then his mouth sort of twisted. And then I was covered in something wet, warm and foul-smelling.

'Oh God,' he said.

When you've just been vomited on, all over your breasts, it's hard to know what to say. I was grateful he'd bent over as he'd done it, so it hadn't hit my face.

Vomity warmth seeped into my cleavage. I stood before Nick Rammage, in my bathers, dripping with pool water and spew. He appeared to be completely frozen.

'Well,' I said, as a chunk of what appeared to be half-digested gummi bear dripped off my right breast and landed on my big toe. 'I know that love-shys aren't supposed to be attracted to large-breasted women, but I didn't know you were so *repulsed* by them!'

Nick made a soft choking sound. Oops. Probably shouldn't have mentioned my boobs. Probably not the kind of thing that a love-shy in the middle of a freakout would find funny.

'S-sorry,' he said, so softly I could barely hear him, as he half turned away and wiped his mouth with the back of his hand. 'I'm so sorry.'

I remembered my conversation with Hamish yesterday. *You have to find a way to talk to him that completely removes all aspects of romance. A situation where romance and sex are totally, utterly, not options.*

There was vomit between my breasts and between my toes. The smell was making my eyes water. If ever there was a situation where romance and sex weren't options, this was it. It was time to put myself in Nick's friend zone.

'Make it up to me,' I said. 'I'm going to have a shower, and you're going to wait here. When I get back, you and I are going to have a chat. Nothing serious. I just want to talk to you. I'm not interested in dating you. I've got this whole personal policy about dating and vomit.'

Nick didn't say anything.

'You owe it to me,' I said. 'What you had for breakfast is currently dripping onto my toes.'

He jerked his head in what looked like a flinch, but just *might* be a nod. I took that as a yes, and sprinted off to the showers.

My team members were there, wrapped in damp towels, huddled together and talking quietly.

'Penny!' Sarah Parsons took a step forward, then wrinkled her nose. 'Are you okay?'

I nodded. 'I just need a shower.'

'What happened?' asked Olivia Fischer, glaring.

Sarah shh'd her. 'What d'you *think* happened?' she said, gesturing at me. 'Penny was sick. Did you want her to throw up in the pool?'

I blinked, and was about to tell them it wasn't *my* vomit,

139

when I realised why they were all so annoyed. I'd won the race, but I'd got out of the pool before the race was over.

'We were disqualified?' I asked, and Sarah looked down at the floor and nodded.

It wasn't fair. I'd won the race fair and square. I was a better swimmer than all the rest of them put together. What if I really had been sick? It was a stupid rule. The Australian women's relay team had been disqualified in the 2001 World Championships because the whole team had jumped *into* the pool before the race was finished, but that's because it was disrespectful and unsportsmanlike. This was an *emergency*!

'Maybe if we talk to Ms Carlson,' suggested Arabella Sampson, 'and explain that Penny was sick...'

'It's too late,' snapped Olivia. 'They've already awarded the Swimming Cup and medals.'

What did she want from me? I wasn't going to apologise for being sick. If it hadn't been for me, there was no way we would have won anyway, so we'd be in exactly the same position. Well, maybe we'd have been in second or third position instead of disqualified, but what did that matter? Winning was the only important thing when it came to racing.

Nick would be waiting for me. I didn't have much time.

'I'm still not feeling great,' I said. 'I might just have a shower and head home.'

Sarah looked at me with concern as Olivia stomped off to get her bag. 'Do you want me to wait for you?'

'No,' I said. 'I'll be fine.'

If I was honest with myself, I wasn't expecting Nick to wait. It'd be easy for him to slip away while I was washing bile from between my toes.

But he didn't slip away. When I emerged, pink and clean in tracksuit pants and a hoodie, Nick was sitting on a bench at the edge of the quadrangle. He was perched up on the back of the bench with his feet on the seat, as he had been the other day.

'Here,' I said, and held out his phone, which I'd been keeping in my bag for him.

He didn't move. I put the phone on the bench beside his feet.

'You waited,' I said. 'Thank you.'

Nick made a shrugging, nodding gesture.

'Do you mind if I sit down?'

No response, which I took as a *yes*. I sat. I didn't look directly at Nick, because I didn't want to spook him, but I could see out of the corner of my eye that he was trembling.

'From the outset,' I said, 'I want to reiterate that I'm not interested in any kind of relationship with you. My interest is purely professional.'

Best to get that out in the open. It might help him let his guard down.

'So,' I said. 'I think you have a problem. I think I know what it is. And I think I might be able to help you.'

Nick didn't say anything.

'You're shy. You seem all cool and aloof on the outside, but it's just a mask. The idea of talking to a girl makes you unbearably anxious, even though a girl is all you want.'

I touched him gently on the arm, and he pulled away as if I'd given him an electric shock. Don't touch the love-shy. Check.

And then he burst into tears. Great hacking, choking, bawling sobs.

'I'm sorry,' he said. 'I just don't think I can—'

'It's okay,' I said. 'Take as long as you need. You'll find I'm pretty patient. I'm not going anywhere.'

I remembered the last time I'd cried like that. It was nearly two years ago. The day Dad told me and Mum that he was gay, and Mum left.

It was a Saturday. I'd just come back from swimming, and I remember the smell of chlorine and the stinging feeling in my eyes as I started to cry. We were in our old house in the suburbs. The back door was open and I could hear birds singing in the garden, and the sound of someone's lawnmower.

Mum didn't say anything, not a word. She just listened as Dad spoke, his voice trembling and tears in his eyes. Then, when Dad stopped and waited for our reaction, nothing happened. Mum just sat there, her hands folded neatly in her lap.

Then she pursed her lips, stood, and went into her and Dad's bedroom. I looked at Dad.

'It's okay,' he said. 'She just needs a minute. She's fine. We'll all be fine, I promise.'

But Mum emerged from the bedroom holding an overnight bag.

'Kelly,' said Dad, standing up. 'Sit down. Let me make you a cup of tea.'

Mum didn't look at him. She just walked out the front door. I heard her car pull out of the driveway a moment later.

She hadn't looked at me either.

I'd cried it out, that afternoon. It had taken about an hour, and afterwards I felt weak and empty. But then Dad and I talked. He answered every question I asked, and I couldn't hate him, or wish he'd done anything else.

I knew Nick would cry it out as well, eventually. And then we'd talk.

It took about ten minutes. Then he was very quiet, his head still buried in his arms. I wondered if he'd fallen asleep.

'Nick?'

He flinched, raising his head and wiping his eyes. 'I th-thought you'd gone.' His breath came in shallow panting gasps, like a dog on a hot day.

I grinned. 'Told you I was patient.'

Nick straightened up. 'Why are you h-here?' He didn't look at me.

'I know you're love-shy,' I said. 'Hamish Berry told me.'

I didn't want to tell him that I knew he was PEZZimist. It might compromise the honesty of his blog posts if he knew I was reading them. It felt sneaky and nosy, but it wasn't as if I were reading his diary. It was a public blog, on the internet for all to see. Surely on some level Nick *wanted* people to read it. Otherwise he'd just write in a journal.

'That...' Nick swallowed, then forced himself to speak. 'That doesn't answer my question.'

Fair enough. 'I want to be a journalist,' I said. 'I think your condition is fascinating, and I'd like to write a story about you. I'm pretty sure I could sell it to a real newspaper.'

Nick looked as if he was about to explode, or possibly vomit again.

'Don't worry,' I added hastily. 'I'd change your name,

and nobody'd ever know it was you. But I think it would help you.'

'H-how?'

'You'll get to talk to me,' I said. 'A lot. And I'm a girl. It'll be like practice-dating. But with no anxiety, because I already know about your condition, so I'm not going to reject you. Plus, as previously mentioned, I'm in no way interested in you romantically.'

Nick was quiet for a minute, but I could see he was thinking about it.

'What would I have to do?' he said at last.

I shrugged. 'Tell me about yourself.'

Another long pause. 'I-I can't.'

'Sure you can. Tell me about your family. Do you have any siblings?'

Nick shook his head.

'Me neither. See? We have something in common.'

Nick seemed to think over the whole idea for a while, then he hung his head. 'I'm sorry,' he said. 'I don't think I can do this.'

'Don't you want to be able to talk to girls?'

His head turned, and he didn't *quite* look at me, but it was pretty close. 'Of course I do,' he said, with a vehemence that I doubted either of us expected. 'I want it more than *anything*. It's all I've ever wanted.'

'So let me help you.'

Nick's face twisted, as though he was in pain. 'There's—'

He broke off, and a bead of sweat trickled down his brow. He was shaking again, his breath coming in those little shallow pants. I saw his knuckles go white as he gripped the bench. He'd gone all pale.

'Nick? Are you okay?'

He screwed up his eyes, and in one explosive breath he managed to speak out loud, in a tangle of words.

'There's a girl. I like a girl.'

I gave him a minute to let his breathing calm down.

'Good,' I said. 'That's good. Can you tell me something about her?'

Nick seemed to relax a little, but he didn't open his eyes. 'She's beautiful. She's small and perfect and has long brown hair like silk. She's gentle and kind and feminine – she doesn't feel as if she has to be like a boy in order to be heard.'

'She sounds amazing.' She also sounded *nothing* like Amy Butler.

'She is.' Nick's face clouded over. 'But it's useless. I'll never be able to speak to her, let alone ask her out. She'll find some alpha male who won't treat her as well as she deserves, and I'll just be alone until the day I die.'

I gave him a flat look. 'You've been watching too much

daytime television. Stop talking as if you're on *Jerry Springer* and start being *you.*'

'But I don't know who I am,' said Nick hopelessly.

'Nonsense,' I said. 'You just have to trust me. I can totally help you. I can help you talk to Amy Butler.'

Nick tensed again. 'How did you know it was Amy Butler?'

I laughed. 'I'm not *blind*. You're always watching her. Plus, she's the perfect girl for a love-shy. Petite, pretty, long hair...'

'How do you know so much about love-shyness?'

I nearly said *your blog*, but caught myself just in time. 'I read a book,' I said, which was also true.

'D-do you know her?' Nick asked. 'Amy?'

I could run into trouble here. I didn't want to tell him I thought his chosen bride was boring and not very bright.

'A little,' I said. 'Not very well. She seems nice.'

Nick sunk into a reverie that probably involved walking Amy down the aisle or rescuing her from the jaws of a crocodile.

'Do you think maybe I could write her a letter?'

'Who?'

'Amy. I-I could say it all in a letter. Better than I ever could in real life. In real life I'll just fall over and die. Or throw up on her.'

'Yeah,' I said. 'Don't throw up on her. Not everyone's going to be as forgiving as me about that.'

A teeny smile flickered across Nick's face. 'So?' he said. 'A letter?'

I thought about it. 'I don't know. What would you say in a letter?'

'How I think about her all the time. How I think she's the most beautiful girl I've ever seen. How I want to be with her always. How I want to spend my whole life with her, just the two of us, cuddled up in our own safe little paradise while the world goes rushing by around us.'

'Um,' I said. 'Maybe don't lead with that.'

'Why not? It's poetic.'

'It's creepy. If someone who'd never spoken to me before sent me a letter saying those things...'

'What?'

'I'd think they were a stalker. Or a serial killer. Or at the very least a bit of a weirdo.'

'I *am* a bit of a weirdo. But I'm not a stalker. Not really. And definitely not a serial killer.'

'I think you need to have had some real contact with Amy before you profess your eternal love for her.'

'But how can I do that? I can't do it at school. There's too much else happening. Someone else might see. A *teacher* might see.'

I blinked. 'Who cares if a teacher sees?'

'It'd be way too embarrassing. I might vomit. Again.'

'What if you saw Amy outside of school? In a more social situation?'

Nick shrugged. 'I don't know. Maybe. I still think I'd be too anxious.'

'But it'd be better, right? Than doing it at school?'

He shrugged his shoulders miserably.

I smiled. 'What are you doing next Saturday night?'

'Nothing. Like every other night.' He sighed, and I imagined him sitting in his bedroom, night after night, gazing out the window at the world going on without him. I shuddered.

'Well, now you are,' I told him. 'It's Sarah Parsons' birthday party, and you're coming with me.'

'No.'

'Come on,' I said. 'It'll be fun.'

Nick clammed up. The hesitant, curious expression that had crept over his face was replaced with stony blankness.

'Come on,' I said. 'How do you expect to get better if you don't try? You *do* want to get better, don't you?'

'I'll never get better.'

'Amy Butler will be there.'

He hesitated.

'You could talk to her,' I said. 'It might be easier in a non-school environment. No teachers to see you.'

He shook his head. 'No. I'd say the wrong thing. I'd

do something dumb. I'd have a panic attack in front of everyone.'

'But don't you see?' I said. 'That's what you're supposed to do at parties!'

'Have a panic attack?'

'Do dumb stuff. Say the wrong thing. Do whatever you'll regret the next morning. Everyone else will be doing it too, except they'll be really drunk so they'll probably throw up at the end of the night. And you've already got that bit out of the way.'

'No.'

'Just promise me you'll think about it?'

'I said *no!*' Nick's voice cracked hysterically. 'You have no idea what it's like to be me. You can't just waltz in, give me a makeover, take me to a party and I'll suddenly realise how beautiful I am. This isn't some cheesy '80s teen film – it's my life, and nothing in it is going to change. So just leave me alone.'

He stumbled off the bench, and ran away.

9

OVER THE WEEKEND, I READ a research paper from the University of Wisconsin about an experiment with rhesus monkeys. Scientists isolated baby monkeys to prevent them from playing with other monkeys. When these monkeys grew up, they turned out to be totally incapable of reproducing on their own. Not because they were sterile, but because the female monkeys wouldn't let the males anywhere near them.

So the scientists artificially inseminated the shy female monkeys. But when they gave birth, they didn't recognise their young as babies. They stomped on the babies, threw them against the walls of the cage, and in some cases tried to eat them.

I thought about Nick, and the things he'd said about *his* mother. She didn't sound like a particularly nurturing figure, but Nick's ideas about relationships were so skewed – maybe she was completely normal, and he was just a spoiled brat gone wrong. A dysfunctional family might begin to explain Nick's love-shyness, but I couldn't just assume that his family was screwed up. I needed to meet them.

I was going to have to put in a bit more work before I'd score an invitation for a playdate. Especially given that after our first proper conversation he'd told me to leave him alone and run away.

Still. I'd talked to Nick, and he'd talked back. He'd seemed...almost normal, except for the part where he threw up on me and the part where he'd cried for ten minutes and all the parts where he came across as a totally creepy stalker. But there had been *moments* when he seemed normal. There had been moments when it was as if we were two friends, hanging out. And I'd enjoyed that. I knew I was there for a purpose; I was mentally taking notes for my article the whole time. But I'd also had fun, just chatting. I talked to a lot of people, interviewing for the *Gazette* and canvassing for the SRC, but this had been different. Gentler, somehow.

I spent most of the weekend recording my recollections and observations from our first meeting. I also made two lists, one of questions to ask Nick about his family and upbringing and thoughts about stuff, and the other of possible conversation starters he could use to make him more comfortable with talking to girls on a casual basis. It was a productive weekend; I even managed to squeeze in a little homework – although it probably wasn't up to my usual standard – as *well* as help Dad and Josh do a jigsaw of Barack Obama's face drawn in tiny coloured rhinestones. The only thing I didn't get around to was my oboe practice, but I was a good enough sight-reader to get by in rehearsal. I noticed Nick hadn't mentioned the vomiting-on-my-boobs incident on his blog. I guessed even he had a reputation to maintain.

On Sunday evening I sat at my computer to do some solid work on the love-shy article.

LOVE-SHYNESS AND PROFOUND ANXIETY IN ADOLESCENT MALES

What is love-shyness? Is it a disease? A collection of complicated phobias and mental illness? Or just a convenient excuse for antisocial behaviour? This investigation will delve into the unknown world of love-shyness, examine its characteristics and symptoms, and chart the progress of a genuine love-shy – through my initial stages of contact with the subject to a process of rehabilitation and eventually a cure.

I sighed. How *was* I going to cure Nick? Conversation starters were all very well, but I had a feeling he'd need something more. The book I'd read had mentioned stuff like 'practice-dating' and 'coeducational living', but it all seemed pretty ineffectual. There was also a website devoted to 'sexual surrogacy', which was downright frightening. Then a whole bunch of posts on the love-shy forum suggested this creepy dating strategy that turned the whole process into a game, with stupid acronyms and everything. Men were supposed to deploy sleazy tricks such as pulling a girl's hair or saying negative things about her in order to emotionally manipulate her into hooking up with them. I wasn't sure if it was misogynistic and sinister, or just pathetic.

At eleven, I turned off my computer, totally grossed out. I was going to need to find my own approach to help Nick.

At recess on Monday, Hugh Forward followed me back to my locker from Maths, badgering me about the budget for the school social. I noticed that the Walt Whitman paperback had been replaced by a new book of poems by Walter Dean Myers. I'd assumed that the Whitman was for an assignment, but maybe Hugh actually liked poetry?

'James O'Keefe says his cousin's band is really good,' Hugh said.

I rolled my eyes. 'Yeah, right,' I said. 'I'm not spending two hundred and fifty dollars to have a bunch of stoners drool and shake their hair around on stage. We should be spending the money on something important, like converting the gardens to sustainable native flora, or a new water tank...'

I trailed off. Nick was standing in front of my locker, headphones on, looking aloof.

'Then what do you suggest?' asked Hugh. 'There's a kid in Year Nine who is apparently a really good DJ. He might do it for fifty dollars.'

I stared at Nick.

'Penny?' said Hugh. 'Hello?'

'Yeah,' I said, still staring at Nick. 'The DJ. Fine.'

Hugh sighed and stalked away.

'Hey,' I said to Nick.

He nodded and looked down at the floor, scuffing his Chuck Taylors against the linoleum.

'Do you want to go outside?' I asked.

Another nod.

We found a bench outside, away from the recess crowds.

Nick took a deep breath. 'I-I'm sorry I yelled at you,' he said. 'I know— Sometimes I can get...a bit melodramatic.'

I thought about his overblown blog posts. 'That's okay.'

'I'm just not used to talking to...people.' It was as though every word he spoke was causing him pain, and he had to pull them out of his mouth like splinters.

'I understand,' I said. 'I know it's difficult for you. But it's good you're trying.'

He sighed, and then words started to tumble out, faster and faster. 'Sometimes I can look at myself and see that I'm being ridiculous, that it's all just willpower and I can change if I want to. If I want it hard enough. But other days everything's dark, and I feel like I'll never find my way out.'

He stopped, shocked that he'd said so much.

'I get it,' I said. 'And I want to help you.'

Nick rocked back and forth a little and tilted his head up to the sky. 'I don't think you can,' he said to the clouds. 'It's just all too much. Too hard.'

'Just try,' I said. 'For a few days. See how it goes.'

He swallowed audibly, but didn't say anything. It was better than an outright *no*.

I found Nick at lunchtime that day, and the next day. The *Gazette* and Debating could do without me for once. We had a break from swimming practice, after the carnival, and I wagged Orchestra and avoided Ms Darling in the corridors.

Nick was starting to seem less anxious around me. His

breathing was normal and he no longer trembled and dripped with sweat whenever I sat next to him. I was sure if he could go to a social event such as a party and see that it wasn't the big deal he thought it was, he'd relax. And maybe even pluck up the courage to talk to Amy Butler. Then he'd realise she was kind of boring, and I could move on my as-yet undefined plan to *really* fix his problem. But Nick remained adamant that he wouldn't be able to talk to Amy, because he'd be too anxious.

'Anxious about *what*?' I asked, on Wednesday afternoon. 'What do you think is going to happen? What *could* happen that would be so very bad?'

'Everything,' said Nick. 'She might laugh at me, or tell everyone and *they* would laugh at me. And then every day for the rest of my life I'd think of it, and burn with shame, right into the depths of my soul.'

'Okay,' I said. 'What if you only had six months to live? And your doctor told you that for those six months, your lifestyle wouldn't be compromised in any way by your health. Would you talk to her then?'

Nick shook his head. 'No way. I'd still be too anxious.'

'So you'd just sit in your room and do nothing?'

Nick leaned forward so his chin rested on his hands. 'I'd steal my father's credit card,' he said. 'Or sell my mother's engagement ring or something. And I'd run away.'

I frowned. 'Really? You'd steal your mother's engagement ring? You don't want to win the lottery or something?'

'I've never bought a lottery ticket. I'd never win. I'm too unlucky.'

'But this is a hypothetical fantasy,' I said. 'You can win the lottery if you want.'

'I'd rather steal from my parents,' said Nick. 'To teach them a lesson.'

I really, *really* had to meet Nick's family. Surely they couldn't be as bad as he was implying. Could they?

'Okay, then,' I said. 'Where would you run away to?'

'Everywhere. I'd travel around the world. I'd stroll along the canals of Venice, and climb the Eiffel Tower, and walk on the moors in Scotland. I'd go to galleries and museums all over Europe. I'd go to London and see every musical showing in the West End, apart from the ones that have music from Queen or ABBA.'

'Alone?'

Nick nodded. 'Alone.'

'That's sad.' I didn't mean *sad* as in *lame*. I meant it made me sad to think about Nick in all those romantic places, surrounded by couples, but always alone.

'Why?' he asked. 'What would *you* do if you only had six months to live?'

I thought about it. And the more I thought about it, the

sadder I felt. Because if I was truly honest with myself, I'd do exactly the same thing.

I mean, I wouldn't steal Dad's credit card or sell Mum's jewellery. And I'd probably go to different places (well, maybe the Scottish moor. And Venice. But definitely not the musical theatre). But I'd want to travel. I'd want to see everything I possibly could before I died. And I'd be alone.

Because I knew that if anyone else was with me, they'd want to do different things. And see different things. And so I wouldn't ever get to have my perfect overseas trip. Everything would be a compromise. I supposed that was what being in a relationship would be like. Always compromising. Maybe it *was* better to be alone.

18:31

I hate being at school, but I've come to hate being at home more. Every day is the same, and the longer I spend in the house, the worse it gets. I lose my appetite, I can't sleep. I get so tired I can't concentrate on anything for more than five minutes, but I still can't sleep. I don't talk to anyone for days, not even my parents. I end up walking just to get away from everyone and everything.

I walk every day, all the time. Round and round our block, so many times I'm surprised there isn't a groove worn by my feet. I count the steps as I walk. It's 1829 steps around the block. 2743 to the shops and back, not that I ever buy anything. 4914 to school. Pace, pace, pace. I step on every single crack, just in case the poem is right and my mother will break her back.

And I think about my girl. I think about her hair and her eyes and her warm shy smile. I think about what might happen if I came across her on my walk. Maybe I would accidentally bump into her, and she'd drop whatever she was carrying. A bag of oranges maybe, or books from the library. And then I could help her pick them up and we could start talking.

Or maybe I'd come across her sitting in the gutter, crying. And I could ask her what was wrong and she could tell me how lonely she felt, and how she needed someone to talk to. And then she could talk to me, and I could listen.

Or she'd be coming out of the florist with a bunch of daisies. And she'd pull one out and give it to me. Guys never get given flowers, which isn't fair because it's not like we don't think they're beautiful too.

This never happens, of course. I've never seen her when I'm walking. But I keep walking anyway, and counting. Otherwise I'd go crazy. More crazy.

'I think you've seen too many movies,' I told Nick on Thursday after school. We were sitting on some steps near the library, away from watching eyes. 'You can't spend your whole life waiting for that perfect moment where you rescue Amy Butler from drowning or her dad accidentally hits you with his car or you get locked on a rooftop together.'

'Meet cute,' said Nick.

'What?'

'It's called a "meet cute". When two characters in a story meet each other and fall in love.'

I stared at him.

'I spend a lot of time on the internet,' he explained.

'Whatever it's called,' I said, 'it doesn't happen in real life. You have to get to *know* people. Love at first sight isn't a real thing, and if it is, it never lasts.'

Nick sighed. 'I know. It's all lies. Sometimes I think there's no such thing as love at all, that it's all made up by Hallmark and Hollywood.'

He looked as if he was going to cry.

'That's not what I meant,' I said. 'There is totally such a thing as love. But you can't waste your life waiting for it to land on your doorstep. You have to go out and make things happen for yourself.'

'And how do you suggest I do that?' he asked, turning a miserable face towards me, but not meeting my eyes.

'Well, there *is* that party I told you about,' I said. 'On Saturday.'

'No,' he said flatly. 'I just couldn't. I wouldn't know what to say to anyone.'

'It's easy. You just go up to someone and say "hi". Then you start a conversation.'

Nick went pale. 'I don't think I'll ever be able to do that. The very idea of having a conversation with a girl makes my blood run cold.'

I laughed. 'Well, I hate to frighten you,' I said, 'but in case you hadn't noticed, *I'm* a girl. And we've just been having a conversation for over half an hour.'

Nick blinked. 'Really?'

'Yep. And you're doing an excellent job. We'll have you kissing girls in no time.'

He scratched his elbow and stared at an illegible piece of graffiti on the step beside him. 'I've never kissed anyone,' he said. 'Or been kissed.'

'Except by your mum.'

Nick shook his head. 'I don't remember my mother ever kissing me.'

'Seriously?' My mother had her flaws, *plenty* of them. But I'd never felt I lacked affection from my parents. Never.

'And what about your dad?' I asked.

'He never kissed me either.'

162

'Have you ever tried telling him about your problem?'

Nick laughed in a colourless sort of way. 'My father doesn't like to talk about personal matters.'

'He never sat you down and gave you the Talk?'

'What talk?'

'You know,' I said. 'The *Talk*. About sex.'

'What?' Nick looked surprised and offended. 'No way! God. No.'

'But you do . . . *know* . . . about sex. Right?'

He made eye contact with me for a long moment, the longest he'd ever looked at me for. 'Yes, Penny,' he said, and I was momentarily surprised that he knew my name. 'I know about sex. I do have the *internet*, you know. I may be an anxiety-ridden emotional cripple, but that doesn't mean I'm a total idiot.'

I laughed, and Nick's face cracked a tiny bit. Just a hint of a smile changed everything about him. His sullen aloofness lifted and he looked boyish and hopeful and . . . kind of beautiful. I could finally see why all the girls thought he was hot. His eyes opened up, and they were soft and greenish-brownish-grey, like a misty morning high up in a mountain forest. Something squeezed inside me. This was new.

Then he saw me watching him and blushed, and the smile was gone and his face was locked away again behind his Nick mask.

'But…' His face screwed up as though he were tasting something bitter, and he closed his eyes for a moment. 'I am…' He swallowed.

'Yes?'

He bit his lip. 'Promise you won't tell anyone?'

I nodded, adding in my mind that the article didn't count, because I wouldn't be using Nick's real name.

'I'm…' His voice dropped to a whisper. 'I'm a *virgin*.'

I couldn't help bursting out laughing. Nick went bright red and started to tremble.

'Nobody can know,' he said, between clenched teeth. 'It'd be too humiliating.'

I shook my head. 'That's your big secret? That you're a virgin?'

Nick glanced around, a hunted look in his eyes. 'Don't say it so loud!'

'Nick,' I said. 'We're in Year Ten. Statistically, only about 40 per cent of the people in our year have had sex. You're in a healthy majority.'

'Does that mean…' His voice cracked. 'Are you…?'

'A virgin? Of course.'

He blinked. 'Really?'

'Really. Teenagers are massively prone to exaggeration. Contrary to popular belief, Con Stingas doesn't have regular sexual relations with Luke Smith's mum.'

Nick seemed ridiculously pleased. *Boys.* They were all the same, more or less.

'I should go home,' he said. 'My mother will be expecting me for dinner.'

'I want to meet your parents,' I said.

Nick barked out a short laugh. 'No way.'

'Why not? They'd probably be overjoyed if you brought a girl home.'

'*No.*'

I'd never heard Nick say anything so firmly. Usually he ducked his head when he spoke, and there was always a faint tremor in the back of his throat, as though he could cry at any moment. But that single *no* had been said with total force and confidence. It only fired up my curiosity even more.

I *had* to see Nick's home and meet his parents. It would be essential to my article, and to my understanding of him as a person. Upbringing was clearly such a major factor in love-shyness. It wasn't enough for him to *tell* me about his parents – I had to make an independent assessment.

It was time for some journalistic sneakiness.

I pulled out my iPhone and pretended to check my email. 'I'd better go too,' I said. 'Dad wants to try this new Moroccan place for dinner.' I made a show of looking off to Nick's right, away from me. 'Hey, is that Amy Butler over there?' I pointed.

Nick's head whipped around, and he peered at the gaggle of girls by the canteen. 'No.'

'My bad.' I zipped up the pocket to my bag and slipped off the bench. Nick didn't seem to notice that I was no longer holding my phone.

When I got home, I made a beeline for my laptop. I logged into my account and clicked on the Find My iPhone button. A map of the city popped up, with a pulsing blue circle that zoomed in until it centred on one suburban home.

'Found you,' I said, scribbling an address on a post-it.

'Going somewhere?' asked Dad. 'We found the most incredible jigsaw of a *poodle* groomed to look like a *dragon*. It's got to be worth at least sixty points.'

'Yeah,' I said. 'Sorry. I'm going to a friend's house for dinner.'

'You're going next door?' He nodded his head towards Rin's apartment.

'No, another friend. His name's Nick. But don't get excited,' I said, as Josh opened his mouth. 'He's *just* a friend. He's helping me with an article I'm writing.'

10

IT WAS AN UNREMARKABLE HOUSE in an ordinary street in a leafy suburb not far from school. It was large, brick, and would have been very elegant when it was built in the 1980s, with lots of windows and a well-maintained lawn. It didn't look like the house of horrors that Nick had darkly referred to.

A middle-aged woman opened the door. She had curly blonde hair and was wearing a simple yet expensive-looking blue dress and well-applied makeup. I thought she resembled a mum on an American soap opera, pretty and bland and nurturing. She seemed mildly surprised to see me.

'Mrs Rammage?' I held out my hand. 'Hi, I'm Penny.'

Mrs Rammage shook it, still confused. 'Are you selling something?'

'Pardon?' I said, laughing. 'No, I'm Nick's friend. He didn't tell you he'd invited me for dinner?' I put my hand over my mouth in mock dismay. 'Oh, I am *so* sorry. He said he'd check with you first. He must have forgotten.'

Mrs Rammage's polite confusion had been replaced with a frown. 'My son invited you here? For dinner?'

I feigned embarrassment. 'He did,' I said. 'But it's *totally* okay, Mrs Rammage. I'll just go home. I wouldn't want to impose on you without any warning.'

Nick's mum continued to stare at me as if I'd told her I was from another planet.

'It was lovely to meet you,' I said, trying to appear polite, responsible and confused all at the same time. 'But I'll just go, shall I? I'm really sorry to have bothered you. Silly Nick.'

I turned and started walking back towards the gate, counting silently in my head. *Say something, lady!*

'Wait,' said Mrs Rammage, and I turned, relieved. I adopted a politely questioning expression.

'Of course you should stay,' she said with a tight smile. 'It's lovely to meet one of Nick's friends. Please come in, I'll tell him you're here.'

She ushered me through the door, and invited me to sit in the living room before she disappeared to find Nick. I gazed around and realised that, despite its normal exterior, all was not okay in this house.

Everything was covered in plastic. There was a clear rubbery runner over the hallway carpet, and the couch was covered in the kind of plastic that movers use to protect fabric. The TV had a plastic cover, and on top of it, two remote controls nestled in styrofoam holders. On the mantelpiece was a collection of blown glass birds with long, thin necks and pointed beaks. They looked cruel. The house smelled of disinfectant and air freshener. It made my eyes itch. The only sound was the loud ticking of an ugly gold clock above the mantelpiece.

The faintest whisper of a presence behind me made me turn. Nick was standing in the doorway to the living room, an expression of total horror on his face.

'Hi, Nick!' I jumped up off the couch with a squeak of plastic. 'I can't *believe* you forgot to tell your mum I was coming over!'

Nick said nothing. He looked like that screaming Edvard Munch painting. Or a sex-doll.

'I like your house,' I said. 'It's very…clean. And you're right, it wasn't hard to find it at all – it's so close to the train station. Are you going to show me your room?'

I advanced towards him, and he backed away as if I were going to stab him with one of the glass birds.

Mrs Rammage glided back in with a tray bearing two glasses of lemonade.

'You kids sit down,' she said. 'I'll let you know when dinner's ready. It won't be long.'

She put the tray on the coffee table and ushered me back to the couch. Nick sat in an armchair as far from me as he could possibly get. He wouldn't look at me.

Mrs Rammage disappeared from the room again, her heels clacking softly on the plastic runner. I wondered if she was going out after dinner. Who wore high heels in their own home?

'So...' I said. 'This would be a good opportunity for practising small talk in awkward situations.'

Nick said nothing. I could hear his breath coming in shallow pants, the way it did when he was especially anxious.

'Look,' I said. 'I'm sorry I came here without your permission. But you need to be exposed to new challenges, otherwise you'll never get better. And I wanted to meet your family.'

Nick leaned forward and took one of the glasses of lemonade. He drained it in one breath, like the desperate cowboy does in the saloon before he goes outside to meet the troublemaker at ten paces. He broke his stoic silence by belching loudly, and blushed.

'Nice.' I helped myself to the other glass of lemonade.

We sat there in strained silence for what felt like hours, until Mrs Rammage came to say that dinner was served.

The dining room on the other side of the hall was just as sterile and weird as the living room. The heavy dark wooden

170

table was set with good white china, silver knives and forks, and embroidered cloth napkins. But the whole effect was spoiled by the plastic tablecloth with its tacky daisy print.

Mr Rammage was already sitting at the table. He was a big man, wearing a suit and tie. (Dad wouldn't have approved. Too big-shouldered and power-suity. Very 1990s.) He nodded at Nick, and then stared at me.

'This is Penny,' said Mrs Rammage. 'A friend of Nick's from school.'

Mr Rammage raised his eyebrows, but didn't say anything. Clearly they weren't a very chatty household.

'It's nice to meet you, Mr Rammage,' I said, holding out my hand.

He hesitated, then stood and leaned over the table to shake it. 'Hello,' he said.

Well, it was more than I'd got out of Nick.

There was an entree of salad with cold ham. There was so much dressing on the salad that each piece of lettuce dripped as I picked it up. My mouth grew fuzzy from the salty dressing and sugary lemonade. Nick ate mechanically, not raising his eyes from his plate. Nobody spoke.

I thought of Rin's family, who were also quiet and polite, but in an entirely normal and human way. This was like having dinner in Stepford. Any minute now Mrs Rammage's robot head would explode and she'd try to kill us all.

'May I please have some more salad?' asked Nick, his voice barely a whisper, his head down.

This was crazy. The salad was right in front of him. Did he really have to ask *permission* to eat more vegetables? My mum used to *pay* me to eat vegetables.

'Of course you may,' said Mrs Rammage, and to my astonishment she stood up, walked to the other end of the table, and served Nick some salad.

'Thank you,' said Nick, still not looking up.

'You're welcome.' Mrs Rammage returned to her seat.

I couldn't believe this. Was this what every dinner was like? Or was it a special performance for my benefit? I half expected Mrs Rammage to burst out laughing, and for Nick to tell me I'd been punk'd.

'Um,' I said loudly, trying to fill the air with the sound of something other than chewing. 'Did anyone see that report on the ABC last week about climate change? I think it raised some really interesting points.'

Nick and Mr Rammage stared at me as though I'd just announced I was about to give birth to a trout. Mrs Rammage stared at her plate as if I hadn't spoken at all.

'Especially about alternative energy sources?' I faltered.

Nick returned his eyes to his plate. A bead of sweat dripped from his nose into his salad.

'Must have missed that one,' said Mr Rammage shortly.

And that was my sole attempt at conversation. Clearly talking during dinner was just Not On in the Rammage household.

The dinner dragged on in silence. After Nick's mum had served us some very overcooked slices of beef with watery gravy, Mr Rammage stood up to turn on the radio. Some loud-mouthed talkback host was asking people about their experiences with overcrowding on public transport. The noise only made things seem more quiet and still in the dining room. I had been chewing on the same piece of beef for over a minute, and was pretty sure it was never going to break down. Could I spit it into my napkin? Would this meal never end?

I glanced at Nick's mum, and saw with horror that she was crying silently. Fat tears slid down her cheeks, taking eyeliner and foundation with them, so her face seemed to be melting. Neither Nick nor his father seemed to notice – or if they did notice, they didn't care to comment.

I was in over my head. Nick's case was too far gone, his psychological damage must be too severe. With a family like this, how could he ever get better? He didn't know what it was like to be normal.

I'd never in my life wanted so much to be at home with Dad and Josh, eating Moroccan food and doing a jigsaw of a poodle dressed as a dragon. What was I doing here?

I managed to force the beef down and straightened my knife and fork to see that Nick and Mr Rammage had finished too. Had they been watching me masticate my way through this culinary disaster? I felt the lump of almost-solid meat making its way slowly down my throat. This was why people turned vegetarian.

'Thanks for dinner, Mrs Rammage.' I swallowed again, just to be on the safe side. 'It was delicious.'

Nick's mum ignored me, still crying into her uneaten roast beef.

Nick seemed frozen. It was clear I was going to have to get myself out of this whole ugly situation. But even though I badly wanted to crawl home and give Dad a giant hug for being so pleasantly functional, I wasn't finished. This was what being a journalist was all about. Sometimes I'd have to put myself in difficult or unpleasant situations. Nellie Bly spent ten days in a mental asylum. I could manage one evening.

'So, Nick,' I said, raising my voice to be heard above the radio. 'You said you could lend me that book? The one you mentioned the other day?'

Nick stared at me. 'W-what book?' It was the first time he'd spoken to me all evening.

'Oh, you remember. You said you had it. In your *bedroom*.'

'I don't remember anything about a book.'

I sighed. 'Let's just go look, shall we?' I stood up and started towards the dining room doorway. I had no idea where Nick's room was, but I was pretty sure he'd follow me.

And, with a clatter of cutlery and a scrape of chair, he did.

'Where are you *going*?' he hissed, as we walked down the hallway.

'Well, which one of these doors is your room?'

Nick hesitated in front of a door, and I grinned triumphantly and opened it.

'No,' said Nick. 'Don't go in there.'

'Why not?' I walked in, flicking on the light.

In some ways it was just an ordinary bedroom. A bed (single), a bookshelf. A desk with a laptop on it. But I immediately noticed other things: neat stacks of CDs on the bookshelf; a collection of what looked like light globes; and a row of Pez dispensers lined up on the windowsill.

pezzimist. Of course.

'Th-the red cockatoo one is worth over three hundred dollars,' said Nick. I could barely make out his voice. He was still hovering in the doorway, beads of sweat on his brow, struggling. He didn't like me being in his space.

I went over to the collection of light globes and my breath caught in my throat.

They were eight tiny little gardens, each inside its own globe. One was a desert, with miniscule cacti rising out of golden sand. Another was thick dark moss, with a cluster of white toadstools in the centre. Yet another held smooth stones with tiny purple flowers peeking up between them.

'Did you *make* these?' I asked.

'They're terrariums,' Nick replied. 'The plants are all real.'

'They're amazing,' I said. 'How do you make them?'

Nick shrugged. 'Patience. I like to grow things, but my mother won't let me plant anything in the front garden in case I spoil the lawn, and the backyard is just plastic. I like being able to make little worlds, apart from everything else.'

Like you, I thought. *A little world apart from everything else.*

'Wow,' I said.

'I'm a weirdo,' said Nick. 'Have you had enough yet?'

I grinned at him. 'Not even close. Are you going to come into your bedroom, or are you going to hang out in that doorway for the rest of the evening?'

Nick slunk into the room like a miserable dog and sat gingerly on the edge of his bed, his posture all tense as if he was ready to spring up and flee. He cleared his throat. 'H-how did you find out where I live?'

'I hid my phone in your bag,' I told him, examining his meticulously alphabetised CD collection. 'I tracked its location online.'

Nick didn't say anything, and I was kind of disappointed.

Wasn't he impressed by my investigative skills?

'Bach, Debussy, Handel, Vivaldi,' I read aloud. 'So you like classical music.' I moved along the shelf. 'And ... Gilbert and Sullivan.'

'I like romantic music,' Nick muttered.

'But no Andrew Lloyd Webber?'

He shook his head. 'Too loud. Hurts my ears.'

'Of course,' I said. 'You prefer the proper traditional musical to the modern rock opera.'

Nick said nothing.

'I don't know much Gilbert and Sullivan,' I said. 'But my parents took me to see *The Pirates of Penzance* when I was little. There was a song about being a very modern mister...?'

Nick didn't look up, but his face brightened and he began to speak very quickly.

'*I am the very model of a modern Major-General,*
I've information vegetable, animal, and mineral,
I know the kings of England, and I quote the fights historical
From Marathon to Waterloo, in order categorical;
I'm very well acquainted, too, with matters mathematical,
I understand equations, both the simple and quadratical,
About binomial theorem I'm teeming with a lot o' news,
With many cheerful facts about the square of the hypotenuse.'

I stared at him. It was the most I'd ever heard him say all

at once, delivered rapid-fire, without a slip or a stammer. I felt like bursting into applause.

'A Very Model of a Modern Major-General,' said Nick. 'Major-General Stanley sings it near the end of Act One. It's really difficult to sing because it's so fast and tongue-twisty.'

'That was amazing,' I said, and meant it.

Nick shifted uncomfortably. 'I still don't remember telling you about a book.'

I rolled my eyes. 'For someone who spends his whole life pretending to be something he's not, you're not very good at picking up lies. I just wanted to get away from the dining room.'

'Oh.'

'Although I would like my phone back.'

Nick fumbled in his backpack until he found my iPhone. He handed it to me, making sure our hands didn't touch.

'Sorry,' he said. 'About dinner. I told you not to come.'

'Don't apologise,' I said. 'It helped me understand you a bit more. Your family is...not exactly normal.'

'No.'

I gazed at the terrariums and thought about how Nick's ultra-cool persona was like a glass wall that sheltered him from the world.

'Nick,' I said. 'What happened at your old school? Why did you leave?'

Nick scratched at his elbow. 'Nothing,' he said. 'Everything. I don't want to talk about it.'

'I need to know.'

He sighed and took off his watch, laid it carefully beside him, then picked it up and put it back on again before he finally started talking.

'There was a girl,' he said. 'She was beautiful, the most beautiful creature I'd ever seen. She was quiet and thoughtful and sometimes when she'd catch me staring at her she'd smile and look away, like she was shy too. I knew that if only I could work up the courage to talk to her, everything would fall into place, and we'd be together forever. I just had to find the right moment. I watched her, trying to figure out her routine. I used to wait for her after school every day, hoping that I'd be able to finally speak to her. And every day she'd walk on by. A couple of times I even followed her home, hoping and hoping that a miracle would happen and that I'd be able to say something. This went on for a month or two.'

Nick took his watch off again and held it in a tight fist, his eyes closed.

'And then what? Did you speak to her?'

He shook his head. 'She told her parents that I was stalking her. I can't believe she did that. I mean, she *smiled* at me. I thought she *liked* me.'

I didn't say anything. Of course she thought Nick was a stalker. What do you call a creepy guy who stares at schoolgirls and follows them home? A stalker. Or worse.

'So her parents called the school and the school called my parents.' Nick's voice broke on the last word, and he started to cry.

'Oh.' I didn't know whether I should try to comfort him, or whether it would make him more anxious. I waited. He pulled his sleeve across his nose and swallowed.

'My parents were so mad. My mother screamed and screamed at me, asking what she'd ever done to deserve a son like me. So they pulled me out of the school, which was good because I think I might actually have died if I'd ever seen the girl again. And then my mother grounded me. She said it was time for me to start acting like a real boy, and that I wasn't allowed out again until I could. And I wanted to say *well then help me find a girlfriend, and I will grow up*, but she didn't. Ever. She never helped me meet girls, never got any of her friends to bring their daughters around, never introduced me to anyone.'

I wanted to ask him why he wanted his mother's help in the first place – didn't most teenagers hate it when their parents tried to interfere with their personal lives? But Nick wasn't *most* teenagers.

'I hated her,' he was saying. 'I hated her so much, and I

couldn't leave the house and she was there all the time, yelling at me and crying and telling me what a disappointment I was. So I started... doing stuff.'

'What kind of stuff?'

Nick paused again, his body convulsing with silent sobs. He shook his head, and took a few gulping breaths.

'I put a dead mouse in the kettle. I cut all my clothes into shreds with scissors. And one night when my parents were asleep, I went into the kitchen and took all the plates and glasses, and built them into towers on the floor, until they reached the ceiling. Then I went back to bed and left it all there for them to find the next morning. My mother thought I was going mad, and told me to stop. I told her I'd stop when she let me out and helped me find a girl. She didn't, so I kept going. One day when she went out to the supermarket, I took all her jewellery from her bedroom and took it to Cash Converters and got nearly three hundred dollars for it.'

I frowned, remembering what he'd said about running away and seeing the world. 'You stole your mum's jewellery?'

Nick nodded. 'Dad called the cops. I spent a night in the cell at the police station.'

'Your father had you *arrested*?' This story was so crazy I could barely believe it. If I hadn't met Nick's parents I definitely would have thought he was lying.

'He came and got me the next morning. Then my mother said that she'd help me, but that I had to promise that I'd try to be the son she wanted, instead of a crazy mess. I agreed. She even wrote out a contract and I signed it. Then she went out for a whole day and came back with bags of clothes and magazines and DVDs. She cut out pictures of cool boys, and put them all in a scrapbook. She bought me all these clothes.' He plucked the fabric of his T-shirt. 'She put me on a diet and made me work out for three hours a day. She showed me DVDs of hot guys and made me practise walking like them, over and over again, for hours. Finally, she said I was ready to be a normal boy, and it was time for me to go back to school.'

'And that's when you came to East Glendale?'

Nick nodded, then buried his head in his arms and made horrible hacking sounds as he trembled. When he'd cried like that outside the pool, it had been okay. He'd been an interview subject, a test case. He'd simply been display-ing symptoms of anxiety. But now...now he was a person. A person who'd been a kid, like me. Except while I'd been growing up with my loving parents, he'd been growing up in a plastic-covered bubble with parents who I couldn't quite believe were human. It made my parents' divorce seem like nothing. At least they loved me.

I wanted to tell him that everything was going to be all

right. I wanted to comfort him. I wanted him to believe that I knew all the answers.

But I didn't. This was *huge*. It wasn't just a matter of a boy who was too shy to talk to girls. Nick had been *abused* by his family. He was broken in ways I couldn't even imagine. I thought of Dad and Josh, and wanted to be safe at home with them more than anything else in the world. And I knew that Nick had never felt like that. For Nick, there was no *home*. There was no *safe*.

I thought of an ostracised rhesus monkey, throwing its baby at the walls of a cage.

It was too much. Nick didn't need an investigative journalist. He needed a *therapist*.

I couldn't do it. I was no Nellie Bly. I was just a teenager.

Nick was still curled over, his face hidden. I knew I should stay with him, try to make things okay, let him know that at least someone in the world cared. But every single cell and atom in my body was humming with fear. I knew about the fight-or-flight response – it had always seemed a cliché. But it was real.

I fled Nick's room, leaving his house, his life and the love-shy project behind me.

I'd made PEZZimist.blogspot.com my homepage when I'd started the project, so it automatically loaded when I got home and powered up my laptop. I hesitated. After tonight, there was no way I was going to work on the love-shy project anymore. I should just stay away from Nick.

I slammed the lid of my laptop closed, picked up the whole thing and shoved it into the back of my wardrobe. I didn't want Nick's horrible life to infect mine. I didn't ever want to see him again. I couldn't do it. I just couldn't.

11

It wasn't difficult to avoid Nick on Friday. At lunchtime I went to my SRC meeting, where we finalised the catering and entertainment for the social. We'd sold tickets to nearly 80 per cent of the student body, so we'd make a tidy profit and I could finally start implementing the canteen recycling program I'd been working on. After school there was a special pre-publication meeting of the *Gazette*, where we finalised the layout and story list for the next edition. East Glendale's star basketball champion needed a knee reconstruction. The Vegan Alliance was picketing the Home Economics room for not offering any cruelty-free recipes. Mr Whiteside was retiring at the end of the semester, after working at the school for forty-eight years.

'What about the front page?' asked Ms Tidy. 'You've been working on something, haven't you, Penny?'

'Um.' I hadn't, although I'd told her I needed to skip the

last meeting because I'd been too busy working on a story. The love-shy story. Which I'd never intended for the *Gazette* in the first place, but was now not going to write at all.

The rest of the *Gazette* committee looked at me expectantly. I couldn't tell them I hadn't done anything.

'Yep,' I said. 'It's nearly done.'

'And...' Ms Tidy raised her eyebrows. 'Can you share the topic with us?'

'N-no,' I said slowly. 'The article is of a very sensitive nature. It's a profile of a student. I can't tell you who it is yet.'

Ms Tidy seemed unimpressed, but it was nearly four-thirty, and I had a train to catch. I'd have to come up with an idea for a front-page story. But it wasn't as though I hadn't done it before. I did it every issue. It could wait.

I'd told Hamish and Rin to meet me at Scuttlebutt at eight o'clock on Saturday night, and we'd head to Sarah Parsons' party from there. That way I could make sure the initial meeting went reasonably smoothly and Hamish didn't say anything too offensive.

The café was more crowded at night than it was during the day, with people sipping coffee or drinking fancy designer beers and eating Turkish bread and dips. I caught sight of Hamish sitting at a table near the kitchen. I cringed inwardly. He was wearing a *tie*, and not in an ironic way. A short-sleeved white shirt was tucked into jeans that, judging from the centre-crease, had been ironed by his mother.

'Hi,' I said, walking up to the table and sitting down.

'What's wrong?' said Hamish, looking concerned. 'It's the tie, isn't it?'

Guess my cringe hadn't been as inward as I'd thought. 'It does look a bit like your mum picked your outfit.'

Hamish quickly removed the tie. It was a clip-on.

'Anything else?' he asked.

'Untuck your shirt. And maybe try messing up your hair. It's very shiny.'

Hamish complied, and looked marginally better. It was the best I could do without a reality-TV makeover crew.

'Um,' said a tiny voice behind my elbow. It was Rin, wearing a very short skirt with white socks pulled above the knee. She looked like a character from *Sailor Moon*.

'Hi, Rin!' I said, standing up. Hamish stood too, and knocked over his chair. Once he'd recovered himself, I introduced him to Rin, and they shyly shook hands.

We all sat down, and I tried to get Rin and Hamish to talk to each other. But they were both pathetic, gazing down at their laps and nodding along to my attempts at conversation. It was like talking with *two* bobble-headed dolls. Except at least the dolls usually smiled.

'So the party should be fun,' I said, lamely.

Rin and Hamish nodded again. I resisted the urge to groan, and checked my watch.

'Is Nick coming?' asked Hamish, with a slightly smarmy look.

Rin's eyes opened wide. 'Why would Nick be coming?' she asked me. 'Did you guys— Are you *dating*?'

'What? No. No, we're not dating, and no, he's not coming.' I glared at Hamish.

'Oh,' said Rin, sounding disappointed for me. She lowered her voice and leaned over to me, her eyes sparkling. 'Maybe you'll meet someone at the party.'

I opened my mouth to tell her I had neither the intention nor the desire to meet *anyone* at the party, but found I had neither the energy nor the heart to disappoint her.

'Right,' I said instead. 'Well, I guess we should go.'

'I might run to the bathroom first,' said Rin.

While she was gone, Hamish reached into his bag and popped a breath mint into his mouth. I raised my eyebrows.

'Better to be on the safe side,' he said. 'I had a kebab for dinner.'

My plan was going as well as could be expected.

Sarah Parsons' party was in its early stages when we arrived, which was good. I tended to get bored once everyone was drunk and making out on the couches or vomiting into the bushes.

There was some reasonably inoffensive and not-too-loud pop music playing on the stereo, and people were gathered in clusters, chatting, drinking and eating corn chips.

I gave Sarah a hug (I didn't really like hugging, but I did realise this was what you were supposed to do at a party) and nearly choked on her perfume. 'Happy birthday!' I said, and introduced Hamish and Rin. Sarah may have been a little surprised that I'd brought *two* dates along – especially one as dorky as Hamish – but she was far too polite to say anything, as I'd expected.

We settled on a couch and I sent Hamish off to get us something non-alcoholic to drink.

'So,' I said to Rin. 'What do you think of Hamish?'

Rin shrugged. 'He's very quiet. But he seems...okay.'

'He told me that he thinks you're very pretty,' I lied.

She blushed. 'Really?'

'Really. And did you see he has blue eyes and freckles?'

Rin nodded, pleased. 'This is fun,' she said. 'I actually know people here. That girl over there is in the Manga Club at school. I can't believe I'm at a party! With boys!'

Hamish came back, inexpertly carrying three drinks at

once and sploshing lemon squash all over his wrist. Maybe it was time for me to give these two some privacy.

I saw Amy Butler across the room. 'Can you guys excuse me for a moment?' I said. 'I have to go and say hi to someone.'

Amy was sitting on a stool at the breakfast bar and swinging her legs, a plastic cup of something orange in her hand. I hoped it was just Fanta, but I doubted it.

'Hi Penny!' Amy gave me a kiss on the cheek. Definitely not just Fanta. 'Are you feeling better?'

I blinked. 'What?'

'It was sooo unfair, you getting disqualified just because you were sick.'

'Yeah,' I said. 'That *was* unfair.'

I thought about the swimming carnival for a moment. A month ago I would have been furious. I would have confronted the principal and written an editorial for the *Gazette*. I wouldn't have rested until I had that Swimming Cup in my hand. But now I couldn't quite bring myself to care. I took it as evidence that I was growing as a person and felt quite proud.

Amy Butler hiccuped, and I considered the possibility that I might be thrown up on a second time in as many weeks.

'So there are, like, *no* cute guys at this party,' said Amy.

I studied the various boys nearby. James O'Keefe was pressed against Caitlin Reece, his hands creeping up under her T-shirt. Con Stingas and Andrew Rogers were having a competition to see who could fit the most Cheezels in his mouth. Max Wendt was showing Perry Chau a video of something on his phone that was, if Perry's delighted exclamations were anything to go by, very lewd indeed.

'No argument here,' I said.

I glanced over to Rin and Hamish. Rin was waving her hands around animatedly as she explained something to Hamish, who kept nervously licking his lips. I sighed.

'Sometimes I think that there are no cute boys anywhere,' I said. 'They're all freaks.'

'There *are* nice ones,' said Amy with a secretive smile.

I immediately thought of Nick. 'Really? Like who?'

Amy screwed up her pretty nose. 'Oh, I don't know. Nice guys who are, like . . . nice. And funny and good-looking.'

Well, Nick fitted all those categories. Most of them, anyway. He was good-looking, and he was certainly funny-peculiar even if he wasn't laugh-out-loud funny. Was he *nice*? He'd waited for me after he'd thrown up on my boobs. Although that might be stretching the definition of *nice*.

'Do you have anyone in mind?' I asked. 'Specifically?'

She gave me a cheeky smile. 'Maybe,' she said.

I couldn't help myself. 'Would you think about dating someone who was . . . a bit different?'

'Like a Year Twelve?'

'No...more different than that.'

Amy leaned her head towards mine. 'You know,' she said softly. 'I kind of have. There *is*...someone. And he's not exactly the kind of guy I thought I would ever like. I mean, he's pretty cute, but he isn't very popular.'

Did Amy like *Nick*? Was that possible? What if they got together? I imagined it for a moment. It'd be a total disaster. He wouldn't be happy with her. She wasn't smart enough for him; they'd never be able to have a proper conversation. And that's what Nick wanted, I was sure of it. He could go on about her long hair and pretty face, but what he really wanted was a soul-mate, right? Someone he could open up to, someone he could be his true self with.

Except...what *was* Nick's true self? Now I'd been to his house and met his parents, I wasn't sure I knew him at all. Would he ever be able to have a conversation with a girl he liked? A relationship? Or was he just too broken?

Why did I even care? I wasn't writing the article anymore.

'I've seen him watching me,' said Amy. 'And at first I was creeped out, because, well, he's a bit weird. But then I looked at him properly, and I thought...maybe. He has beautiful eyes.'

Nick *did* have beautiful eyes. Grey and soulful, with very long lashes.

'So do you think he likes you?'

'Oh, I'm sure he does,' said Amy. 'And I think maybe because he's quiet, and I'm quiet too, he wouldn't want to talk all the time the way some boys do.'

It *was* Nick! She liked Nick! Of course, Nick was quiet because he was shy, and Amy was quiet because she didn't have much to say. But still. She *liked* him.

I wasn't sure how I felt about this.

'And he'd never cheat on me,' continued Amy, 'because I'm so much prettier than most of the girls he'd be able to get.'

'I don't know, Amy,' I said. 'If he's so shy, how do you know he'd open up around you?'

'I just know,' she said. 'And anyway, he's not shy around his friends.'

Wait. 'His friends?'

'Yeah, he's fine with them. Always chatting and laughing. Unless he's looking at me. With those eyes.' She sighed happily.

'Um,' I said. My Jenga tower of assumptions was swaying. 'So who is this guy, Amy? With the eyes?'

Amy leaned over and whispered boozily into my ear, '*Youssef.* Youssef Saad. I *know* he's a dork, but at least he's a Year Ten dork, so that's better than dating a dork in my year. Do you really think I should go for it?'

'Sure,' I said, suddenly feeling a bit strange. 'Could you excuse me? I have to visit the bathroom.'

'Wait,' said Amy. 'Is it true that you're going out with Nick Rammage?'

'*What?*'

'Kate Pittman said she saw you guys sitting together at lunch, two days in a row. And he never sits with anyone.'

I nearly fell over. People thought Nick and I were *dating*?

'I told her it was probably just something for the school paper,' said Amy. 'Nick doesn't really seem your type, and doesn't he have a girlfriend at another school?'

'You're right,' I said. 'It was just something for the paper.'

I stumbled away. Did it make me a bad person that I was relieved Amy didn't like Nick? Was it that I didn't think Amy would make Nick happy? Or didn't I *want* him to be happy? And why was I thinking about him so much, anyway? The love-shy project was terminated.

And Youssef Saad *was* a really nice guy. He'd take care of Amy. Good for her.

Rin was chatting to a few girls over by the TV. She seemed perfectly comfortable, laughing and swaying from side to side with the music. I couldn't see Hamish anywhere.

I sighed and went back to the couch. I didn't feel like talking to anyone. Usually I tried to chat to everyone at a party, in case someone dropped some particularly interesting piece of gossip that I could use in the paper, but my heart just wasn't in it.

A daggy '80s song started playing, and someone turned up the sound. Girls squealed and dragged boys into the middle of the room to dance.

'Hey, Penny.' Hugh Forward sat down next to me on the couch. Brave, considering how totally he had humiliated himself at last year's cast party. He was wearing a brown corduroy jacket with a tweed cap. Probably to keep his insane hair under control, but it worked, in a grandpa kind of way.

'I suppose you're making some keen observations about the nature of adolescent interaction,' he said. 'I'm sure I'll read about it someday in one of your books.'

He was clearly joking, yet surprisingly close to the truth. 'Something like that,' I said.

Hugh cleared his throat.

'Aloof, aloof, we stand aloof, so stand
Thou too aloof, bound with the flawless band
Of inner solitude; we bind not thee;
But who from thy self-chain shall set thee free?'

I stared at him.

'Christina Rossetti,' he said, a little flustered. 'I thought about what you said the other day in the library, about how we don't study much writing by women. And I realised I'd never read any poetry by women, which is weird, because I've read a lot of poetry. So I'm rectifying the situation.'

That was unexpected. And...impressive. 'How are you finding it?'

'Excellent,' he said. 'I'm loving Christina Rosetti and Emily Dickinson and Dorothy Parker. Anne Sexton's a little full on, though.'

I nodded knowingly, although I'd actually never read anything by any of them. Perhaps I wasn't a very good feminist after all? But I really wasn't a poetry kind of person, although I didn't want to admit it.

'I think we spend too much time praising women for how they look,' Hugh went on, 'and not enough time praising what they say. However, as you already know I'm a big fan of the things you say, I will also add that you look very nice tonight.'

'Thanks,' I replied, although I knew he didn't mean it. I was wearing jeans and a dark blue shirt. I didn't see the point of getting dressed up to hang out in some lounge room with a bunch of kids I saw every day at school.

'I haven't seen you around much lately,' Hugh said. 'You've missed a few SRC and Debating meetings.'

Great. He'd come over to guilt-trip me. 'I've been busy.'

'Really? Busy with what?' Hugh paused. 'Or...who?'

What business was it of his? I'd only missed a couple of meetings. 'Stuff,' I said, in what I hoped was a dismissive tone of voice. 'The paper.'

'Of course. How's the paper going?'

I shrugged, and idly wondered what I should write about for the lead story. Maybe I *should* write that editorial on the swimming carnival after all. Although maybe I just needed a new assignment. An investigative feature was still a good idea, even if love-shyness wasn't the right topic. Maybe I should go undercover, like Nellie Bly. Where could I go? The inner chambers of our local council? A suspiciously steroidy gymnasium? One of those super-religious schools where they don't let the students read *Harry Potter*?

I realised Hugh was staring at me. 'What?'

'I asked you about the paper, and then you just shrugged and stared off into the distance.'

'Oh,' I said. 'Right, yes. The paper's great. Just generating some new story ideas at the moment.'

'Awesome.'

'Yep.'

'So are you going to the social? I'm glad we sorted out all that stuff with the decorations budget.'

'I suppose so,' I said. 'I'll have to cover it for the paper.'

I wondered what exactly it was that he wanted. Was it about our upcoming Debating final? Or was he just being polite because I was sitting on my own?

'Er,' said Hugh. 'Do you want to dance?'

'At the social? I'll probably be too busy with *Gazette* stuff.'

'No, here.'

'What?'

'Dance. With me. Now. Here.' He nodded his head towards the dance floor area.

This was unexpected. And he didn't seem drunk. 'Um, no thanks. I don't really dance.'

'Oh. Okay.'

We sat uncomfortably for a minute, and I wondered why I'd turned him down. Dancing might have been nice. I tried to remember what we'd been talking about when he tried to tongue me in the ear at last year's cast party, but couldn't. I did remember he'd been wearing a grey argyle vest, though. And a cream shirt. It had made him look as though he should have been playing a banjo in a sepia photograph. And I remembered laughing. I think I'd been enjoying our conversation, until he ruined it with the tongue thing. Boys.

'So,' said Hugh. 'I'm going to get another drink.'

He stood and left, and I stayed on the couch. He wouldn't be coming back. I should have agreed to dance with him. But I didn't want him to try to kiss me again, and it wasn't like he *liked* me. He'd probably just felt sorry for me because I was sitting here on my own.

I wondered what would have happened if I *had* been able to convince Nick to come. Would he have spoken to anyone? Would he have found out about Amy's crush on

Youssef and broken down? Or would he have finally relaxed and enjoyed himself? There were plenty of other girls here who would have wanted to talk to him.

I imagined Nick in his room, surrounded by his Pez dispensers and romantic music CDs and terrariums. Perhaps he was making a new one, gently packing damp earth and moss into the delicate glass.

'Penny?' It was Hamish, standing a little too close to me. I could smell alcohol on his breath.

'Hey,' I said. 'Are you having fun?'

'Can I talk to you?' he said, swaying slightly. 'Outside? I need your advice.'

'Sure,' I said, and followed him outside. Fairy lights were strung across the back porch, and a few couples were ensconced behind bushes and on loveseats. Hamish led me to the edge of the porch and sat down, his legs hanging over the side. The air was warm and smelled of jasmine. It would have been quite romantic, if I was the kind of person who believed in romance, and was there with someone other than Hamish.

'What's up?' I asked.

'Um,' he said. 'Thanks for inviting me to the party.'

'You're welcome,' I said. 'Have you been talking to Rin? She's lovely, right?'

'Yeah,' said Hamish. 'She's nice.'

Excellent. At least one of my plans was working. I waited for Hamish to continue. Did he want advice about Rin? How to ask her out on a proper date? Or her phone number?

'I really appreciate what you're doing for me, Penny,' said Hamish. 'It's very kind. Not many people are that kind.'

'It's nothing,' I said.

Hamish swayed again, and his shoulder bumped against mine. He must have drunk quite a lot. I tried to shuffle away subtly. I didn't want *another* shy guy to throw up on me.

'Hamish? Are you okay?'

'I'm okay,' he said. 'I'm good, actually. Really good. Everything feels right, don't you think? Tonight?'

'Sure.'

'The weather is lovely, people are lovely, these little lights are lovely.'

'Uh-huh.'

'You're lovely.'

Oh, crap.

And then Hamish was pressed up against me, pushing his face into mine. It was disgusting. He made a sort of moaning noise and slobbered all over my mouth.

'Hamish, *no*.' I squirmed away and wiped my chin.

He looked dismayed. 'But you said you'd help me.'

'I will,' I said. 'I am. But I'm not going to *make out* with you.'

'Then why did you invite me here?'

'I didn't,' I said. 'You asked me to come out here with you.'

'Not out here, to the *party*.'

'Oh,' I said. 'I was trying to *help* you be less shy.'

'So kiss me.'

'No.'

'Please? Just for a little while.'

'*No.*'

'What if I gave you fifty dollars?'

I stared at him, outraged. 'Then I'd feel like a hooker.'

Hamish looked as if he might cry. 'I just want to *touch* a girl.'

'You will,' I said. 'But you can't just *jump* on them like that. You have to ease into it. And less tongue. *Much* less tongue. The object of kissing is not to open your mouth as wide as you can and try to swallow a girl's head.'

'Show me. Show me how to do it properly.'

I rolled my eyes. 'Let me make this very simple for you, Hamish. I'm not interested in you. I will never be interested in you. I brought you to this party, yes. But I brought someone else too, remember? Rin? Rin doesn't have a boyfriend. Why don't you go inside and talk to her? And perhaps try to have a conversation and hold her hand before you suffocate her with your face.'

I went inside without waiting for a response.

Hugh Forward was on the dance floor, slow-dancing with painfully skinny Olivia Fischer. I scowled at her. I'd often wondered how her tiny frame had enough energy to get to the other end of the swimming pool, and now she was expending all that energy dancing and flirting with boys. I felt sorry for Olivia, really. She looked hungry. She was like a Hungry Hungry Hippo, except with no hips and extra helpings of ho.

I shuddered. I really *was* a bad feminist. And how could I be jealous? I'd turned Hugh down. It wasn't as if I *liked* him, even with his cute vintage outfit and his sensitive quotes from female poets. I needed to stop hanging around with so many hormonal teenagers – it was starting to rub off on me.

I had a sudden, unpleasant flashback to Hamish trying to kiss me. What would I have done if Nick had tried that? Would I have pulled away and told him it would be unethical for us to become romantically involved?

I'd had enough. I went over to Rin and the girls from the Manga Club. 'I've got a headache,' I told her. 'I kind of want to go home.'

Rin nodded. 'Let's go straight away. Shall we call a taxi?'

I'd expected her to stay at the party, and send me home on my own. But she didn't. We walked out the front and she speedily rang for a cab.

'Thanks so much for bringing me, Penny,' she said. 'Are you okay? Is your head all right?'

'I'm fine,' I said, touched. 'Just tired, I think. And you're welcome. I'm glad you enjoyed yourself.'

'Oh, I *did*. Everything was *wonderful*.'

She was so starry-eyed and glowing, I felt bad I hadn't been able to orchestrate anything successful between her and Hamish. Then again, she totally deserved better than him.

Dad was still up when I got home, curled up on the couch reading something by Dostoyevsky and drinking herbal tea. I sat down by his feet.

'Did you have a good time?' he asked, not glancing up from his book.

'Yep,' I said, without much enthusiasm.

Dad nodded. I played with the tassels on a cushion.

'Dad?'

'Hmm?' He turned a page.

'What would you do if your doctor told you that you only had six months to live?'

'I'd get a second opinion.'

'I'm serious.'

Dad closed his book, marking his place with a finger. 'If my doctor told me I had six months to live?'

'And your lifestyle wouldn't be impeded by your illness.'

Dad considered it. 'I'd make sure I had enough money set aside to take care of you.'

'And what else?'

'I guess I'd use the rest to travel.'

'Really?' I wasn't a loner loser freak like Nick, after all. Everyone wanted to travel. Who didn't want to see as much of the world as possible before they had to leave it?

'I'd go to Machu Picchu. And Angkor Wat. And New York, because I know how much you want to go there—'

'Wait,' I said. 'I'm there too?'

Dad laughed. 'Of course you are,' he said. 'I'm not going anywhere without you.'

'But what if I wanted to do different things to you? Go to different places?'

'We'd figure something out.'

'But it's your last chance to do what you want. Do you really want to have to compromise?'

Dad seemed puzzled. 'Well, there'd be no point seeing all those places unless I had someone to share them with.'

I undid my shoelace, and then did it back up again.

'Penny?' Dad touched my shoulder. 'Are you okay?'

I nodded, then straightened up and smiled at him. 'Don't you want Josh to come, too? On our round-the-world tour?'

'Would that be okay with you?'

'Of course!' I said. 'You know I like Josh.'

'I know.'

'And...well, isn't he part of our family now?'

Dad smiled – and I think he actually blushed.

I took his hand and squeezed it. 'You know, Dad, if you ever want to ask Josh to move in here with us...it's fine with me.'

Dad looked surprised, then leaned over to give me a hug.

'I love you, kiddo,' he said.

'I love you too,' I replied, and I meant it. I wondered if Nick had ever said those words. Or whether anyone had ever said them to him. I wondered if anyone ever would.

I couldn't help myself. I needed to know that Nick was okay, that he hadn't done something stupid. I'd just check his blog this one last time. Then I'd give up.

08:27

There's a party on tonight. I've been invited, not by the hostess, but still. An invite is an invite. I haven't been invited to a party since I was six.

I'm going to go. I *must* go. I *can* control this thing.

What should I wear? I've pulled every item of clothing out of my wardrobe, and can find nothing. I can't wear what I've worn to school before. I need special party clothes.

What are special party clothes?

Nick *had* wanted to go to the party? That meant that he didn't hate me. Well, that was something.

13:18

I've just spent three hours looking at YouTube videos of teen parties to get a feel of what it will be like. Will there be alcohol? Should I drink any? Would I be expected to provide my own alcohol? What's the protocol? The last time I went to a birthday party, there was a cake with candles and Pass the Parcel and Pin the Tail on the Donkey. I took a present wrapped up in shiny yellow paper, and a card in a purple envelope. Then I had a panic attack at the front door and had to be taken home. Should I take a gift? A card? A packet of chips?
I've already showered three times today. I don't want to smell bad. I might put on some more deodorant.

16:02

What if someone tries to talk to me? I'll say the wrong thing, and they'll learn I'm not worth speaking to. Then I'll just be on my own and everyone will stare at me and whisper and know that I'm the one, the loser who everyone hates. I won't even be invisible anymore, I'll be naked and exposed and they'll laugh and jeer and it will be like summer camp all over again.

I can't go.

I can't.

I can't do it.

18:29

I have to go. I *will*. I need to do this. I'm going to have another shower to calm my nerves, then get dressed and go.

21:48

I didn't go.

I wanted to. I had eight showers today, washed and dried my outfit twice, and laid it out on my bed. Then when I came back from my last shower, I froze in the middle of my room, wearing a towel around my waist. I couldn't do it. I couldn't get dressed. It was like I'd been paralysed. I stood there for an hour, shivering.

I'll never get better. This is it. This is my life. Nothing will ever change.

I switched off my computer, feeling a bit sick. I wished I'd been stronger, braver. I wished I'd been able to help Nick. I wished I hadn't fled from his house the other night. I wished I'd never gone there in the first place. I wished I'd never heard of love-shyness.

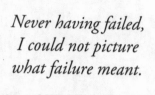

Never having failed,
I could not picture
what failure meant.

NELLIE BLY

12

As i headed for my locker after Maths on Monday morning, Ms Tidy stopped me in the hallway. 'How's everything going, Penny?'

I shrugged. 'Fine.'

'Are you sure?' she said. 'You seemed a little distant in Friday's meeting.'

'Sorry,' I said. 'I've been working on that new story.'

'Of course,' said Ms Tidy. 'The mystery story. Look, Penny, maybe you could take over the story on the Home Economics picket as well. Arabella's writing really isn't up to scratch. And just in case this feature you're planning doesn't work out. If it does, then we'll run it on the front page and the vegan picket can go on page four. In fact, I've already emailed you Arabella's notes. Is that all right?'

I smiled. 'Of course.'

'Great,' said Ms Tidy, brightening. 'The other thing is, I'd really like to see a draft by the end of lunch today, so I can run it by the principal's office. Sensitive issue, you know how it is.'

'Of course,' I said. 'I'll do it now.'

Rin came bouncing up to my locker as I was putting away my books. 'I had *so* much fun at the party,' she said. 'Thank you so much for taking me!'

'Not a problem,' I said. 'I'm glad you enjoyed yourself.'

'I did!' Rin sighed happily. 'I wish I could go to a party every weekend.'

I shuddered. Sounded like my idea of hell. 'Well, you know the social is coming up soon. Do you have a ticket?'

Rin nodded. 'I told my parents we'd be going together. That's okay, isn't it? They like you because you're responsible and have your whole career planned out.' She rolled her eyes.

'Um, yeah,' I said. 'Sure. That's fine.'

Rin clapped her hands. 'What are you going to wear?' she asked. 'Do you think anyone'll ask me to dance?'

'I'm sure they will,' I said. 'Look, Rin, I can't really talk right now.'

Her face fell a little. 'Oh.'

'Sorry,' I said. 'I have to write this article for the paper. But I'll see you later, okay?'

Rin nodded and gave me an impulsive hug. 'Oh!' she

said. 'I almost forgot. Did you finish reading the manga I gave you? Because I have the latest volume of *Battle Vixens*, if you want to borrow it.'

'That'd be...great.' I'd completely forgotten about the books Rin had lent me.

'Ace!' she said, and skipped off.

I closed my locker door to find Hamish standing behind it. I started. 'Could you try to be a little less creepy?'

'I want her number,' he said.

'What? Whose number?'

'Rin's.'

I blinked. 'I thought you liked *me*.'

Hamish shrugged. 'But she likes manga,' he said. 'Plus I can't be bothered playing your hard-to-get game.'

My mouth fell open. 'My *what*? I'm not playing any kind of game! I'm not hard to get – I'm not *available*.'

'Whatever. So can I have her number?'

'No,' I said, mostly because Hamish was being a creep, but also because I hadn't actually saved Rin's number to my phone. 'If you want to ask her out, you should give her *your* number.'

'Are you crazy?' he said. 'What if she laughs at me?'

'Then the seas will boil and a plague of frogs will rain down from the sky,' I said. 'Now if you'll excuse me, I have to get to the library.'

I turned on my heel and stalked down the hallway, only to be waylaid by Hugh Forward. 'What is it *now*?' I snapped.

Hugh raised his eyebrows. 'I just need you to sign off on the social budget so we can put in the catering order.'

I took a deep breath and resisted the urge to push him out of the way. 'Can it wait until lunchtime? I'm kind of busy right now.'

'They need it by midday,' said Hugh. 'Come on, it'll only take a minute.'

I sighed and followed him to the office, where the secretary spent far too long searching for the right form and a stamp.

'Looking forward to the debate?' asked Hugh.

'Sure,' I said shortly, glancing at my watch.

'I hear St Catherine's is the other school in the final. They should be pretty easy to beat.'

'Yep.'

Hugh cocked his head. 'Are you okay?' he asked. 'You seem a little preoccupied.'

'Well, I *was* in the middle of something when you dragged me here,' I said.

He chuckled. 'You really are in a bad mood today,' he said. 'Worse than usual.'

What was that supposed to mean? *Worse than usual.* I wasn't normally in a bad mood. I wasn't in a bad mood *now*, I just had to write this stupid article for Ms Tidy. Who cared if the Vegan Alliance wanted to picket the Home Ec room? Home Economics was an elective, so if the vegans didn't want to learn how to make an omelette, they should take metalwork or graphic design.

'Here we are,' said the secretary, producing a piece of paper. I scribbled my name on it and left Hugh to finish all the administrative nonsense. I was halfway up the stairs to the library when the bell went for third period. I groaned. I'd have to write the article at lunchtime.

I headed to the library as soon as the lunch bell rang. I could easily dash off the Vegan Alliance article and have it to Ms Tidy by the end of lunch.

I trawled the National Institute of Food Technology's website, and found some statistics about the proportion of vegetarian dishes made in Home Economics classrooms. Arabella had already collected some quotes from the picketers, and a response from Mr Delaney, the Home Ec teacher. I just had to pull it all together. If I'd had more time I would have done some more in-depth research about civil rights and possibly the differences between public-school Home Economics curriculums and, say, the programs at Jewish or Muslim schools, or schools with a high percentage of Hindu students. But I didn't have time, and frankly it wasn't as if anyone would notice if I put in a little less effort than usual.

'Um.'

It was Nick looming over me. My heart started to hammer. 'Hey,' I said, feeling strangely awkward.

He stood there for a moment, biting his lower lip. 'Do you want to take a walk?'

I looked at my computer screen. I'd written one hundred and fifty words. But I could finish it later. The principal didn't really need to see it, and it was only going to layout this afternoon. It wouldn't actually go the printer for at least another week.

'Sure.'

We wandered through the school grounds, not speaking. What did he want? Was he mad at me? Was he going to cry again? Was he about to beg me to promise I wouldn't tell anyone about his crazy family? No fear there – I didn't even want to *think* about them. Every time I did, I could see Nick's mother crying into her dry roast beef, while Nick's father ignored everyone and listened to the radio. It made me feel sick.

Nick stopped by the bench where we'd had our first conversation, and sat down abruptly. I did the same. We sat there in silence for a while.

'I wanted to thank you.'

Thank me? For what, inviting myself over to his house and witnessing his miserable crazy family? I looked across at him, but he was staring at the ground.

'I didn't . . . I'd got used to the way things were. It wasn't until you showed up that I realised . . . how bad everything is. How wrong.'

'Oh.' I had no idea what to say. I couldn't tell him it'd be all right. It wouldn't. That family wasn't going to change anytime soon. And it wasn't as though Nick could leave them. You can't choose your family, and you can't make them go away just because they're insane.

'I thought I'd be in trouble because you came over. After you left I waited in my room for them to come up and tell me I'd done something wrong. But they didn't come. And, I realised that I'd done something *right*. Something normal. I'd invited a friend over for dinner – or at least that's what they thought. And that was something normal people do. And even though I didn't actually invite you over, it still made me feel . . . like I could do some other normal things.'

I nodded encouragingly.

'But it's hard. And I tried to go to that party you told me about . . . ' He shook his head.

I couldn't tell him that I knew what had happened – he still didn't know I was reading his blog. So I just kept nodding.

'And I realised that you *have* helped me. I can talk to you – I'm doing it now. I've never done that before. It's weird how much it helps to talk about stuff. I thought it'd make everything scarier, more real, but it actually makes things easier. Like, if I can talk about it, then maybe I can *do* something about it.'

I'd helped Nick. I'd *helped* him. The project was working. A vision of a feature article popped into my head, in the *New Yorker* or the *Monthly* or *Vanity Fair*. I'd call it 'The Love-shy Experiment'.

'But,' said Nick, 'you can't fix me.'

Why not? It was working so far, wasn't it? He'd just said it was.

'I think I need… something more intense. More serious.'

It was as if Nick were breaking up with me. Which was silly, because we weren't dating – and never would. I wasn't his type and, anyway, I didn't want to be dating anyone.

'So I made an appointment to see a counsellor.'

'Oh,' I said. I thought about it for a moment. 'Good for you.'

It *was* good. I couldn't fix Nick entirely. He needed professional help, and I wasn't a therapist. But I could still follow his journey, document it, support him. The article was back on!

'It's tomorrow,' he said. 'After school. At the community clinic. And, um...'

His cheeks went pink.

'Do you want me to wait for you?' I asked. 'Be there when you come out?'

He nodded, relieved. 'Yes, please.'

There was a noise from over near the basketball courts, and Nick's head popped up like a startled bunny's. James O'Keefe and Rory Singh were playing one-on-one basketball, yelling some pretty horrific things about each other's mothers. Nick flinched.

'Oh,' I said. 'The Teenage Boy in his natural habitat. What a beautiful thing.'

'It isn't *my* natural habitat,' said Nick.

'No,' I said. 'You wouldn't like sport much, would you?'

Nick shook his head. 'I just don't get it,' he said, talking very fast all of a sudden. 'I don't get the *point* of running around and sweating and grunting and hitting other boys. It just looks painful. I can't think of anything worse than all that *effort* for nothing. I mean, what do you get out of it? The opportunity to rub your sweaty body up against some other guy's? *Gross.*'

I laughed. This was good. He was talking in full sentences. And he certainly had a point regarding the sweaty boys and the grunting. 'You're definitely not gay, then.'

'No,' said Nick. 'I don't like boys. Not for anything. Not even to talk to. Boys are loud and violent and scary.'

'Do you ever wish you were a girl?'

Nick shrugged. 'Sometimes. But when I do I wish I was a lesbian. Because I'd never want to be with a guy. Guys are horrid.'

'A male lesbian,' I said. 'Fair enough.'

'I kind of wish I was attracted to boys,' said Nick.

'Really?'

Nick shrugged. 'At least if I was gay I wouldn't always have to make the first move. Someone might try hitting on *me* for a change.'

I frowned. 'But Nick, girls hit on you all the time. Girls *faint* in class so you'll notice them. Any sane girl would want to go out with you.'

'Do you?'

'Um,' I said, feeling my cheeks flush. 'No. Of course not. Definitely not. *No.* But I don't want to go out with anyone, so don't take it personally. But whenever one of those girls *does* come up and talk to you, you act like you're too good for them. You don't *seem* shy. Everyone thinks you have a girlfriend at your old school.'

Nick went very quiet, and I knew he was thinking about his old school, and why he moved.

James bellowed and tackled Rory to the ground, although

not in a particularly aggressive way. It looked like standard boy-silliness to me, but it seemed to be upsetting Nick, who winced every time they swore or did something violent.

'Come on,' I said. 'Let's keep walking.'

Nick and I headed across the oval towards the creek that ran along its furthest edge. We weren't technically allowed down there as it was out of school bounds, but there weren't any teachers around, and Nick seemed pretty comfortable – he wagged school all the time. We walked in silence, but it didn't feel particularly awkward. I decided to wait until he said something. Let him make the next move, as it were.

It took ten minutes. The branches and undergrowth opened up suddenly into a pretty green patch of grass, fringed with yellow buttercups that went right down to the edge of the creek, where two ducks circled lazily in the sluggish current of the creek.

'Oh,' said Nick softly. 'How lovely.'

'Do you want to sit?' I asked, indicating the green patch. It looked soft and comfortable.

'Where?'

'Here,' I said. 'On the grass.'

Nick made an incredulous noise. 'On the *ground*? You must be crazy. There could be syringes, or dog mess, or *anything*.'

I raised my eyebrows. 'Dog *mess*?'

'Just think of the *germs*!' He stopped, looking embarrassed. 'I'm doing it, aren't I? Being ridiculous and melodramatic.'

'A little bit.'

Nick took a deep breath, and closed his eyes for a moment. 'Sorry,' he said. 'I'm trying to be more normal.'

'That's good,' I said. 'You're doing a good job.'

'It's nice of you to pretend that.' He smiled in his fluttery, nervous way. 'But I'm still not sitting on the grass.'

'Why are you so afraid of sitting on the ground?' I asked, as we turned and headed back towards school.

'Mysophobia.'

'Fear of germs?' I guessed. 'How many phobias do you have, exactly?'

'I'm trying to collect a full set.' I could see he was trying to be funny, but his face drooped miserably.

'Is that why your house is covered in plastic?' I asked. 'Is your mum a germ-freak too?'

He nodded. 'She never let me play outside when I was little, and always sprayed her hands with hand sanitiser after picking me up or touching me.'

Yikes.

'But what about gardening?' I asked. 'You like making your little terrariums, but you won't sit on the grass because there might be dog poo?'

Nick looked uncomfortable. 'I use potting-mix for the

terrariums,' he explained. 'It comes in a sealed plastic packet, so I know it doesn't have any bugs or dog... mess. And I wear gloves and wash my hands with antibacterial soap and then have a shower.'

For a moment panic rose inside me, the way it had at Nick's house. I wanted to run away from him and all his crazy problems. It was too much to fix. He'd never get better.

'Did you ever read *The Secret Garden*?' Nick asked suddenly. 'When you were a kid?'

'Um,' I said. 'Yes, I think so. With that horrible bossy girl and the boy in the wheelchair?'

'The girl kind of reminds me of you,' said Nick.

I felt stung. 'I'm not horrible and bossy.'

Nick gave a little huffing chuckle. 'Well, you're not *horrible*,' he said. 'But neither is Mary. Not really.' He gave me a sly smile. 'Not once you get to know her.'

I wasn't sure how to respond to that.

'Anyway,' he said, 'I love the way they talk about nature in that book. Like it's something wild and beautiful and powerful. I love the descriptions of Mary and Colin lying in the grass and meeting animals and getting dirt under their fingernails and really *growing* things. Bringing life into the world.'

Nick's eyes were bright, and he had a faraway, peaceful expression on his face. 'I want that,' he said. 'I want to feel the dirt under my fingernails. I want to be outside in a garden, with the sun on my face and the smell of things growing all around me. I want to do that and be *happy*, instead of worrying about *clostridium perfringens* and *listeria monocytogenes* and *vibro cholerae*. I want to get better.'

'You will,' I told him. 'You will get better.'

'I know,' said Nick. 'You're like my Mary, bossing me around to make me be less pathetic, and I'm like Colin, all weak and afraid of the world at first, but growing stronger and braver every day.'

I frowned. 'Can't I be the other one? The other boy who has the magic nature power and talks to robins?'

Nick gave me a long look paired with an almost sarcastic smile. 'No,' he said with another chuckle. 'You're definitely Mary.'

When I read Nick's latest post that afternoon after school, I wanted to squeal with happiness. Progress! I was making progress. It was working!

17:58

I'm not sure if today was the worst day of my life, or the beginning of something that might be good.

It started to rain as I walked home. I love the way the

world smells when it rains, like everything is new again. I love the way raindrops gather on nasturtium petals like beads of mercury.

I don't know. Can she help me? She says she can. The thing is, I don't know if I can even imagine it. The idea of it, having a real girlfriend, being able to hold a girl and talk to her and even maybe one day have *sex* with a girl that I truly love. I've spent so much time daydreaming about it, but it's kind of like daydreaming about flying or having superpowers. It seems something that is totally outside the realm of possibility.

I see other people doing it all the time. People walking together and holding hands and looking happy and com-fortable. And I just can't imagine it ever happening to me, other than in my dreams.

But maybe. Just maybe.

13

On tuesday, I barely heard a word any of my teachers said all day. I was sure I was more nervous than Nick was about his counselling appointment. Mr Gerakis called me back as I left English, and asked if I was okay.

'I'm fine,' I said. 'Why wouldn't I be?'

'You've seemed very distracted lately.'

I shrugged. 'It's a busy time of year. The Debating final is coming up, and SRC's organising the social.'

'How many extracurricular activities do you do, Penny?'

I counted. 'Swimming, Band, Debating, SRC and the *Gazette*. Five.'

Mr Gerakis raised his eyebrows. 'Five is a lot. Perhaps you should consider dropping one or two to make more time for your studies.'

Was he crazy? 'I'm sorry if I wasn't paying attention

today, Mr Gerakis. I didn't sleep well last night. But I assure you, I'm excellent at managing my time. There really isn't a problem.'

He didn't seem convinced, but I had to get to Italian, so I gave him a reassuring smile and left.

I perched on a swing in the playground outside the community centre and took some halfhearted notes for the love-shy article. I hated waiting. I wondered what Nick was talking about in there. Would he talk about me?

My phone chirped. It was a text message from Rin, asking if I wanted to come to her house for dinner. She probably wanted to talk to me about Hamish. I tapped out a quick reply to tell her I was busy. I had to support Nick – I didn't have time for matchmaking. I'd introduced her to Hamish, given them an opportunity to get to know each other, and the rest was up to them.

Nick reappeared after an hour and came to sit on the swing next to mine. He shut his eyes and let out a long, shaky breath.

'How did it go?' I asked after a few moments had passed.

'Okay. Very hard, but okay.'

He kicked his heels against the tanbark and leaned back in the swing, letting the sunshine melt into his face.

'Do you...want to talk about it?' I asked.

He shook his head. 'There's just so much...stuff. That I always thought was normal.'

'What do you mean?'

He swung in silence for a moment. 'When I was eight, I told my parents I wanted a Lego pirate ship for Christmas. I'd seen it advertised on TV and I wanted it more than anything. My father said I could have it if I played sport every Saturday for the rest of the year.'

'And did you?'

Nick nodded. 'I chose Little Athletics, because there were no balls and I didn't have to be in a team. I still hated it, though. The other kids all laughed when they had to delay a race because I hadn't finished the previous one yet. The only time I ever got a ribbon was when all the kids except me and two others got disqualified for not staying inside their lanes. And I still came third.'

I'd done Little Aths too. I don't think I'd ever *not* got a ribbon. 'But you got your Lego pirate ship, right?'

Nick dug his feet into the tanbark, halting himself midswing. 'Oh, I got it. On Christmas Day.' He smiled bitterly. 'Every single brick in place.'

'Wait, what? They put it together?'

'They stayed up on Christmas Eve and put the pirate ship together, so I wouldn't make a mess.'

'That's just *wrong*.'

'That's not all,' said Nick. 'They superglued it together.'

I stared at him in horror. 'Your parents *superglued* together a Lego pirate ship before they gave it to you.'

'Yes.'

'And you thought this was normal.'

Nick shrugged. 'I thought it was mean at the time. I just didn't realise other people would find it so shocking.'

'So what did she say? The therapist, I mean.'

'Um.' Nick's knuckles whitened as he gripped his knees. 'She thinks I should...' He took a deep breath. 'She wants us to have counselling together as a family. And that maybe if that doesn't work I could go and live in a residential care facility until I finish school and can either live on campus at university or get a job where I can support myself. She says I need cognitive behavioural therapy. I don't really know what that is. She also says I could try anti-anxiety medication, but she wants to see if I can get better without it first.'

He drew another deep, shuddery breath.

'Wow,' I said, aware that as a reaction it was rather lacking.

'Wow,' repeated Nick. 'Yeah. Wow.'

'Do you think your parents will do it? Have counselling?'

'I don't know. I think they'll be angry with me when they find out I went to see her.'

Nick sat for a moment, looking like a lost little boy.

'So,' I asked, trying to keep my voice gentle. 'How do you feel?'

'Terrified. I always thought I knew what my life would be like. I'd always live with my parents, because I'd never be able to get a job. I'd always be shy and useless. Nothing would ever change. But now...now it's all wide open. I don't know what's going to happen, who I'm going to be.'

'Who do you want to be?'

Nick's eyes grew distant and a flicker of a smile touched the corners of his mouth. 'I don't know,' he said. 'Anyone but me.'

'Rin stopped by,' said Dad, looking up from Dostoyevsky. 'I said you'd call her when you got home.'

'Thanks,' I said. 'I'll do it later.'

'Are you okay?' He put down the book and stood up to give me a hug. 'You look tired.'

'I'm fine,' I said, breathing in his Dad-smell and closing my eyes for a moment. 'Had a long day.'

'What was it tonight?' Dad pulled back from the hug and studied me. 'No wet hair, so it wasn't swimming. Debating? SRC?'

'Working on an assignment for the paper.' It wasn't quite a lie, but I still felt bad for not telling Dad everything.

'You work too hard,' he said, ruffling my hair.

'So do you,' I retorted. 'What are you doing home so early? Isn't it Tuesday?'

'Meeting was cancelled. I made pasta. Yours is in the oven.'

'You *cooked*?' I reached up to feel his forehead. 'Is everything okay?'

Dad shrugged. 'I wanted bolognese, and La Cucina isn't open on Tuesdays.'

I gave him a suspicious look, but pulled my plate out of the oven and took it to my room. It was surprisingly good.

I shot a guilty look at my empty music stand and unopened oboe case, then opened my Chemistry textbook to the problems we were supposed to do. But my eyes glazed over and lines for the love-shy article kept popping into my head. Now that Nick was getting professional help, my article had all sorts of exciting new angles. I wondered if there was a way I could interview his counsellor, or whether that would be unethical. I pushed the Chemistry textbook aside and started making notes.

Nick bailed me up the next morning at recess.

'I need to talk to you,' he said through clenched teeth.

'Sure,' I said. 'Do you want to go outside?'

'Not here,' he muttered. 'After school. I can't talk here.'

'Okay, I'll see you at that bench,' I said, bemused. I watched him hurry off, his shoulders hunched and his head down, without his usual fake-swagger. It was as though he was really shaken about something. Had he told his parents about the therapist?

I wondered about it all through my classes, and bolted out to the bench as soon as the last bell went. Nick was already there; he must have skipped class again. He seemed about to have another panic attack. His breath was all panty again and tears rolled down his face as his body shook with silent sobs. What had happened? I imagined Nick's father grinding one of his terrariums to dirt and glass shards under his heel.

'Calm down,' I said. 'What's going on?'

'It's – it's—'

'Tell me,' I said. 'Actually, breathe first. Then tell me.'

Nick took a gulping breath. 'It's Amy,' he said, all in a rush. 'She – she...' He squeezed his eyes shut.

What had she done? Had he spoken to her? Had he realised how boring and shallow she was?

'Nick,' I said. 'What happened with Amy? Did you guys talk?'

Nick shook his head. 'I can't – I can't ever talk to her again.'

'Again? You never *did* talk to her.'

He glared at me through his tears. 'Well, now I never will.'

'Why? What happened?' Had Amy got together with Youssef?

Nick breathed deeply for a moment, his face stricken.

'She cut her hair.'

I blinked, then laughed. He shrank from me as though my laughter were some kind of poison.

'Don't mock me,' he said. 'Don't you *dare.*'

'But I don't understand why you're upset,' I said. 'Just because a girl you like cut her hair?'

'You haven't seen it.'

'Does it look bad?'

'I can't even begin to explain,' he said. 'Just tell me something. You're a girl.' He eyed me as though this was a bit of a revelation.

'I believe so, yes.'

'Why do girls cut their hair short?'

'It's easier to look after.' I inadvertently reached up to feel my own short hair. 'And it's cute on some girls. Pixie-like. Some faces are suited to short hair.'

'Boys' faces,' said Nick. 'Not girls'. I hate it when girls cut their hair. They're so pretty with it long, and then they get it cut and all the other girls flock around and tell them how *cute* they look. It makes me sick. Why do they lie like that?'

I frowned. This wasn't a side of Nick I was particularly

charmed by. 'How do you know they're lying? Maybe they really *do* think it looks cute.'

'How can they? It ruins a girl's prettiness. It makes her look disgusting, like a boy. The prettiest girl can turn dog-ugly just by having her hair cut.'

I scowled at him. '*I* have short hair, you know. In case you hadn't noticed.'

'So?'

'So you basically just jumped up and down and told me I was dog-ugly. If you ever want to get a girlfriend, then follow this red-hot tip: don't tell a girl she's dog-ugly. It won't get you very far.'

Nick waved a dismissive hand. 'You don't count.'

'Why not?'

'You just *don't*.'

'But Amy Butler does.'

'Did. Amy Butler *did*. Not anymore.'

'Because she had a *haircut*?'

Nick burst into a fresh flood of tears.

'Listen to yourself!' I said, clenching my jaw. 'You get all high and mighty because the girls think you're hot, but then won't want to talk to you when they find out you're shy. And you call *them* shallow.'

'They *are* shallow.'

'And you don't think it's shallow to suddenly not like the

girl of your obsessively romantic dreams, just because she got a haircut?'

'That's different.'

I folded my arms. 'How is it different? Enlighten me, because I'm *very* curious.'

'Those girls don't *understand* me,' he said. 'They'd judge me if they knew what I was really like. They wouldn't be able to see past my condition.'

'Like you can't see past Amy Butler's haircut.'

'No,' he said. 'I can't help being love-shy. But Amy did that to herself. She *chose* to do that. It's like she doesn't *care* about looking pretty and attracting the right boy.'

'Well, maybe she doesn't.'

'Then she's just lazy.'

I couldn't believe what I was hearing. Amy was a bit boring, sure, but nobody deserved to be talked about that way. 'Maybe *looking pretty and attracting the right boy* isn't a priority for Amy. Maybe she'd rather concentrate on swimming, or getting into university, or doing something to make the world a better place.'

Was I talking about Amy or myself?

'But why can't she do those things and look pretty at the same time?'

I shook my head. 'You sound like a creepy misogynist. Women don't exist just to look pretty. Women are *people*, and they want things and need things the same way that men do. We're not *dolls*.'

'I'm not a misogynist,' Nick said. 'It simply isn't fair that girls get to be beautiful, and then just throw it away. Boys aren't *allowed* to look pretty, so their only option is to look at pretty girls.'

I wanted to smack him in the face. I wanted to tell him that he spent too much time on loveshyforum.com with all the other weirdos... except Nick still didn't know that I knew that.

'Do you want to look pretty?' I asked. 'Then look pretty! This is the twenty-first century, Nick. If you want to wear makeup and a dress to school, then yeah, people will think you're weird, but they already think that, so what's the difference?'

'I don't want to wear a dress,' Nick muttered, looking sullen.

'Well, *I* don't want to be treated like a doll or an object,' I said. 'And I'm sure Amy Butler doesn't either.'

Nick swallowed and gazed at his shoes for a long moment. 'You're right,' he said at last, with considerable effort. 'You're right. I shouldn't talk like that.'

'Damn right you shouldn't,' I said with a frown. I was pretty sure this conversation wasn't over.

14

'Hey,' I said, sitting on the bench beside Nick at recess the next day.

Nick jumped, then nodded without looking at me and took off his headphones.

'What are you listening to?' I asked.

'Stuff,' he said. 'You know.' He floundered. 'Er. Rock and roll?'

I raised my eyebrows. 'What are you *really* listening to?'

'I am the very model of a majorly mental basket-case,' he said with a wry smile.

I laughed. 'Gilbert and Sullivan still working for you, I see. How are you?' I asked. 'Anything to report?'

'We were supposed to do fitness testing in Biology,' said Nick. 'Run around the racetrack and then measure resting heart rate. I wagged.'

'You really don't like physical exercise,' I observed.

'I hate it. And I hate touching the equipment.' Nick shuddered. 'All those sweaty germs. I failed PE in Years Seven, Eight and Nine. When I came to this school, I forged a note from my doctor saying I had a heart condition and had to be excused.'

'You should be a girl,' I said. 'We can always say we have our period.'

Nick blushed bright red at *period*. Then he sighed. 'I wish I *were* a girl. You have it so easy.'

I narrowed my eyes. It seemed we were going to continue the previous day's conversation. Still, Nick was making good progress. He'd have probably thrown up on me again if I'd mentioned the word *period* a week ago.

'The grass is always greener,' I told him. 'The downside to being able to say you can't do PE because your period pain is so bad, is that sometimes it's true.'

'Girls still have it easier,' said Nick. 'Girls don't have to play sport in order to be popular. You don't have to get a job, you can just stay at home and raise children and spend your husband's money. You—'

My mouth hung open. 'I'm sorry?' I said. '*You don't have to get a job, you can just stay at home and raise children and spend your husband's money?*'

'It's true,' said Nick. 'My mother doesn't work.'

236

'Well, mine does,' I said. 'And you know what else? She does the same job as a man, but gets paid, on average, 30 per cent less, because she's a woman. She's also statistically more likely to get overlooked for a promotion.'

'Women can't get the draft.'

Was he insane? 'Neither can men! Conscription was abolished in the '70s. The same decade, by the way, that gave women the vote in Switzerland.'

'Women get to sing the good bits in choirs. Bach, Handel, Beethoven, Mozart. All the most beautiful parts are for the sopranos.'

'All of those choral works were written by men,' I said. 'And the soprano parts were mostly written for *boy* sopranos.'

Nick seriously knew nothing about the world, or women.

'And girls don't bully,' he said. 'They don't fight. They're not violent.'

I stared at him until he blushed.

'What?' he said.

'Are you serious? You think girls don't bully, or fight, or be violent?'

'Well, they don't. Girls are calm and play quiet games and are nice to each other.'

I felt genuinely angry. 'You're nuts. Do you hear yourself?'

'I *am* nuts,' said Nick, suddenly cold. 'We've established that already. I'm nuts. I'm mental. Deal with it.'

'No,' I said. 'You're not going to blame this ridiculous misogyny on your condition.'

'I'm not a misogynist,' Nick said, his brow knitting. 'I *love* women. That's part of my whole problem.'

'Your problem,' I snapped, 'is that you see girls as these perfect, pretty objects for you to worship, instead of seeing us as *people*. Come on.' I stood up.

'Where?'

'I need to show you something. I think you need to understand a little more about girls.'

Nick seemed alarmed.

'Don't worry,' I said. 'I'm not going to make you talk to any of them.'

I crossed my arms and looked impatient until finally he climbed to his feet and followed me across the courtyard. We skirted the edge of the cricket field, Nick hunched over defensively, his eyes on the hurtling balls.

'What?' he muttered, when he saw my amused look. 'I don't want to get hit in the head. I could get a concussion.'

Between the cricket oval and the pool were two basketball courts. We wandered over to the closest one.

'Observe,' I said. 'Boys playing basketball.'

Nick looked disgusted.

'They're aggressive, sure,' I said. 'See how Rory Singh is trying to block James O'Keefe's access to the ball. But that's his role in the game, he's supposed to block James and stop him from scoring. And he's willing to put his body on the line to do it. Look.'

'I don't want to look,' said Nick. 'I hate it here. Can we go?'

'Just pay attention,' I said. 'This is important. Now, James is pretty pissed off, right? He looks like he wants to punch Rory in the face. And Rory looks like he wants to tackle James to the ground.'

Nick nodded.

'Do you think he will?'

'I don't know. Probably.'

'Let's see, shall we?'

We watched the game. Despite Rory's valiant attempts, James's team was better, and just as the whistle blew, one of the other boys sunk a final three-pointer, and it was over. I made a mental note to have a word to the coach, because it was clear none of those boys had been introduced to the concept of strategy.

'A pretty humiliating loss,' I said to Nick. 'But what do the losers do? They shake hands with each member of the winning team. Now watch James and Rory.'

After the handshake, Rory gave James a playful shove, and then they walked together to the side of the court, where they grabbed towels and water and slumped onto the bench.

'They don't seem so angry now, do they?'

Nick shook his head. 'But that's my point,' he said. 'They're all normal and friendly now, but put a ball between them and they want to kill each other.'

I put my hand on his shoulder and he flinched. I pulled away. 'Let's go look at the other court now.'

The girls' game was still going. Nick flushed to see all the singlet tops and bare thighs.

'Watch these girls,' I said. 'Specifically, that one over there with the blonde ponytail.'

I pointed to Olivia Fischer, who was standing so close to Kayla Morgan that a less erudite person than myself would have described Olivia as being 'all up in Kayla's grill'.

'What about her?'

'Look at her hands.'

Nick frowned. 'What do you mean? Her hands are...hands. She doesn't seem to be doing anything inappropriate with them.'

'Look closer. Look at her fingernails.'

'Is that...elastoplast?'

I nodded. 'Why do you think Olivia is wearing elastoplast over her fingernails?'

'I don't know. So she doesn't damage them? I know girls don't like to break their nails.'

I snorted. 'No,' I said. 'It's not so she doesn't damage

them. Officially it's to stop her from accidentally scratching Kayla when she grabs for the ball. Girls' basketball is physical and rough – just like boys' basketball. Girls are not calm, quiet and nice on a basketball court. And untaped fingernails are weapons.'

Nick was taken aback.

'And if you ask me, unofficially it's to stop Olivia from scratching Kayla's eyes out after Kayla takes a three-pointer.'

Olivia slammed into Kayla. Kayla fell to the ground, and Olivia 'accidentally' trod on her hand. Nick flinched. The referee's whistle blew and Oliva was fouled off the court.

'Now look at her mouthguard. Can you read the words on it?'

'It says...*bite me*?'

'Right. Not so nice.'

Without Olivia in the game, Kayla owned the court, shooting two- and three-pointers at will to take her team to an easy victory. I turned to Nick. 'Remember what happened after the last game?' I said. 'The boys all shook hands and were friends again. Do you think Olivia will do that?'

He turned wide eyes on me, hopeful. 'The girls are shaking hands too,' he pointed out.

I raised my eyebrows. 'Olivia's probably going to lay into Kayla in the changing rooms, because Kayla got her fouled out of the game.'

'I think I need to sit down.'

We walked away from the court, over to a bench in the shade of a large gum tree.

'Not all girls are like Olivia,' I said. 'And not all girls are...what did you say? *Calm and play quiet games and are nice to each other*. Girls are people, just like boys. Everyone is different.'

Nick stared at me as if I'd thrown a puppy in front of a train. 'But *most* girls aren't violent.'

'When I was five,' I told him, 'there was a girl called Holly Hamilton who didn't like me. She used to pull my hair and grab my sandwiches off me and throw them into the dirt and stamp on them. And she told me that if I told a teacher about what she was doing, she'd cut off all my hair.'

Nick looked rather green. 'What did you do?'

'I went home after school one day and cut off my own hair.'

'And then you told a teacher?'

I grinned. 'And then I pushed Holly Hamilton over in the playground and kicked tanbark into her eyes.'

Nick was quiet for a moment, then said, 'You know, Penny, I'm quite frightened of you.'

I laughed. 'But do you see my point? Girls don't have it easier. We don't get bullied less, we're not less violent. Girls are just as horrible, mean and selfish as boys. More so, because we bully psychologically as well, and it doesn't stop in primary school. Girls are always needling each other about their clothes, their hair, whether they're having too much sex, or not enough. You can never win, if you're a girl. You're either frigid or a slut. Square or a loser. Slacker or try-hard.'

'But if you're popular everyone likes you.'

I watched students drift through the school grounds. You could spot the popular ones from a mile away, all golden and shining.

'You know how people call popular girls "It Girls"?' I said. 'Well, being popular is more like being It. Like in chasey. You get all the attention – everyone's focused on you. But you're always running around on your own apart from everyone else. It's much more fun being part of the crowd, running away from whoever's It.'

'I've never played chasey.'

I wasn't surprised. 'Just remember that popularity isn't something easy. It's something you have to maintain. It's hard. It can suck your whole life away.'

'But you're not like that. And you're popular.'

I shrugged. 'Not really,' I said. 'People respect me because they know I'm smart, but that's not the same thing as being popular. Not *A-list* popular.'

'But couldn't you be A-list popular? If you wanted to be?'

'I suppose so. But I have no designs on popularity. I don't

really care for the competition of high school.'

'So not all girls are mean and violent. You're not.'

'No. There are plenty of lovely, caring, emotionally genuine girls. There are plenty of shy girls. There are plenty of girls who don't want to date a jock or a stoner. My point is, you can't go around saying boys are like this and girls are like that, because it doesn't work that way.'

Nick looked confused.

'Men aren't from Mars,' I told him. 'And women aren't from Venus. When you get down to it, there are some people who are nice, some people who aren't, and a whole lot of fuzzy grey in between.'

Nick wove his fingers into his hair and scratched thoughtfully. 'I'm sorry,' he said at last. 'You're right, of course. I know that. It's just... easier to think of girls as this great unattainable Nirvana that I'll never be able to reach. Because that way...'

'That way you can just put it all in the too-hard basket without even trying?'

'Yes,' he said. 'I'm sorry.'

'That's okay.'

'No,' said Nick. 'It's not okay. I'm acting like a dick, and I'm really sorry. I just— It's hard, but I'm going to change. I was being a silly sausage, and I'm sorry.'

I blinked. 'A what?'

He smiled faintly. 'It's what my therapist says I'm allowed to call myself. Because calling myself an idiot and a terrible person and an emotional cripple is just making me more like those things. So when I do something that I'm not supposed to, or react in an unhealthy way, I'm allowed to call myself a silly sausage. But nothing worse.'

'Fair enough,' I said.

Nick looked at me for a moment, a little frown between his eyebrows. 'Can... Can I ask *you* a personal question?'

'Sure.'

'What are you afraid of?'

'What do you mean?'

'What frightens you? What makes you anxious?'

'Wait,' I said. 'Are you asking me what makes me feel *fear*, or what makes me feel *anxiety*? They're different. Fear makes you want to be with others, but anxiety makes you want to be alone.' Or so I'd read in the love-shy book.

'Either. Stop avoiding the question.'

'I wasn't trying to avoid it. I was just *clarifying*.'

'So now it's clear.'

I thought about it.

'Nothing,' I said. 'I can't think of anything.'

Nick raised his eyebrows. 'You're not afraid of anything.'

I shrugged.

'Spiders?' asked Nick.

'Nope. I mean, I don't want to get too close to a whitetail or redback, but daddy-long-legs and huntsmen are fine.'

'Heights?'

I shook my head.

'The dark?'

'I find the dark peaceful,' I said. 'I miss it, living in the city.'

'What about getting needles? Everyone hates getting needles.'

'Doesn't bother me.'

'I don't believe you,' said Nick. 'I'm afraid of people, specifically girls, but I'm pretty frightened of boys too, to be honest. I'm frightened of my father *and* my mother. I'm frightened about germs and getting sick. I'm frightened of throwing up on people. I can't bear spiders or mice or moths or cockroaches. I sleep with the light on. I hate going to the dentist. Or the doctor, or anyone else who might make me take my clothes off or stick something into me.'

'Well, I'm not,' I said. 'I guess I'm just well-rounded.'

'You're in denial, that's what you are.'

'I'm not! I just don't have any phobias.'

'What about losing?'

'What?'

'Imagine if you came last in a big swimming race? Or lost a debate? Or didn't get elected for SRC?'

I remembered the heart-hammering terror I'd felt

when Perry Chau had nearly beaten me in that Year Eight Debating final. I'd only won by two points. 'It wouldn't happen.'

'Or what if you got a mark that wasn't an A?'

'Wanting to be good at stuff isn't a phobia,' I said. 'I simply have high personal standards.'

'Fear of failure *is* a phobia,' said Nick. 'It's called *atychiphobia*. Fear of losing.'

'Well, I don't have that. I just like winning.'

'What if you failed Year Ten? What if you didn't get into journalism at uni?'

The bell jangled for the end of recess, and I felt suddenly ill-at-ease. What subject did I have next? Was there homework I hadn't done? I didn't like the way Nick was messing with my mind.

'Stop it,' I said. 'None of that would ever happen, because I wouldn't *let* it happen.'

'No,' said Nick. 'And I'll never have a nervous breakdown over talking to a girl. Because I won't let *that* happen.'

'But that's different,' I said, feeling my face heat up. 'You're *avoiding* your fears and problems. I'm in control of my life. That's what makes us different.'

'Maybe,' said Nick. 'But what if you can't fix me? You can't control *me*.'

I didn't have a reply to that.

'Penny!'

It was Ms Tidy. Her hair was particularly *un*tidy, and she looked worried. 'Penny, is everything okay?'

'With me? Of course. Everything's fine.'

Concern was written all over Ms Tidy's face. 'You didn't—' she started.

What was she so upset about? Had I forgotten...

The article. Damn.

'I'm so sorry,' I said. 'It totally slipped my mind. I'll do it today, I promise.'

Ms Tidy shook her head. 'We did the final compile and sent it to the layout team yesterday,' she said, her concern giving way to annoyance.

'But... the article...'

'Arabella finished it.'

I blinked. 'So... there'll nothing by me in the paper?'

This had never happened before. I'd had a minimum of one article in the *East Glendale Secondary College Gazette* every month since Year Seven. And now a whole issue would go to the printer with nothing. Not so much as an editorial note or a book review.

'I'll do something,' I promised. 'I'll slip it in before it goes to the printer next week. I'll make it fit.'

'Are you *sure* everything's okay, Penny?' asked Ms Tidy. 'Nothing's happened to upset or distract you?'

Everything had happened, but I couldn't tell her that. 'I'm fine,' I said. 'I really am sorry.'

'You have a lot of extracurricular commitments,' said Ms Tidy. 'I'm sure everyone would understand if you dropped a few to make more room in your life.'

'No,' I said. 'I really am fine. It won't happen again. I'll be at the next newspaper meeting, I promise.'

'But—'

'I have to go,' I interrupted, and scurried away down the corridor.

'I need to get a job,' said Nick, the next day. 'My therapist wants me to start talking to more people – especially more girls. And she says a structured interaction like serving someone at a cash register is a good way of practising.'

'That sounds like a great idea,' I said. We were sitting in our usual spot outside the science labs, away from the lunchtime bustle.

Nick didn't look so sure. 'I'm scared of touching money.'

'Scared that other people's greed will rub off on you?'

'Scared that other people's *germs* will rub off on me. Did you know that 94 per cent of banknotes in Spain carry traces of cocaine? And faecal bacteria and *staphylococcus* are found on 42 per cent of American notes?'

'Where do you *get* these statistics from?'

'Yet another charming example of my epic mentalness.' Nick's lips curled in a self-mocking smile.

'Silly sausage,' I told him, and he shrugged.

'My therapist has given me some exercises to do about the germ thing,' he said. 'I have to pick up some rubbish and then not wash my hands for an hour. On Sunday I have to go the whole day without a shower. And I have to shake hands with someone and not wash my hands afterwards.'

His shoulders hunched up in an embarrassed cringe.

'Was that a request?' I asked. 'Do you want to shake hands with me?'

'No,' said Nick quickly. 'And yes. This is harder than it should be.'

'Because I'm a girl?'

He nodded. 'But at least I know your hands are cleaner than a boy's.'

I held out my hand. Nick swallowed and closed his eyes for a moment, taking a deep breath. Then he reached out and took my hand.

I expected it to be clammy and nervous, but it wasn't. Nick's hand was warm, and very soft, but not limp. I squeezed his hand a little, and to my delight he squeezed back, in a proper handshake. I grinned at him, and he dropped my hand.

'See?' I said. 'That wasn't so hard, was it?'

Nick bowed his head, but he was smiling. His ears were pink and he was so utterly pleased and proud of himself that it was all I could do not to throw my arms around him and give him a big hug. One step at a time.

I arrived home to discover the soggy towel and bathers that I'd forgotten to rinse on my bedroom floor. Great. Now my whole room smelled of damp and chlorine. I sighed and tossed them into the laundry, then checked Nick's blog and loveshyforum.com. Nothing new. This was a good sign. Now he had me to talk to, Nick didn't have to post.

Dad stuck his head around the door. 'Can I come in?'

I nodded, and he came in and sat on my bed. Was this going to be another lecture about how I should be talking to my mother?

'So I got a call from your school today,' he said, picking up a pink highlighter and popping the cap off and on.

'Oh?'

'Some of your teachers are...concerned. About your recent behaviour.'

I blinked. 'What recent behaviour? Is this about the swimming carnival?'

'That was mentioned, yes. And apparently you've been skipping classes, and neglecting your extracurricular activities.'

Morons. Couldn't the concert band or debating team function without me?

'Am I in trouble?'

'No, sweetheart, of course not. Your teachers just want to make sure you're okay. As do I.'

'I'm fine.'

'Sometimes I think you take on too many projects,' he said. 'Debating, SRC, the newspaper, swimming, oboe. Maybe you could drop a thing or two. Especially since your studies are getting more intense as you approach Year Eleven.'

I rolled my eyes. 'Dad, I'm fine. I'm not under too much pressure. I can handle my extra commitments. But they're called "extracurricular" because they're not compulsory. I missed a couple of SRC meetings. Who cares? It's not like we ever do anything important anyway.'

'I haven't heard you practise your oboe lately.'

'I've been doing it when I get home from school,' I lied. 'You're still at work.'

Dad put down the highlighter and looked uncomfortable.

'What?' I said flatly. 'What's going on?'

'The teacher I spoke to suggested you see the school guidance counsellor. She's got some time on Monday morning.'

'No.' This was ridiculous. There was nothing wrong with me! I was just busy working on an assignment. I bet this never happened to Christiane Amanpour.

'When I said "suggested"...' Dad trailed off.

'They're *forcing* me to see a guidance counsellor?'

'No, not *forcing*, as such...'

'So what happens if I don't go?'

'You'll have to drop your extracurricular activities.'

15

'Would you like to order?'

I looked up from my phone. 'Um, no thanks,' I said. 'I'm waiting for someone.'

The waiter nodded and left me alone.

It was Saturday night, and I was waiting for Nick. We were going on a date. A practice-date. He'd resisted the idea at first, but I'd threatened to turn up at his house again for dinner, and he caved pretty quickly.

But now he was fifteen minutes late and I was afraid he'd bailed on me.

I tapped my fingers on the table. I'd actually made quite an effort, wearing a *dress* (rare for me) and even mascara and lipstick. We'd arranged to meet at La Cucina, a cute little Italian restaurant in the city. Dad and I ate there all the time, so the waiters knew who I was. And it wasn't so flash or crowded or noisy that it would freak Nick out.

My stomach rumbled. There was crab ravioli on the Specials menu, and I hoped Nick would arrive soon so I could order it before the chef ran out.

Twenty minutes late.

Twenty-five.

I sighed and decided to order the ravioli anyway, and eat it on my own. I was signalling the waiter when – miracle of miracles – the door to the restaurant opened and Nick appeared, carrying a small plastic bag.

My stomach turned over. He'd come! He'd actually turned up!

I waved. Nick ducked his head and sidled past the other diners to our table, where he sank into his chair with a sigh of relief. He was nicely dressed in a black shirt and dark blue jeans, and his hair was as floppily cool as always. A table-ful of older girls looked over at him appraisingly, and I felt rather proud to be seen with such a hot guy. But now he was up close, I could see the sheen of sweat on his pale forehead.

'Are you okay?' I asked.

Nick nodded. 'I think so. I nearly didn't make it.'

'Frozen again?'

He ducked his head again. 'And I had to sneak out, because I didn't want to tell my mother where I was going.'

'Why not?'

'Too embarrassing. She'd probably cry.'

I had a sudden flashback to Nick's mum crying into her leathery beef and tried not to shudder.

'But you're here now,' I said, handing him a menu. 'Which is wonderful. A big step. Well done.'

He blushed and seemed pleased, then the faintly mocking expression took over. 'One small step for everyone else, one giant leap for Nick Rammage, Emotional Cripple.'

'Silly sausage,' I said.

'One giant leap for Nick Rammage, Silly Sausage,' he said, and allowed himself a genuine smile. I smiled back.

'I brought you something,' he said, passing me the bag. 'I didn't have any wrapping paper. But I wanted to say thanks.'

It was a Pez dispenser.

'It's the Cowardly Lion from *The Wizard of Oz*,' Nick explained. 'Because you helped me find my courage.'

I thought my smile might split my face in half. 'Thank you,' I said, feeling unbelievably touched.

The waiter returned, and we ordered. Nick pulled a small stack of white cards out of his back pocket.

'Are you making a speech?' I asked.

'My therapist gave me some ideas for conversation topics that I could try out.'

The debater in me couldn't help but respect a guy who brought note-cards along on a date. 'Great,' I said. 'The floor is yours.'

'Um,' he said, looking down at the first card nervously. 'What are your plans for next year?'

I grinned, and we started to talk. Nick's left eyelid twitched every time the conversation lulled, but all in all it went well. He asked me questions and seemed to be genuinely interested in my answers, pausing thoughtfully before commenting on my reply. I could almost believe I was on a real date, with a normal boy. It was quite nice, really.

'So, why journalism?' asked Nick. 'You could do anything, surely. Why not become a lawyer and earn heaps of money, or a politician and rule the world?'

I picked up my fork and studied it. 'Journalism's exciting,' I said. 'I don't ever want a job where I get bored. Where the only challenge is getting the next promotion. I want to travel and see amazing things and meet amazing people. And I want to share that. Most people don't think enough, don't wonder about what the outside world is like. I want to *make* people think. Make them ask questions. I want to change the rules, do things that no one has ever done before.'

I told him all about Nellie Bly, and how she had not only changed opportunities for women writers, but had also changed journalism itself.

'What about you?' I asked. 'What do you want to do when you leave school?'

Nick thought about it. 'I don't know,' he said. 'I never thought I'd be able to do anything. Now...' He closed his eyes, looking overwhelmed. 'I'd like to do something where I could be outside. Work with plants. Landscape gardening or something.'

'That sounds nice,' I said, and then, because he seemed a bit more comfortable, I decided to throw him a challenge. 'So have you given any thought to coming to the social next Friday?'

Nick screwed up his face and buttered a piece of bread. 'I don't think I want to go,' he said. 'I'm not sure I'm ready.'

I put on my *I'm disappointed in you* face. 'Well, I think you *are* ready. Look at you, talking to a girl, in a restaurant. There are candles on the table. It's almost romantic!'

'Yeah,' said Nick. 'But this is different. It isn't...a *social*.'

'You'll never get better until you face your fears. And you chickened out on Sarah Parsons' party. You owe me.'

Our food arrived and Nick looked relieved.

After dessert, I leaned back in my chair with a contented sigh.

'That was good,' said Nick, licking the last bit of sorbet from his spoon. 'Really good.'

It must have been really good, I thought, after being served stringy overcooked rubbish every night.

'Shall we go for a walk?' I suggested. 'I'm stuffed to the gills and could use a little fresh air.'

'Okay.'

We wandered through the city, peering down alleyways and into the windows of interesting little shops.

'What's it like?' Nick asked. 'Living in the city?'

'I love it,' I told him. 'I love the food and the energy, and having everything so close. I know that no matter what time of the day or night, there's always something happening, in a laneway or a tiny theatre or a cavernous art gallery. There's always music and people and life.'

'Where did you live before?' asked Nick. I glanced over at him to see if he was referring to his conversation cards, but he was gazing at the lit windows overhead.

'A normal house in the suburbs,' I said. 'Nothing special.'

'Why did you move?'

'My parents broke up.' I didn't really want to talk about it.

'I'm sorry.' It really sounded as if he was. 'And you live with your dad now? Do you still see your mum?'

We passed a busker playing 'Candle in the Wind' on a ukulele. 'No, she moved to Perth for work.' And then, because I wanted to be honest with Nick, I added, 'Or at least that's the official story. The real reason is that she freaked out about my dad being gay and ran away.'

Nick blinked. 'Your dad's gay?'

I realised that even though I knew pretty much everything about Nick, he didn't really know much about me. I nodded.

'But *you* didn't freak out,' he said. 'You stayed with your dad. You could have gone with your mum, couldn't you?'

Not when she left without me. I shrugged. 'Dad didn't do anything wrong. He was just being honest about who he is. Sure, I was surprised. But it wouldn't be fair to be angry at him for being honest.'

'That's . . . amazing,' said Nick. 'I think I would have been more selfish about it. Angry that my family had broken up. If I'd had your family, of course,' he added. 'I expect I wouldn't have nearly so many problems if my parents had broken up when I was little.'

'Maybe not,' I said.

'But I mean it,' said Nick. 'A lot of people wouldn't be so understanding. You're a good person, Penny.'

I felt a warm glow spread through my body. 'Thank you,' I said, genuinely flattered. I smiled up at Nick, and he smiled back, and for a moment I felt just like an ordinary girl on a date with an ordinary boy.

'Do you miss your mum?' he asked.

'No,' I said shortly, but I knew that despite my resolution to be honest with Nick, I was lying.

We paused before a florist's shop with a wild, tangled green window display.

'Penny?' There was a little tremble in Nick's voice. 'How does this work in real life? With a real girl?'

I was a little stung. 'What am I, your imaginary friend?'

'You know what I mean. Tonight has been good and I feel a lot better about the idea of... going on a date. But how do I do it for real?'

'You find a girl you like, then you ask her to go out to dinner with you. Or to a movie. Or bowling. Or to a Pez dispenser exhibition.'

'But what happens *then*?' asked Nick.

'What do you mean?' I said.

'What happens *after* I ask her out?'

I blinked. 'You go out.'

Nick frowned. 'But then what? At what point in the date do you move things forward? Should I try to hold her hand? Kiss her? Do I open doors for her? Buy her dinner?'

'You have to figure it out as you go,' I said. 'You can offer to pay for her dinner if you like, but it's probably better to split the bill on the first date, as we did tonight. And the other stuff... you just have to read her signals.'

'Like what?'

'Like, if she's leaning forward and laughing and making lots of eye contact, then she probably likes you, and you could try holding her hand.'

I couldn't believe that I was actually giving Nick dating advice. It wasn't as if I were the most experienced person in the world at dating. But I'd seen plenty of cheesy rom-coms with Dad and Josh, so I knew the basic rules.

'And kissing?'

'I don't know,' I said. 'I guess you just know if it's appropriate. You should be able to sense it.'

Nick didn't seem convinced. 'But *then* what?'

'Well, if you decide it's appropriate, then you kiss her.'

Nick traced his finger over the lettering stencilled on the shop window. 'But *how*?'

'How do you kiss her?' I was beginning to get out of my depth. I'd never kissed anyone either, not really.

'Um,' I said. 'You know. You just kiss. Press your lips against her lips.'

'I know *that*,' said Nick. 'But then what happens? There must be more to it.'

Was there more to it? Was *I* going to screw it up? Was there stuff I should know about kissing? I thought back through all the romantic comedies, and to last weekend and the incident with Hamish.

'I guess you just try to be gentle,' I said. 'Don't slobber on her. Don't lick her face.'

'Tongue?'

'Probably not the first time.' I was a bit nervous about

where this conversation was headed. My palms were growing sweaty, and I wiped them on my skirt.

'And what do I do with my hands?'

Nick's face was totally open and interested, without any trace of anxiety or shyness. His hair flopped over his forehead and his eyebrows crinkled in his cute questioning way. Maybe he really *was* getting better.

'I'll show you,' I said, and moved a little closer to him.

Nick looked uncertain.

'Come on,' I said. 'I promise I won't bite.'

I stepped in close to him. He smelled very clean, like laundry detergent and soap. I could feel him tense as I got closer. I took one of his hands and put it behind me, around my waist, and his other around behind my back, so his arms encircled me.

'I think it's a bit like this,' I said, moving even closer. I could feel his heart beating so fast it was making his chest vibrate. His breath came in shallow gasps.

'Um,' he said, and swallowed.

'And then,' I said, my voice very soft. I tilted my face up towards his and put my arms around his shoulders. 'I think it goes something…like…'

I closed my eyes, leaned upwards and pressed my lips against his. His mouth felt soft and cool. I tightened my arms around him, but didn't feel him do the same to me.

He was pretty nervous, I supposed. I let my lips open a little and leaned forward even further, pressing myself up against him. He felt solid and comforting, and my stomach squirmed in a really, really good way. I let my eyes open a teeny crack to see how he was responding.

Nick's eyes were wide open. I pulled away. He was frozen, an expression of total horror on his face. I stepped back.

'What's wrong?'

He shook his head.

'I'm sorry,' I said. 'Was that too much? Too soon? I was only trying to help.'

That wasn't entirely true. I'd kissed Nick because I wanted to. I did want to help him get better, but I was beginning to suspect it wasn't for lofty journalistic reasons. I wanted him to get better so we could be together. I wanted Nick to fall in love with me, the way . . .

Oh.

Was I falling in love with Nick?

He finally spoke. 'How *dare* you?'

'What?'

He was white, and shaking. 'How *dare* you do that to me? How *dare* you touch me like that. *Kiss* me.'

The happy squirming in my stomach had been replaced with an ugly, sick feeling. 'What do you mean?'

'You can't *do* that,' said Nick. 'You can't be all supportive and listen and talk to me like I'm not a total freak, and then try to screw me up by playing games.'

'I wasn't,' I said. 'I wasn't playing games.'

'Oh, so I suppose you did it out of the goodness of your heart. To *help* me.'

I nodded, not trusting myself to speak. An elderly couple passed us on the street, avoiding eye contact.

'Or, or, or maybe you did it because you secretly *like* me,' said Nick.

I do, I thought. *I do like you. A lot.*

'Except you don't,' said Nick. 'You can't. You're just like all the other girls. All those horrible blonde girls who laugh and giggle and throw their hair around as if they're interested, but then as soon as I speak, they're out of there faster than you can blink. Am I really that repulsive to you?'

'You're not repulsive to me at all,' I managed.

But he wasn't listening.

'You don't *know* me,' he said. 'You act like you do. You act like you understand. But you don't. How can you know me after talking to me for a few days? You know *nothing*.'

'I do know you,' I told him, feeling as if I was going to cry and hating myself for it. 'I do.'

'You don't. You're just as bad as all the rest of them. You're just like them. I thought things were changing. I thought I was getting better. But I'm still standing knee-deep in the water. It's still too cold. I still can't go in.'

I grabbed his arm and he flinched. People were watching us from inside the cocktail bar on the other side of the street. 'Nick,' I said. 'I'd never throw stones at you. I promise. You can take as long as you like to dive in. I'll wait.'

Nick stared at me as though I were a monster. 'What did you say?'

'I said I'll wait.'

'No,' said Nick. 'That wasn't what you said.'

His face was suddenly cold and distant. I'd never seen him look that way before. He didn't look frightened or weak or anxious. He looked furious.

'You said you'd never throw stones at me.'

Uh-oh.

'How did you know that was what I was talking about when I said the water was cold? How did you know that boys threw stones at me at camp? *How did you know?*'

I spread my hands. 'Nick, I'm sorry. I was going to tell you.'

'*How did you know?*'

'The love-shy forum,' I said. 'That's how I found you. You were reading loveshyforum.com in the library and then I found your blog and wanted to find out who you were, so I talked to every boy in our year level. For a while I thought it was Hamish, but then I realised it was you.'

Nick blinked. 'In the library?' he said. 'That was *weeks* ago. You've been stalking me since then?'

'Not *stalking*. Observing. Understanding. Sympathising.'

'I don't need your sympathy.'

'Empathy, then,' I said. 'Look, it's no big deal. But I *do* know stuff about you. I *do* know you. Because I've read what you said on your blog.'

'I can't believe you'd violate my privacy like that! It's like reading my *diary*.'

'It's a *website*. A *public* website. When you post stuff on a public website, it's public. I never violated your privacy.'

'My posts are anonymous,' said Nick. 'When you crossed that line into real life, *that*'s when you violated my privacy.'

'Well, I'm sorry,' I said. 'And I'm sorry I tried to kiss you.'

I wasn't sorry I'd kissed him. I was sorry he hadn't kissed me back. This was all going wrong. Nick's face flickered from cold to hurt and landed on cruel.

'As if I care,' he said. 'And anyway, I can't believe you'd ever think I'd go for you anyway. You're so not my type. You have short hair that makes you look like a boy and you're not even pretty.'

'Hey,' I said. 'Back off. I wasn't trying to upset you, okay?'

'No,' said Nick. 'It's not okay. And where do you get off

being so all-knowing about people and relationships? You've never had one either. I bet you've never kissed anyone yourself until now.'

I glared down at a squashed cigarette butt on the footpath, feeling tears prick at my eyes.

'You act like you're so much better than me,' he continued. 'Like I'm this freakish charity case and you're my therapist, like you've got all the answers. Like you're perfectly adjusted and happy in your life.'

'I *am* happy,' I said. 'My life is just fine, thank you.'

Nick had come over all nasty, red blotches standing out on his cheeks.

'You're not happy,' he said. 'You hide behind all the crap you do at school, the SRC and Debating and swimming and that stupid newspaper. You've got this crazy idea that having a good career is the only thing that matters. Well, it isn't. People matter, too.'

'I know people matter,' I said. 'I have people.'

'Do you?'

'Of course I do,' I said. 'I have Dad, and Josh.'

'But you don't have any actual *friends*,' he said. 'You spend your life running around being busy, to hide the fact that you are actually totally lonely. You don't let anyone in. You never admit you're wrong about *anything*. People look up to you, and you get invited to parties and you're reasonably popular. But that's not the same thing as having friends. You're just as bad as I am.'

I had no words to reply to him. I wanted to yell and scream and call him a lonely loser freak.

But I couldn't. Because I was a lonely loser freak as well. Nick was right. I *was* just as bad as he was.

16

Ms ARMSTRONG ASKED ME TO call her Janet. I didn't. I didn't call her anything. She sat behind her desk wearing an understanding and compassionate expression. But that was her job. She didn't really care.

'We merely want to make sure you're not under too much pressure, Penny,' she said.

I didn't say anything. The third rule of interviewing also worked if you were the interviewee. Hopefully she'd chat for the whole half hour, and then I could escape.

'Is everything all right at home?'

I managed a tiny nod.

'Have you fought with any of your friends?'

I didn't have any friends. I'd had one, but then I tried to kiss him and ruined everything.

Ms Armstrong sighed and made a few notes on a piece of paper. 'Penny,' she said, crinkling her brow. 'I can see that you don't want to talk, which is highly unusual, knowing what I do about you. Your teachers say that you seem distracted during class, and they're concerned that you're struggling with the pressure of your extracurricular commitments. You've missed multiple meetings of the SRC and the *Gazette*, you're unresponsive in class, you haven't been to a band rehearsal in a fortnight, and there was that whole business where you were disqualified from the swimming carnival. If you're not willing to give me an explanation for your erratic behaviour...' She paused to see if I did want to give her an explanation. I didn't.

'Well, then you leave me no choice. I've spoken to your teachers about reducing your extracurricular load, and I'm afraid I'll have to tell them you won't be returning to the orchestra or the swim team. You may attend your Debating final tonight, but after that your team will need to find a replacement for you. As you've been elected to the SRC, we can't make you give that up, and Ms Tidy has requested you speak to her directly about whether or not you will continue working on the *Gazette*.'

Could she really do that? Make me give everything up?

'Are you sure there's nothing you'd like to talk to me about?' asked Ms Armstrong.

I hated her for trying to blackmail me into talking about my feelings. Well, it wouldn't work. I stared stonily at the corner of her desk.

'Then I think that's all for today,' she said, sliding her piece of paper into a manila folder. 'Thank you, Penny.'

I made my way to my locker and stood frozen in front of it, staring at the lock.

'Did you forget your combination?'

Rin had crept up beside me. She was wearing her hair down instead of in her usual pigtails, and it made her look older.

'Penny? Are you okay?'

Why did everyone keep asking me that? 'I'm fine,' I said. 'Just busy.'

'I brought you the latest *Battle Vixens*.' She produced a small book with a silver-haired girl bearing a sword on the cover.

'I don't want it,' I said. 'I haven't even read the other ones.'

Rin looked confused. 'Oh, sorry, I thought you had. You said—'

'I have to go.' I had the sudden overwhelming feeling that I was going to cry, and I couldn't. Not in front of Rin. She'd be all concerned, and that'd just make everything worse. Because I'd know she didn't mean it. I'd know she was only doing it so I'd invite her to the next party.

'Do you want to come and sit with us at lunch today?' she asked.

'No,' I said. 'I don't want to sit with you at lunch today. Just leave me alone.'

I turned and walked away, but not before I saw Rin's bottom lip tremble, and her eyes fill with tears. But it was better this way. Before I'd got involved with her and Nick, nothing had ever gone wrong. I was meant to be a loner.

I wagged Maths and sat by myself in the library, staring at the scratches on a desk that proclaimed that DAMO LOVES PETE'S MUM and that KT IS HOTTT. I tried not to think about love-shyness or friendship or stupid Ms Armstrong the guidance counsellor. When the lunch bell rang, and students started to file into the library, I tried to shrink into my chair. I knew everyone was looking at me. Judging me. I'd had enough.

I pushed my chair back, picked up my bag, and walked out of the library and straight out the front gate of the school. I didn't care if anyone saw, or if I got detention. I was going home.

I stayed on the couch in my pyjamas for the rest of the day. Dad came home just after five, but I didn't get up.

'Penny?' he said. 'Are you okay?'

I flipped a page of Truman Capote's *In Cold Blood*. 'I'm not feeling well.'

'Do you want anything? Ginger tea?'

'I'm just really tired.'

'Do you want me to stay home tonight? I have that Plumbers Association Gala Dinner thing, but I can cancel.'

I shook my head. 'I'm okay.'

Dad nodded and wandered into his room. My phone chirped a message and I glared at it. Whoever it was, I wasn't interested.

Chirp, chirp.

Then it buzzed around on the coffee table with a call. I ignored it. It chirped again to indicate there was voicemail. I turned it off. The home phone rang.

Dad came out of his room, an indigo and silver tie loose around his neck, and picked up the phone.

'Penny?' he said after a moment. 'It's someone called Hugh. He wants to know when you're planning on turning up to your Debating final.'

Crap. I glanced at my watch. The debate started in half an hour. I could still make it.

I hauled myself off the couch and dashed to my bedroom, hunting around for some clean clothes, then gave up and pulled on the jeans and T-shirt I'd been wearing that morning.

'Dad?' I yelled, trying to find a matching sock. 'Can you please call me a cab?'

I slid into my seat at 5:59 with a sigh of relief. Hugh shot me a look with some very expressive eyebrows. Aylee Kim, our second speaker, glared at me.

'Where *were* you?' she hissed, but then the adjudicator rang a bell and Hugh stood up to a polite smattering of applause.

'Ladies and gentlemen,' he said. 'Over the next ten minutes, I will demonstrate how foreign aid doesn't help the most vulnerable people in developing nations. Moreover, it actually causes harm.'

I looked down at the stack of empty note-cards in front of me. Luckily I was the best speaker in the Eastern Region – I'd have no trouble winging this one. I took a sip of water and picked up a pen, ready to take notes.

Maybe if I debated really well, Ms Armstrong wouldn't make me give up Debating. Maybe I could just decimate the opposition, prove how totally on-the-ball I was with everything, and it would all be right again. I could have my extracurricular activities back.

Otherwise what would I do all day? Where would I go at lunchtime? Sit with Rin? Not after the way I'd acted today. I'd be surprised if Rin ever spoke to me again.

Hugh was still talking, but I couldn't hear him anymore. All I could hear was Nick's voice, over and over again.

You're just as bad as I am.

But I was *involved*. I participated in school activities – I practically *ran* all the school activities. How would they put out the *Gazette* without me? Didn't they realise the Debating team wouldn't make any regional finals if I wasn't there? I mean, Hugh was a fine first speaker, but Aylee had a tendency of chewing her hair which totally put the judges off, and she wasn't particularly good at rebuttal. And who would play first oboe in the orchestra?

And sure, sometimes I might have been a little distant. But I was a *journalist*. We had to be objective. Nellie Bly had to be firm and hard-hitting just to get people to listen to her in the first place. There was no room in journalism for wishy-washy softness – we had to be ruthless and cutting-edge. Did Nellie Bly have heaps of friends? I didn't think so. She didn't get married until after her great journalistic adventures. She was happy being alone.

She did have a monkey, though. His name was McGinty. I wondered if I could get a monkey. Or maybe a puppy. Something that wouldn't judge me.

I looked up. Hugh had sat down and a girl with braces from the opposition was saying something about earth-quake victims in Haiti and 'so-called administration fees'.

I wondered if she had any true friends. If she'd ever tried to kiss someone. If they'd kissed her back.

'Millions of children in Malawi, Burundi and Kenya are going to school because of government aid,' said Braces Girl. 'Vaccination programs are wiping out diphtheria, tetanus and river blindness.'

I knew what Nick would say. *You spend your life running around being busy, to hide the fact that you are actually totally lonely.*

Hugh scribbled on a piece of paper and passed it to Aylee, who handed it to me.

GOVT AID = STATE BRIBERY

I blinked and stared at it. Hugh nodded meaningfully at me, and I nodded back. It was probably a good time to start paying attention.

I thought about Nick's light-globe terrariums. I could see why he liked the idea of a tiny, safe, beautiful world. A world where you could be completely alone and nobody could touch you or hurt you. A world where you could just be *you*.

Aylee nudged me in the ribs. It was my turn? Really? Already? When did she talk? Had I missed it?

I stood up and looked at the panel of judges, and the crowd of people waiting to hear me speak.

'Knock 'em dead,' whispered Hugh.

My throat was suddenly dry. I looked down at my stack of note-cards. On the first one, I'd written:

That foreign aid should be administered by NGOs rather than states.

That was the topic? I realised in horror that I had no idea whether we were on the positive or negative side. I hadn't been listening. I turned to the next note card. It was blank. They were all blank.

I heard Nick's voice in my head. *Fear of failure* is *a phobia. It's called* atychiphobia. *Fear of losing.*

It was a dream. It had to be a dream. Maybe I could just walk out and wake up in my bed. What was it you were supposed to do when you couldn't wake up from a dream? Blink? Jolt? I bit my tongue too, just for good measure, but nothing worked. I wasn't waking up.

This was real.

This was real and I'd spent the first thirty seconds of my talk blinking furiously and jiggling up and down.

'Penny?' whispered Hugh.

I cleared my throat. 'Should foreign aid be administered by NGOs rather than states?' I said. 'That's what we're here to find out. Or is it?'

I scanned the room, hoping that it would seem like an impressive pause.

'Maybe we are asking the wrong question,' I continued.

'Maybe what's really at stake here is *people*. Should we be helping people?'

Hugh was staring at me as if I were insane. Maybe I could do this. Maybe it'd be like the impassioned speech that comes at the end of the movie, where the lawyer or politician or whoever throws away their notes, speaks from the heart and saves the day.

'Helping people is supposed to make you feel better,' I said. 'Altruism is supposed to be one of the greatest strengths of humanity. You help someone. Their life becomes better. You feel good about yourself. But what happens when that system fails? What happens when you try to help someone, but you just make everything worse?'

My voice sped up and heightened in pitch. My heart hammered. But I couldn't stop.

'And they're unhappy, so they say things to you. Mean things. Untrue things. But then you start to wonder if those things *are* true. Maybe you *are* afraid of failure. Maybe you *don't* have any friends. Maybe you *are* lonely.'

I was crying now. The judges were exchanging mutters and concerned frowns. Hugh was desperately trying to catch my eye. The opposition looked as though they weren't sure whether to be worried or jubilant.

'So...' My voice cracked and was punctuated with little sobs. 'So maybe you shouldn't have helped them at all.

Maybe if you'd just left them alone, then they wouldn't be angry and you wouldn't have realised how terrible everything is.'

What was I doing?

'I'm sorry,' I said, staring down at my cards, hoping that magically some notes would appear to save me. They didn't.

The clock said I had seven minutes left. I couldn't do it. 'I'm sorry,' I said again, this time to Hugh and Aylee.

And I dropped my note-cards and ran out of the room.

I sat out on the fire escape taking big gulps of air and crying. What was wrong with me?

The door behind me banged open.

'What the hell was that all about?'

I shook my head and tried to tell Hugh that I didn't know, but I couldn't get the words out.

'What's wrong with you, Penny?' he asked, his voice full of disappointment. 'It's like you just don't care anymore. About school. About anything. Are you really so much better than us that you can't be bothered preparing for a debate final?'

That only made me cry harder. I hated the idea that I'd let people down. I was the reliable one! No matter how rubbish everyone else was, I could always bring it home and save the day. Not anymore, it seemed. I'd got my team disqualified from the swimming carnival. I'd been kicked out of the orchestra. I wasn't allowed to debate anymore – not that any team would have me now. I'd missed my last two deadlines for the paper, and for what? Following a boy around, pretending to have all this journalistic integrity, all because I had a dumb crush.

I hated myself.

'I'm so sorry,' I croaked out between sobs. 'I don't know what to do.'

There was a confused silence from Hugh, and then, 'Move over.'

He sat down next to me on the fire escape. 'It's okay,' he said. 'We all choke occasionally. It's what makes us human.'

'I don't,' I said. 'Not ever.'

'Not ever except for today.'

And a few other times lately that I could think of. I put my head in my hands.

'To be honest,' said Hugh, 'I'm kind of relieved to learn that you're human like the rest of us. It gives me hope.'

'What do you mean?'

Hugh paused, and I looked up at him. Was he blushing? 'You know. That the rest of us have a chance. That you won't always be the best at everything. That maybe one day someone else will get the front page story on the *Gazette*, or come first in a swimming race, or play the oboe solo, or be class captain, or get the best-speaker award at a debate.'

I sniffed. 'Well, you got your wish. I'm not allowed to swim or be in the band or the debate team after tonight.'

'What?'

'I had to see the school counsellor. She says I'm over-committed and that's why I keep dropping the ball.' I swallowed another sob. 'And after tonight I think maybe she's right.'

Hugh was quiet again.

'Aren't you glad?' I asked. 'That now you'll be the best debater?'

He didn't reply.

I started to cry in earnest again. 'Do you really all hate me that much? That you want to see me lose? Is that all I am to you? Just someone to beat?'

'Isn't that how you see us?' asked Hugh.

I opened my mouth to deny it, but he was right. I did see everyone else as competition.

'But if I'm not the best at everything,' I whispered, 'what will be left of me? Why would people like me then?'

'People don't like you because you're the best at everything.'

I let out a wet laugh. 'People don't like me at all.'

'Nonsense,' said Hugh. '*I* like you.'

I studied him. He'd started off the debate with every hair in place, but it was reverting to its usual wild, curly state.

He had a weird mole on his right cheek, like a beauty spot, and his ears stuck out a little. But his eyes were dark and gentle, and they looked at me in a way that made me feel a little nervous.

'Why?' I asked, my voice barely audible.

'You're curious and interesting and very, very funny – even if you don't always mean to be. You care about the world, and you're fiery and ambitious and you don't let anyone walk all over you. And you're ridiculously smart, which is intimidating for some people, but it's a big turn-on for me.'

Turn-on? Hugh went bright pink and turned away. 'Now stop fishing for compliments,' he muttered.

I felt myself smile soggily, and suddenly everything didn't seem as bad. Perhaps I was just being a silly sausage and needed some perspective.

'Is that why you stuck your tongue in my ear at the cast party last year?' I asked. 'Because my incredible intellect turns you on?'

Hugh blinked. 'What? I never stuck my tongue in your ear.'

'Yes, you did. Just before Jamal came out of the bathroom wearing nothing but a feather boa and a pair of Ray-Bans.'

Hugh frowned, then gave a yelp of laughter. 'I really didn't,' he said. 'I was leaning over to ask you something, and you jumped sideways to avoid Jamal's...well, you remember. And you kind of ear-butted me. You nearly broke my nose.'

That wasn't how I remembered it. 'What were you going to ask me, then?'

Hugh went a little pinker. 'Never mind.'

We sat there awkwardly for a moment, then Hugh said, 'He's not worth it, you know.'

'What? Who?'

'Nick Rammage.'

I felt as though someone were squeezing my throat. 'What?' I croaked. 'How do you know about Nick?'

Hugh rolled his eyes. 'Everybody knows,' he said. 'You wait at his locker and then wag Debating or SRC to go and sit with him every single day.'

My mouth hung open. 'But...' I said. 'No. It's not what you think.'

'Really? Because I think you were drawn to his carefully cultivated air of mystery, the way all the other girls are. And for once he actually talked to someone, and that made you feel special, and you ended up falling for him.'

I stared at him.

'How close am I?' he asked.

I was about to tell him that he was wrong, that he had totally misinterpreted the situation, that he didn't know the details. But...

'Pretty close, actually,' I admitted.

Hugh seemed somehow disappointed, as though he hadn't wanted to be right. 'He's just a phony. You know that, don't you?'

'Yeah,' I said. 'I do know that.'

'Good. Because if you're going to throw away everything you're good at, you should at least do it for someone who isn't such a poseur.'

'He's not a poseur,' I said. 'He's just... he has a lot of stuff going on. It's complicated.'

Hugh looked away again. 'Are you in love with him?'

Was I? I cared about Nick, I wanted him to be okay. I wanted to talk to him and for him not to be angry at me anymore. But love?

'No,' I said, and a wave of relief swept over me. 'I don't think so.'

I wasn't in love with Nick. I'd had a stupid crush, and had done stupid things. But Hugh was right – I'd just been flattered that he paid attention to me. That the most unattainable boy had wanted to hang out with *me*.

Hugh nodded. 'Good,' he said. 'Good.'

Then he stood up. 'We'd better get back inside and find out how badly we lost the debate.'

He offered me his hand. I took it and he pulled me to my feet.

> *I have never written a word that did not come from my heart. I never shall.*

NELLIE BLY

17

I FLOPPED ONTO MY BED, FEELING emotionally exhausted.

For a moment I thought about going next door to see Rin, but it was nearly ten at night. And anyway, who was I kidding? Rin wasn't my friend. She just felt sorry for me.

Was that what everyone thought? That I was some poor pathetic loser? Did I just get invited to their parties because they felt sorry for me?

Or maybe I was nothing more than some high-school-paper hack, hanging around all the beautiful people, always observing, never belonging. Dreaming of serious journalism, when really all I was destined for was some raggy sensation-alist tabloid whose greatest scoop was whether or not Katie Holmes was pregnant again.

I wished I'd never gone into the library that day. I wished I'd never heard of love-shyness.

I heard the front door open. 'Penny? Are you home?' Dad's head peered around my door. 'Are you okay?'

'No.'

'May I come in?'

I shrugged. Dad came in and sat down on the end of my bed.

'What's going on?' he said.

'Everyone hates me.'

Dad raised his eyebrows. 'I'm sure that's not true. What happened?'

I sat up and explained everything. About Nick and the love-shy article and Hamish and Rin and everything. Dad listened, his head on one side.

'Well, you've certainly been busy,' he said at last.

'I don't ever want to go back to school again,' I said. 'And I don't want to be a journalist anymore. I think I might get a job selling fish.'

'Fish?'

'Fish. Wrapped in newspaper. That's all it's good for.'

Dad smiled. 'I reckon there's one or two things you should try before you give up entirely and run away to become a fishmonger.'

'Like? What should I do?'

Dad looked at me. 'Do you want my honest opinion?'

I nodded. Dad got up and left the room, returning a

moment later holding the cordless phone and a post-it note. He stuck the post-it on my desk and handed me the phone.

'I think you know what my honest opinion is.'

I bit my lip. Dad dropped a kiss on my forehead and left my room, shutting the door gently behind him.

I crawled off the bed and sat at my desk with a sigh. I wanted to turn on my computer, but I didn't. I didn't want to be close to the internet, in case I was tempted to read Nick's latest post. I didn't want to see it. I wasn't interested anymore. It would probably be about me, and I didn't think I could take any more cruelty.

I stared at the wall, where I'd pinned up a card containing the Nine Principles of Journalism. I sighed. I'd probably broken them all. Number seven stood out particularly. *Its practitioners must maintain an independence from those they cover.*

I hadn't maintained any independence from who I was covering. Not even a little bit. I'd got involved. I wasn't an independent monitor. My loyalty wasn't to my readers. It was to myself. At some point, I'd stopped talking to Nick for the lofty purposes of research and journalism, and started talking to him because I wanted to.

Because I liked him.

I'd been such an idiot.

It was ridiculous, because I *didn't* like him! I was in the

289

middle of some kind of grotesque, romantic fantasy where I'd rescue Nick from his self-made prison, and he'd be eternally grateful and love me because of it.

That was wrong. It was kind of creepy.

But I *did* want to help him. Because if I could help him, then maybe I could help myself, too. We both thought we were safe in our little glass terrarium worlds, sheltered from cruelty and judgement and spite. But we were also sheltered from the *good* things, too. Such as love and friendship and feeling as if we belonged somewhere.

I wanted to help Nick out of his glass globe.

The problem was, I'd been doing it all wrong. I'd been trying to break the glass of Nick's terrarium to let him out, as though it were a prison. But if you break the glass, all the plants are suddenly exposed to the world and they die. It wasn't a prison; it was more like a protective shell.

I had to coax Nick out slowly, show him that he could grow and flower in the outside world. That it was tough for *everyone* out here, but because we could work together and draw strength from each other, we could grow bigger and better and brighter than we ever could if we stayed inside our little glass globes.

I knew what I had to do.

I turned on my laptop and navigated to pezzimist. blogspot.com. And then did something I'd never done before, in all my visits to Nick's blog. I clicked the Comment button.

I filled in the required fields, and paused at the Username box. Then I smiled a little and wrote *POPtimist*.

22:14

Hi. It's me.

I am the opposite of shy.

Things don't make me anxious. I'm never nervous. I have a good life where both my parents love and support me. I have no trouble speaking to members of the opposite sex. But I've never been in a relationship. I've never really kissed anyone (although there have been a few embarrassing attempts).

I've never been in love. I can't imagine being in love. I can't imagine letting myself go, losing control. Giving myself over to someone else so completely that I'd feel a part of them. I don't think I could do that.

I am rational. Cynical. Aggressive. Fearless. Ambitious. Confident. I don't want anyone to ever see that I'm weak. And it means I push people away. I don't let people get close to me because I don't want them to beat me, or to see me fail.

So even though I have a very different life to you, I think we might be in the same boat. We're both alone. Even though I am the opposite of shy, I think we have more in common than I ever could have imagined.

291

I'm sorry if I hurt you. I really didn't mean to. The thing
is, and it really frightens me to admit this – I did want to
kiss you. I didn't do it to play games or to hurt you. I did
it because I like you. Because I've been reading your posts
and getting inside your brain, even though you didn't
know it. And then in real life you were so different and
anxious and nervous, but as we got to know each other
you started to relax. And I liked that. I liked you.
So I'm sorry. And I hope you'll forgive me.

I hit Post and then closed down the browser and chewed my
lip for a moment before picking up the phone and dialling
the number written on the post-it Dad had stuck to my desk.

'Hello?'

I took a deep breath. 'Hi, Mum.'

'Penny? Is that you? Is everything okay? Is your father okay?'

I didn't say anything for a moment. She'd asked after Dad.
She thought I was calling because something had happened
to Dad. And she was worried. I could hear it in her voice.

'Penny? Are you still there?'

'I'm here, Mum. And everything's fine. I'm fine, Dad's
fine. We're all fine.'

But I didn't feel fine. It had been two years since I'd
called my mother 'Mum'. Two years since I'd heard her say
anything about Dad. I couldn't help it. Tears slipped down

my face, big fat tears that had been waiting behind my eyes for two years.

'Are you sure you're okay?'

I sniffed. 'Mum,' I said. 'I miss you.'

Mum was quiet for a moment too, and then I heard her voice, all quiet and wobbly because she was crying as well. 'I miss you too, Penny. I miss you every single day.'

I took a deep breath. 'And Dad? Do you miss Dad?'

Mum was quiet for even longer. 'Of course I miss your father,' she said. 'Of course I do.'

'Then why don't you come *home*?' I said. 'Come back. And you and Dad can be friends again. I even think you'd like Josh.'

'I can't, Penny,' said Mum. 'I still love your father. I don't want to see him with someone else. And I have a new life here now. But if you wanted to, you could come here. You do know that, right? There's always room for you here, and I know you're starting Year Eleven next year but we could find you a really good school...'

'Thanks, Mum,' I said. 'But I don't want to live in Perth. I like it here. I like living with Dad and I like my school and...'

I was going to add '*my friends*', but I thought about Nick and it felt as though something were squeezing my heart.

'But Mum?' I said. 'I'd like to come and visit. Maybe in the holidays?'

'I'd like that very much, Penny,' said Mum. 'Very, very much.'

We talked for a bit longer. Mum told me about her job, and about the beach down the road from her house. It sounded nice. I told her about school, and even about Nick and the love-shy project, and my Debating meltdown.

After I'd said goodbye to her, I lay down on my bed and had a proper cry. It felt good, letting go of stuff that I'd been holding on to for years. And once I'd let it go I couldn't figure out why I hadn't done it sooner. Eventually I calmed down, and felt kind of wobbly still, but strong. I turned back to my laptop. It was time to write.

18

I DIDN'T WANT TO GO TO the social. I didn't want to see all the people I went to school with who weren't my friends. And they weren't. Oh sure, they respected me. But they weren't my friends. I'd never hung out with any of them just... normally, at their house, or out to see a movie. Only for extracurricular stuff and big parties that everyone was invited to. I hated the fact that everyone knew I had no friends.

I hadn't spoken to Rin, Hugh or Nick all week. I hid in the library at recess and lunch, and kept my head down in all my classes. It wasn't that I didn't want to talk to them – I was just scared of what they might say. Scared they might reject me.

I wasn't really needed at the social anyway. Someone else from the paper could take photos of the best and worst outfits – that was all people wanted to read about. Nobody had cared about the piece I wrote last year on the spiking of the punch, and the effect that alcohol has on the teenage brain. Or the piece the year before about the meningitis epidemic that hit after everyone made out with everyone else. There was no point in being a journalist, all people wanted was gossip and trash.

So I wasn't going. I didn't even go to school on Friday. I stayed home in my pyjamas and watched daytime TV. When Dad and Josh arrived with about seventeen different types of curry, garlic naan and a jigsaw puzzle of the Eiffel Tower recreated in cheese, I dragged myself off the couch and settled happily at the table with a steaming plate of saag paneer.

I'd told Dad about my phone call with Mum. He knew I was still pretty upset about everything that had happened, and he'd clearly told Josh too, because there were no probing questions about my love-life, and no raised eyebrows about my pyjamas and unbrushed hair. We chatted about stupid things and laughed. Josh told us about how he'd tried to help the old lady in his apartment building to take her rubbish out, and that she'd called the police and accused him of being a thief and stalker. Dad told us about how one of his contractors had picked up a Portaloo from a film-set, but not checked to make sure it was empty first, and had driven the film's star actress all the way to the sewage processing plant, locked inside.

I was considering a second helping of chicken makhani when there was a knock at the front door. Dad and Josh both looked at me, so I poked my tongue out at them and went to answer it.

It was Rin. She was wearing an explosion of pink and white lace with a short tutu skirt, and about forty strands of pearls around her neck. Her hair was all twisted up and curled around her ears, and she wore dainty pink slipper-like heels.

'You look amazing, Rin!'

'You weren't at school today,' she said, taking in my pyjamas and curry-stained fingers. 'Are you okay?'

'I'm fine,' I said. 'I just didn't really feel up to school today.'

'But you're coming to the social, right?'

I glanced down at my pyjamas and fluffy slippers. 'Um. No. Not feeling very social.'

Rin frowned. 'But you *have* to come,' she said. 'You organised the whole thing! It's not the social without you. And anyway, my parents are only letting me go if I can go with *you*. They think you're responsible and a good influence on me. And the thing is...' She took a deep breath. 'The thing is, Hamish kind of asked me to go with him.'

'Hamish did *what*?'

Rin nodded, blushing. 'He asked me for my phone number last week at school, and then he called me on the weekend and we talked for like an *hour*. Did you know he's really into manga? Anyway, he asked if I wanted to go with him. And I said yes! I mean, I know he's strange and talks about weird stuff all the time. But he's just shy. Like me! And he's into anime and has seen all of Miyazaki-san's films. And I *like* him. And I want to see him at the social, and dance with him and then maybe he'll kiss me and be my boyfriend, but I can't do that if I can't go to the social, and I can't go to the social if *you* don't come with me.'

Wow. Hamish and Rin. That part of the plan had actually worked. But I still couldn't go. There was a chance that Nick might be there. Or might not be there. And I would feel anxious either way. I thought back to the conversation Nick and I had had about fear. I'd told him that nothing made me anxious or afraid. What a terrible lie.

'I'm sorry,' I said. 'I just can't.'

Rin's sweet and shy expression hardened, and her lips pursed. She grabbed me by the upper arm and steered me back into my apartment.

'Hi, Mr Drummond,' she said grimly. 'Hi, Josh. Please excuse us for a moment.'

She frogmarched me into my bedroom and flung open my wardrobe door.

'Hmm,' she said, flicking through shirts and jeans. 'There isn't much to work with here. You get in the shower, I've obviously got a lot to do.'

I blinked. And then I did as she said. It had been a very long time since anyone had told me what to do. It was kind of refreshing. Making my own decisions and bossing other people hadn't always worked out well for me. Maybe it was time for me to be bossed around for a while.

When I came back into my bedroom, Rin was standing over a pile of clothes, holding a purple chiffon monstrosity I'd worn as my cousin's bridesmaid a few years ago.

'I hope you're not seriously expecting me to wear *that*,' I said. 'It looks like a shower loofah.'

Rin smiled. 'Of course not.' She reached inside the dress and yanked out the purple slip I'd worn under it. 'You're going to wear *this*.'

'What?' I said. 'But it's *underwear*.'

'Trust me.'

Rin found my one and only non-sports bra (conveniently also purple, as it had been purchased for the aforementioned wedding), and some black leggings and ballet flats. While I was getting dressed, she vanished back to her own apartment, and returned carrying a gold cardigan-shrug thing, a tonne of jewellery and a giant sack of makeup. She put gold stuff on my eyelids, and applied mascara and eyeliner, and then gave me some purplish lip gloss. Then she put a handful of apricot-scented gunk into my hair and scrunched it around.

'There,' she said when she was satisfied. 'Look in the mirror.'

I felt like a little kid playing dress-ups, and I was sure I was showing too much cleavage. What if someone said something? Or a boy stared at my boobs? They were always prominent, and now they were on *display*. It was too embarrassing.

What was wrong with me? I was sounding like Nick. His anxiety and fear of embarrassment had rubbed off on me.

'What do you think?' asked Rin, beaming.

I looked again at my reflection. The thing was... I felt like an idiot, but a *pretty* idiot. Not romantically pretty, the way Nick liked. Not beautiful. I didn't have long flowing hair or starry eyes, or lips like rosebuds, or alabaster skin. My figure wasn't willowy or slender. But I was still pretty, in a confident, no-nonsense kind of way. Maybe even kind of... sexy? I looked different, but I still looked like me. Rin had turned me into a pretty, little-bit-sexy, interesting version of myself. I smiled at her. Maybe living inside a glass globe really wasn't all it was cracked up to be.

'We'd better go,' I said. 'We're already late.'

Rin squealed and clapped and threw her arms around me. 'Yay! Let's go! Let's go!'

Our SRC decorations budget had been spent well, if 'well' means 'on pink and black helium balloons'. The problem with school dances was...well, they were always lame. No amount of hired lighting and silver streamers could ever hide the fact that you were spending a Friday night at school, in the Ben Chifley Memorial Hall, surrounded by teachers.

But everyone was doing their best to pretend they were having a good time. The social had been in full swing for a couple of hours by the time we arrived, and people had got over their too-cool-to-dance-ness and were wriggling and bumping hips on the dance floor, as the Year Nine kid perched on the stage and did a pretty respectable job as DJ.

Judging from the amount of smeared mascara, stained lips and pashing going on in dark corners, the punch had definitely been spiked.

'Oh!' said Rin. 'I see Hamish!'

I did too. His outfit – a long-sleeved white shirt and black pants – was actually bordering on cool. Simple, but when you were as much of a dork as Hamish, simple was best. He spotted Rin and his eyes widened. She did look pretty spectacular.

Rin started towards him, then hesitated and looked back

at me. 'You go ahead,' I said. 'It's not like I don't know any-one here. I'll be fine.'

Rin kissed me on the cheek and bounced off.

I sidled to a quietish corner of the room and tried to dis-appear. I'd just stand here. Observe. I'd be fine. I only had to stay for an hour or so, then I could slip out. Rin could get home without me.

'Um.'

I turned. It was Nick. He looked amazing in a black suit with a skinny tie and Converse sneakers. He smiled at me, and if I hadn't noticed the sheen of sweat on his brow and the slight tremble of his hands, I'd have thought he was totally in control. What was he doing here? Had he really managed to come to the social? The *Year Ten Social*, the most anxiety-inducing event of the year, even for non-shy kids?

'You came,' I said. 'You're actually here.'

Nick nodded. 'It was totally easy.'

'Really?'

'Sure.'

I narrowed my eyes. 'How many showers did you have today?'

Nick shrugged. 'Only four.'

'And how long did you stand outside before actually coming into the hall?'

'Maybe an hour.'

'But it was *totally* easy.'

'In a manner of speaking.'

'Well done for making it in,' I said, and I meant it. I'd barely been able to manage it myself.

'Thanks. I think I might be having a heart attack.'

I chuckled. 'You'll be fine.'

We smiled and stared at the floor for a minute.

'I read your comment,' said Nick. 'On my blog.'

'Oh?'

'Thank you. For saying all that.'

'I just wanted you to know I was sorry. *Am* sorry.'

'I appreciate it. I shouldn't have said...those things. About you. I was hurt.'

I nodded, and we continued our floor-staring routine.

'I thought about not writing the article,' I said. 'About love-shyness. I don't want to make you any more uncomfortable, or meddle any more in your personal life.'

Nick frowned. 'Oh,' he said. 'I-I think you should write it.'

'Really?'

He nodded. 'You've gone to so much trouble,' he said. 'We've *both* gone to so much trouble. And I think it would help...if people knew about love-shyness. Maybe people might understand us better, and not always see us as being trenchcoat-wearing stalkers.'

'Okay,' I said, smiling. 'That's good. Um. Because I wrote it the other night.'

Nick laughed, and shook his head. 'Why am I not surprised?'

I felt myself blush. 'I brought a copy,' I said. 'If you want to…'

'Are you kidding? I'm dying to read it.'

I grinned. 'Wait here,' I said, and scuttled off to retrieve my bag, which I'd stashed under the drinks table. When I returned, Nick was still standing on his own, looking a little awkward and uncomfortable. But he smiled when he saw me, and I was pleased that his smile didn't make butterflies twinkle around my stomach anymore. I just felt…happy.

I handed him a manila envelope. 'I hope you like it,' I said. 'I think it's…good.'

'I expect nothing less than excellent.'

I felt nervous and pleased. 'You know, I think it *is* excellent. It's the best thing I've ever written.'

Nick peeked inside the envelope. 'This is the school newspaper.'

I nodded. 'I took the story to Ms Tidy and she redid the whole layout so it would fit. It got back from the printer yesterday.'

'What happened to *The New Yorker* or *Vanity Fair*?'

I shrugged. 'You have to start somewhere,' I said. 'Joseph Pulitzer's first job was as a mule-hustler in Missouri.'

'Interesting,' he said. 'I can see how you could find some common ground with mules. And Nellie Bly?'

I grinned, unreasonably pleased that Nick remembered who my favourite journalist was. 'She got her start by writing an angry letter to a sexist newspaper columnist.'

'Well, that's definitely more up your alley.'

'Definitely.'

He raised his eyebrows. 'So the *East Glendale Secondary College Gazette* isn't such a bad start.'

'No,' I said. 'Not so bad at all.'

Actually, I was pretty sure it was the best issue of the *Gazette* ever published. There were some great articles in there. Articles that weren't even written by me. Arabella Sampson's piece about the Vegan Alliance picket was really good. I saw her standing near the DJ with Max Wendt, looking as if she'd explode if he didn't ask her to dance soon, and made a mental note to congratulate her.

Nick tucked the envelope under his arm. 'I'll read it later,' he said. 'When I'm alone.'

I nodded.

'I have a job interview tomorrow,' he told me. 'At Coles. I'm terrified, naturally.'

'You'll be fine,' I said. 'I know it.'

'Maybe. And look—' Nick held out a hand. 'The four showers took care of most of it, but if you look closely…'

He had a thin crescent of dirt under each fingernail.

'I planted nasturtiums and rosemary and wisteria,' he said, looking as if he might burst with pride. 'Outside, in the backyard. I cut out a square of the astroturf. There were worms and bugs and goodness knows how many million bacteria, but I did it! And the *smell*, Penny. The smell of the earth when you turn it up and pour water on it…' His eyes shone. 'It's the most beautiful thing…'

'Nick,' I said. 'That's wonderful.'

We grinned at each other like a pair of lunatics. Around us, couples were clustering together for a slow dance. I could see Clayton Bell making out with the Year Nine boy he'd brought as his date, and Peter Lange was blissfully wrapped around his girlfriend from St Aloysius, who was wearing a very short black dress with electric pink binary code all over it. Over by the snacks, Amy Butler was smiling shyly as Youssef Saad whispered in her ear. I shook my head a little. Maybe I'd been wrong about Amy, too. Maybe she wasn't as boring as I'd assumed. Maybe she was just shy.

'I still don't want to go out with you,' said Nick. 'I'm sorry. I wish I did. But…'

'But I'm not your type.'

'No.'

'That's okay,' I said. 'I don't think you're really my type either. I'm not sure what my type is.'

'You need someone you can have a good argument with, without them bursting into tears.'

I laughed. 'You're probably right. I do like to argue.'

'So,' said Nick. 'Do you think we can be friends?'

I looked over at Rin dancing with Hamish. She gave me a little grin and wave. Hamish turned and waved at me as well. I seemed to suddenly have quite a few friends. It felt good.

'Definitely,' I said. 'Friends.'

'Good,' he said. 'Because I don't think I've ever had a friend before, and I'd like to give it a shot.'

'Me too.'

Nick held out his hand. 'Well, friend,' he said. 'Would you like to dance with me?'

I took his hand. 'Yes, friend,' I said. 'I would.'

We moved out onto the dance floor and Nick put trembling hands on my waist. I could smell his laundry-detergent-and-soap smell. He smiled nervously at me, and I was pleased to notice that the smile didn't make me feel quite as wobbly and excited as it had before. It still made me feel a *bit* wobbly and excited, but in a slightly wistful way. I supposed this was what nostalgia felt like.

'You're doing an excellent job,' I murmured in his ear.

Nick swallowed. Every blonde skinny girl in the entire

room was staring at me with dagger-eyes of envy. I allowed myself to feel a little bit proud, and let my head rest on his shoulder.

It was fun, dancing with Nick, and I hoped I'd dance with a few other boys. Maybe Hugh Forward would ask me again, and this time I'd accept. Or maybe I'd just throw convention to the wind and ask *him* to dance. That seemed like a good idea. The night stretched out, full of conversation and friends and laughter.

***

'Penny? Is that you?'

When I got home, Dad and Josh were still up, sitting on the couch watching *Iron Chef.*

'How was it?' asked Josh.

I grinned. 'Good,' I said. 'Really good.'

'Dance with any cute boys?'

I blushed. 'Maybe.'

Hugh Forward had asked me to go to the movies with him next weekend. It might be nice to hang out with him and talk about something other than SRC and Debating.

I pulled the *East Glendale Secondary College Gazette* out of my bag and handed it to Dad. 'It's what I've been working on,' I told him. 'It's why I've been so stressed.'

Josh turned off the TV and leaned over to Dad so they could both see the front page. Just under the masthead were the words *The Secret Garden: Helping the Love-shy Bloom*, and, below that: *by Penny Drummond*.

As they settled down to read, I snuck into my room and closed the door. I was looking forward to hearing what they thought of my article. I was looking forward to seeing what Nick thought of it. I was looking forward to hanging out with him, as well as with Rin and maybe even Hamish as well. I was looking forward to calling Hugh and getting to know him as a person and a friend, instead of my competition. I was even looking forward to more Friday night jigsaws with Dad and Josh.

But most of all, I was looking forward to finding another story.